"You don't have to be afraid of me, Cammie."

"I'm not." But she was. Not afraid of him, but afraid of the feelings Brett stirred inside her.

As the music continued to play, Brett softly brushed his lips over her cheek, then rested them against her temple. He gently stroked her back, up and down in a slow, sultry rhythm. After a time, he pulled away and studied her eyes, then slowly, slowly lowered his mouth....

Fortunately, the song ended before the inevitable happened, forcing Cammie out of her stupor. When the disc jockey thanked everyone for coming, she didn't know whether to be relieved or disappointed. Maybe a little of both.

Brett hesitantly released her and handed her the discarded jacket. "Let's go before they turn on the house lights."

Cammie was still in a trance when they entered the glass elevator, the nagging cautions running through her head at breakneck speed.

Never underestimate his power....

Dear Reader,

Several years ago, I set off in my rather large RV to move my mom from Texas to Pennsylvania, pulling her car along behind me. This was no big deal as I'd once towed a stock trailer full of horses behind the motor home through the mountains of Tennessee. As long as I didn't have to back up too often, I managed.

On the return trip to Texas, my good friend—who'd accompanied me on that little journey—remarked that I should hire on as a tour bus driver for some country music star. Since I had a husband and three kids back home, I decided this was not a good plan. However, that comment spurred the premise for what eventually became *The Closer You Get*.

I've always been a fan of country music singers, particularly those sexy cowboy crooners who can make a woman swoon with a simple love song. Those gorgeous guys served as inspiration for Brett Taylor, the hero of this book. He's strong, beautiful, talented and somewhat tortured. It only made sense to bless him with a temporary female bus driver who is immune to his charms—sort of.

I truly enjoyed writing Brett and Cammie's roller-coaster journey on the road, and I sure hope you do, too.

Happy traveling!

Kristi Gold

The Closer You Get

KRISTI GOLD

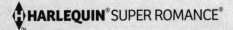

HARLEQUIN® SUPER ROMANCE®

Recycling programs
for this product may
not exist in your area.

ISBN-13: 978-0-373-60757-0

THE CLOSER YOU GET

Printed in U.S.A.

ABOUT THE AUTHOR

Kristi Gold has a fondness for beaches, baseball and bridal reality shows. She firmly believes that love has remarkable, healing powers and feels very fortunate to be able to weave stories of love and commitment. As a bestselling author, a National Readers' Choice award winner and a Romance Writers of America three-time RITA® Award finalist, Kristi has learned that although accolades are wonderful, the most cherished rewards come from networking with readers. She can be reached through her website at http://kristigold.com or through Facebook.

Books by Kristi Gold

Other titles by this author available in ebook format.

To my stellar friend Judy,
who served as my copilot and coconspirator in the
making of this book.
And to the country crooners who populate my playlists
and whose songs have provided many years of
listening pleasure.

CHAPTER ONE

BRETT TAYLOR STOOD at the open door, remaining partially concealed while mentally plotting his course from the tour bus to the rear entrance of the coliseum. As usual, it was nearly impossible to sneak past a crowd during a stock show, particularly when you were parked in wide-open spaces in broad daylight.

The sights, sounds and smells of the ongoing carnival resurrected long-ago recollections, memories of funnel cakes fried in oil, candied apples doled out by the dozens, whirring rides mixed with piercing screams. A crazy, carefree atmosphere—a world away from the life he now knew.

He couldn't recall the last time he'd eaten a corn dog or sat suspended on top of a Ferris wheel. Too long ago to remember. What he wouldn't give to have his arm thrown over his best girl's shoulders, dumping forty bucks in a matter of minutes just to win a stuffed bear so he could earn a sincere smile and a sweet kiss. Unfortunately, he didn't have a best girl, or any girl in his life for that matter. He hadn't for a while now. But he did have a show to put on.

He slid the familiar photograph into his back pocket, the same as he always did before each and every performance. A reminder of what he had lost, and could never recover. Only one of the many sacrifices he'd exchanged for fame.

As soon as he descended the stairs and stepped out onto the lot, the shouting and shoving commenced, sending his security team into action, their beefy arms attempting to hold the crowd at bay.

"Over here, Brett!" echoed from a dozen different places, followed by numerous blinding camera flashes. The normal procedure meant paper pushed into his face, a pen or two narrowly missing his eye. He'd been known to sign T-shirts and cowboy boots, sometimes even legs and arms. He drew the line on certain body parts, including the occasional bare breast.

His height allowed him to peer over most of the crowd and zero in on the targeted entrance while attempting to shake a few of the bobbing hands among the sea of people. A fearless teenage girl shoved her way forward and tried to polish his trophy buckle with her palm, prompting a guard to restrain her.

Fans were good, though. Fans were a part of the life. But some days he wasn't in the mood to be probed and prodded like one of the sideshow exhibits on the crowded midway. Today was one of those days.

He glanced at his watch, and realizing he was already five minutes late, he signaled the guards with a subtle look that he was ready to move on. These fans would have to wait until after the concert.

Then she caught his attention.

A little blue-eyed girl stood at the end of the row just a few feet away from the bedlam, clasping a bunch of red roses in a fist too small to hold them intact, the stems crooked as if they'd been crushed in the human swell of anticipation. She wasn't much more than six years old, looking sweet and hopeful, probably the purest sight he'd seen in a long time. He just couldn't pass her up.

He crouched on her level while random sounds of approval came from the bystanders. Intended or not, pausing to speak to a child earned him a few extra points. It also filled him with regret when he thought about the weathered photo secured in his back pocket. A photo he always carried with him onstage.

"Are these for me?" he asked. She nodded and handed him the bouquet, her smile as soft as the petals.

A proud-looking man offered him a small blue book. "Mind giving my daughter your autograph? You're all she talks about, sunup to sundown."

"No problem." And it wasn't, at least not in this case. "What's your name, sweetheart?"

She twisted a lock of baby-fine golden hair around a chubby finger. "Megan."

Brett's smile came naturally now. "Pretty name for a pretty girl."

She shrugged and returned the smile, revealing deep dimples creasing her cheeks. He could appreciate little-girl innocence, before the little girls grew up and wanted more from him than just an autograph.

He laid the flowers across his thighs, took a pen from the father and quickly scrawled his name on one of the pages.

"Could you date it?" the man asked.

Brett shot him a wry grin. "I'm not sure of the date."

"The sixteenth."

His hand froze in place. March 16. He hadn't even realized it, at least not consciously. Maybe that was his brain's way of protecting his heart.

How many years had it been? Eight? No, nine. Nine years ago his world had come to a halt, ironically coinciding with his big break and the chance of a lifetime. So far he'd been unable to completely recover from the loss, even when he should be counting his blessings. After all, he'd finally realized his dream, at the cost of giving up another.

Shoving the sadness back beneath the surface where it belonged, he handed the child the book of memories and gently kissed her cheek, then straightened and accepted her father's handshake and thanks.

The little girl grasped him around the knees, stared up at him and said in an angel's voice, "I love you, Brett."

At least someone did.

When she released him at her dad's insistence, Brett strode past the remaining fans and into the back entrance of the arena, working his way past the catch pens containing massive, snorting bulls, the railing lined with cowboys spitting the occasional stream of tobacco onto the ground. Several of the men—stars in their own right—grunted greetings. Others shook his hand as he passed by. He fought the urge to borrow a horse and ride away like an Old West hero. But he wasn't a hero. He was only a man, and a flawed one at that.

The guards pushed open a heavy metal door, led him down a corridor and then up the stairs into a wire jungle, huge speakers and intricate sound equipment the wildlife within. Dust from the rodeo arena, blended with smells of smoke and manure, settled into his nostrils. He coughed and traded the roses for a bottle of water offered to him by one of the crew. Sweat beaded on his forehead that he swiped away with the back of his arm before readjusting the black felt hat.

After fitting the guitar strap over his shoulder, he walked to the outskirts of the stage where he could see a few eager faces. He attempted to draw energy from the spirited roar, the passionate applause. It should have been enough to sustain him, but lately, it wasn't. He felt restless, as if something big was brewing inside his soul. He couldn't quite put his finger on it. But as sure as he knew every word of his songs by heart, he somehow knew his life was about to take a turn. That prospect worried him. Change wasn't always good.

He tucked away his intuition and drew a deep breath, prepared to give it everything he had in spite of his sour mood. They expected the best. He had sworn from the day he'd publicly performed for the first time in a run-down Texas dive, he would be the best. His music, the only part of himself he was willing to share, forced him to play dual roles in the scheme of things—the man and the performer.

Tonight he was the performer.

That thought thrust him on the stage to work his magic like an illusionist as he willed his all-too-human persona to disappear. In its place came the reluctant superstar.

Destined for greatness. Undeniably gifted. Many a woman's fantasy.

"Ladies and gentlemen! Give a big Houston welcome to one of country music's finest, Brett Taylor!"

THE MASSIVE BUS LOOMED majestically before her, a black raven with distinctive blue eyes and outstretched wings spanning one side. An appropriate greeting. For Camille Carson, this particular vehicle symbolized long-awaited freedom.

After the taxi driver deposited her bags on the lot and drove away, she lugged her oversize duffel to the entrance, the black nylon tote thrown over her shoulder bumping against her ribs in time with her pounding heart. Her head kept telling her to settle down; she'd seen buses before. Driven so many she'd lost count. But none had been quite as fancy as this.

The top half displaying the raven was bronze, the bottom black with a bronze stripe swirling a path over the division of the two tones of color. And in the corner above the dark rear window, the initials of the owner etched in beige block text: *B.T.* Just seeing the letters sent a succession of tingles down Cammie's spine.

She could blame those tingles on the weather, but the Texas spring morning was warm, sunny and clear with no real wind to speak of. A good day for driving. After a quick mental pep talk to restore her composure, she rapped on the heavy door.

When the latch released, Cammie's heart skipped into her throat. She wasn't sure who she might encounter, but the face before her looked familiar and welcoming.

"Hey, kiddo," Bud Parker bellowed as he hurried down to the pavement and swept her off her feet with a roughness that belied his gentle nature.

After he put her down, she tugged at her shirt and laughed. "And hello to you, too. It's been way too long, Bud."

He grinned. "You're mighty right about that, little girl."

Cammie stepped back and studied his face. Still the same Bud, except for a bit more visible gray tingeing his brown hair and goatee, his face a little fuller. Over time, a kinship had developed between the two, bonding them like siblings for more than fifteen years. And now he seemed incredibly happy.

"I believe impending fatherhood suits you, Parker," she said. "So how's Jeanie feeling?"

"She's restless as hell and ready for our kid to make an appearance, which is scheduled to happen in a week if it doesn't happen before then. My being home should help." Bud affectionately patted her cheek. "I think you've gotten even prettier since the last time I saw you."

Cammie lowered her eyes and twisted a tress of hair into a spiral, a habit she'd long since abandoned in childhood. Oddly, Bud had a way of making her feel like that shy, all-knees-and-elbows kid from years past. "Are you going to let me in now?"

"After you," he said with a bow, moving aside so she could climb the three steps into the interior cab.

Bud took Cammie's three bags and piled them on the passenger seat, then scaled the remaining step leading into the living area of the elaborate home on wheels. "Come on up. The guys will be back in a minute."

He showed her to a plush white leather sofa that took up most of one interior wall. As soon as Cammie lowered herself onto the cushions, Bud dropped down beside her, his kind expression fading into a blanket of concern. "Are you sure you want to do this, Cam?"

Good question. "I have to. Until the business picks up again, someone needs to make some money."

"Jeanie and I have a few dollars put back—"

"Yeah, Bud, that would go over real well with Granddad. He considers charity blasphemous. He won't even go to the bank for a loan, hardheaded man."

"Jed's like a second father to me, Cam," he said. "Hell, you're both like family. I'd do anything for you guys."

"I know."

Uncomfortable over the course of the conversation, Cammie took a look around, amazed at how so much could be crammed into such a small space. The place was relatively neat with the exception of a thin layer of dust and a few water rings etched into the side table to her right. The bus held all the amenities of a small apartment, decorated in a way exclusive to an owner with good taste, and a lot of money.

The far wall housed a recessed liquor cabinet displaying a couple of bottles of top-grade whiskey. An intricate stereo system, two flat-panel TVs and DVD player were built into the inlaid paneling next to that. Underneath, two white leather-covered benches framed an oak table where a pile of pennies and several crumpled beer cans sat adjacent to abandoned hands of cards.

The scent of a driver's most important staple— strong coffee—wafted from the galley kitchen to her left, barely masking the residual odor of cigars.

Stainless-steel appliances sparkled without any sign of wear and tear, leading Cammie to believe they'd rarely been used. Nor would she be putting them to use. Driving the bus, yes. Cooking, no way.

She leaned forward and glanced down the corridor, nodding toward the closed door at the end of the hallway. "Is that where he sleeps?"

"Yeah, his stateroom." Bud stood and walked past the refrigerator to a division equivalent to the bulkhead on an airplane. "There's only one berth in this middle compartment right here, which is where you'll sleep. It's got a TV on the wall and it's pretty comfortable."

"As long as it has a mattress, I'm good." She pointed at a remote control set in a bracket hanging from the wall. "What's that?"

Bud smiled. "That's high tech at its best. It controls the two slides that expand the front cabin, and all the stereo equipment. It's pretty easy to operate."

Easy was good. "The bathroom?"

"It's opposite your berth and there's a washer and dryer next to that. The shower's kind of small, but it's workable."

"Who needs a large shower when you have the means to wash clothes?" She did have one major concern. "Do I have to share the bath with the star?"

Bud shook his head. "Nope. He has his own, along with a fancy steam shower. He might even let you try it out if you ask nicely."

Not going to happen. "I assume the band members have their own bus."

"Yeah, lucky for you. Sometimes they travel together on this one, but they sack out on their bus."

"Who drives for them?"

"His name is Dennis, but don't expect to see him too often. He's kind of antisocial. I think it's because he gets tired of the guys. They can be kind of crude, but basically they're a pretty decent group."

Having spent most her life around tactless men, Cammie definitely related to crude behavior. She strolled toward the driver's quarters and studied the high-backed seat she would be occupying for the next month. "How does he feel about having a female driver?"

"I'm not sure he's figured that out yet."

She faced Bud and frowned. "You didn't tell him?"

He sent her a sheepish smile. "I told him your name's Cam Carson."

Cammie leveled a hard stare on him. "So help me, Bud, if my boss thinks a woman's place is anywhere but behind the wheel, you're in deep—"

A noisy commotion filtering in from outside suspended Cammie's tirade just when she was about to get going. The door released and a sudden flurry of voices invaded the territory, including a few common curses. Cammie stepped back into the main quarters, Bud following behind her. A literal band of merry men tromped up the entry steps, but by the time the last one stepped into the bus, the once-jubilant atmosphere had grown silent, interrupted only by the steady hum of the idling diesel engine.

Cammie regarded the disconcerted group now gathered in the small space next to the driver's quarters, looking like confused clowns crammed into a phone booth. They seemed somewhat perplexed over why this woman was on board. Alone. With Bud.

"It's okay, come on up, guys," Bud said. "Just wipe the suspicious look off your faces and meet my replacement for the next few weeks."

Bud stepped back to make room for the men, then gestured toward the closest member. "This is Pat Jordan on bass guitar, vocals, and senior member of the band. Pat, Camille Carson."

"Just call me Cammie," she said.

Pat smiled and tipped his baseball cap up and away from his silver hair. "Glad to know you, Cammie."

Bud nodded to the man standing beside Pat. "Doug Jones on drums."

"I answer to Bull, ma'am." His wide grin exposed a toothpick protruding from shiny white teeth framed by a sandy-colored beard and round face. His intimidating stature hinted at how he'd come by his nickname.

"And this is Roland Williams on keyboards and steel guitar," Bud said. "He prefers to be called Rusty."

The clean-shaven redhead squeezed between the two men and gave her a brief salute.

"And finally, the newest member, Jeremy Black, guitar and fiddle."

Cammie looked over Rusty's shoulder and met the shy eyes of a boy who couldn't be older than twenty, his blond hair pulled low into a ponytail. He hung back from the group as if his presence was an intrusion, simply raising his hand in acknowledgment. She could relate to his discomfort.

She afforded them a welcoming smile while she wondered over the absence of the star of the show. Probably holed up in the hotel room with some buxom babe. "A pleasure to meet you all."

"You can close your mouth now, boys," Bud said. "I know she's a damn sight prettier than I am, but she can drive the hell out of a bus. I taught her everything she knows."

Rusty gave Bud a playful punch on his way toward the sofa to take a seat, Bull and Jeremy following behind him to claim a place at the booth. "That's reassuring."

"Haven't killed you yet, have I?" Bud said.

Pat eased forward. "Sorry we look so surprised, Cammie. Bud here told us you were coming but—"

"What Pat's trying to say is they weren't planning on you," Bud interrupted. "They were expecting someone with hairy arms who dips snuff and pitches pennies."

Pat shot Bud a go-to-hell look. "Not that it matters you're a woman, mind you. We're just not used to having a girl on board." He addressed his cohorts with a shrewd grin. "At least not for more than a night."

"That's okay," Cammie said. "I'll try to stay out of the way. In fact, you probably won't even know I'm here."

"Oh, we'll know you're here," Rusty said. "And so will *he.*"

He, as in Brett Taylor. Well, *he* could just get used to it. And *he* was apparently coming into the bus, she decided when the door opened again.

Cammie's first view consisted of the top of a dark head bent down to allow his six-foot-plus frame into the passage. When he looked up, she noticed right away he was in need of a shave, at least two days' worth of stubble covering his sculpted jaws. A crescent cleft engraved into his chin set off a sensual mouth that released extraordinary sounds when he sang, generating endless emotions. He wore a pair of threadbare jeans and a faded black T-shirt, not the usual trappings of success, but she sure couldn't register any complaints considering the perfection of the fit.

Yet the cut-glass blue eyes and raven hair were affirmations of the stunning good looks of a man said to have "squeal appeal." And a reputation as the consummate heartthrob of country music.

Some performers had charisma, some had phenomenal talent. Brett Taylor had it all.

Cammie stepped behind Bud, silently admonishing herself for sinking into wilting-flower mode, yet she couldn't quite gear up to face him when considering the possible fallout. The rest of the group just stared at their boss as if he'd grown a second head.

"What are you guys looking at?" he asked.

Bud pulled Cammie forward with a little more force than necessary. "This is Camille."

Brett leveled his unearthly blue eyes on her, letting it be known he had no qualms about using them to his advantage. "Pleased to meet you, ma'am," he said, followed by a blatant size-up from her sneakers to the sunglasses perched atop her head.

Cammie tugged at the hem of her flannel shirt and wished someone would turn the air conditioner up to arctic mode. "Same here," she muttered, but failed to look directly at him, or least not at his face. For some reason her gaze drifted to his thumbs now hooked in his pockets. Not a bad idea at all.

She forced her attention to his eyes and held out her hand. He took it without hesitation, his gaze fixed on her in a try-to-resist-me look.

"How long will you be visiting?" Brett asked with a smile that exuded sensuality and a hint of amusement.

"She's not a visitor," Bud said quickly. "She's my sub until Jeanie has the baby."

In those few moments following Bud's declaration, Cammie felt certain, as her grandfather always put it, you could hear a fly spit. No one moved, much less spoke.

Brett's smile faded. "You're going to drive my bus?"

"Yes, I am," she said with more confidence than she felt at the moment.

"All by yourself?"

Cammie found that utterly insulting. "Unless you plan on helping, but it might get crowded with both of us in the driver's seat."

The guys laughed, which seemed to irritate the star. "What kind of credentials do you have to take this on?" Brett asked.

"She's good," Bud said. "I've been with her when she's driven. She can handle it. She's been on the long haul."

Cammie tried not to choke on the lie. True, she'd driven a bus most of her adult years for her grandfather's Tennessee charter company, but only on jaunts from Memphis to Nashville or Knoxville with chattering seniors, not a superstar stud among them.

Feeling the need to defend her skills, Cammie went into spontaneous résumé recitation. "I hold a commercial license with a passenger endorsement and I've been driving tour buses since I was barely in high school. Contrary to popular belief, women are quite capable of getting in and out of tight spots, handling dipsticks, even the human variety—"

Bud discreetly pinched her arm to silence her. "I'll

guarantee you'll feel safe and sound with Cammie," he said. "If it doesn't work out, I'll come back early."

Brett didn't bother to hide his skepticism. "I'll take your word for it, Bud. But if she screws up, then we'll call you." Without further comment, he headed down the aisle without even a backward glance.

"She's starting immediately," Bud called after him. "That okay with you?"

"Yeah," he muttered before disappearing into his quarters and closing the door behind him.

Cammie massaged her throbbing arm, then turned and kicked Bud in the shin, drawing laughter from the other men.

He winced and scowled. "Why the hell did you do that?"

"Because that pinch hurt, dammit." She unclenched her fists and rubbed her fingertips across the indentations her nails had left in her palm. "Not to mention, your boss obviously isn't too thrilled with my presence. Forty-five feet isn't a lot of room if you're spending weeks on the road with someone you don't like or trust."

"Don't sweat it, Cam," Bud said. "Just give him some time to get used to the idea. Besides, he's probably in shock because you didn't try to tear his clothes off."

"That's true," Rusty said. "If you ignore him you'll get along just fine. He gets tired of all those girls crying and falling at his feet."

Bull stretched his legs out in front of him and sighed. "Hell of a life."

"And take my word for it, Cammie," Pat said. "After two days with this group, you'll learn to hate us, too."

Cammie grinned. "I doubt that."

She also doubted that she would ever rip Brett Taylor's clothes off in some fit of uncontrollable lust. Yes, he was unbelievably gorgeous. Incredibly tall. Great body with a gifted voice to match. She'd learned the hard way that the facade didn't make the man. It could be oh-so-easy to fall for the image without ever knowing what you were getting beyond the external packaging. Brett Taylor was just that— a package deal. A carefully conceived commodity, marketed, promoted and sold daily like prime stock. How well she knew that concept.

So why all the effort to catch her breath when he'd looked at her? Not too late to turn and run.

Ridiculous. She refused to be blown away by this particular kind of man. Been there, done that and didn't plan to ever do it again. Once bitten and all that jazz.

Cammie wrung her hands. "Where are we heading?"

"Austin," Bud said. "Then it's on to San Antonio and Corpus Christi before we head north to Fort Worth. When we leave there, I'll ride on to Oklahoma City with you where I'll catch a plane back home. After that, you're on your own."

On your own. The very first time in Cammie's life when that was essentially true. Even as she'd attended college, she'd still been under her grandfather's thumb. Now all the decisions would be hers to make. The thought was exhilarating.

Except she somehow sensed everyone had glossed over the real Brett Taylor. He obviously found her unsatisfactory as an employee. He would simply have to get over it. She could stand her ground and take on the best, a trait inherited from her crusty grandfather and stubborn grandmother, the people who'd raised her after the tragic bus accident that had claimed her parents' lives.

"What now?" Cammie asked.

"Let's grab some food to go, then we'll be on our way," Bud said, motioning her toward the exit.

When they stepped onto the parking lot, Cammie heard more muffled laughter coming from inside. "They think I'm a joke."

"Nah," Bud said. "They think they're going to have one hell of a time explaining you to their wives and girlfriends."

"Does that include Brett Taylor, too?"

"He doesn't have either one. Says he's not interested in settling down."

"I know the feeling. Maybe we'll get along, after all. He keeps his distance, I'll keep mine, and all will be well in the world of country-music touring."

Bud grinned. "Just one more thing, Cammie."

Suspicion hit her full force. "What thing?"

"He has a serious weakness for brunettes."

She considered cowboy charm and laser-blue eyes. Nice-fitting jeans and black felt hats. The perfect smile and the perfect line. She waved her hand in a dismissive gesture. "I can handle that because I have no weaknesses when it comes to men, especially arrogant, high-strung singers." Not anymore.

"Give it time, little girl," he said. "I still remember running the boys off when you were in junior high. The fact that you wouldn't have anything to do with them made them want you all the more. Someday some lucky guy will come along and you won't be so quick to pass him off."

"Don't count on it, Bud."

He patted her cheek. "One day you'll find someone you can't resist."

"And when I'm eighty years old and still single, scouring the senior centers looking for a decent man, I'll drive up in a bus and make you eat your words."

Bud belly-laughed and hugged her hard. "Right now I'm going to eat some greasy bacon and some eggs."

"Sounds good. I'm starving."

Cammie linked her arm through Bud's and tugged him in the direction of the hotel. When she glanced back at her temporary home, she noticed the slightly parted curtains and caught a glimpse of the face that undoubtedly stole millions of hearts on a nightly basis. And for a moment she even thought she saw him smile.

BRETT YANKED THE curtain closed with a vengeance. Man, this was all he needed. A woman on board. Now they'd have to watch their language. He couldn't walk around in his underwear anymore. Or maybe he could, if she'd return the favor.

A not-so-subtle surge of downward blood flow coursed through his body and landed smack dab behind his fly. He fell back onto the bed and studied the recessed lights. The thought of this Cammie person running around in skimpy panties had caused his body to react like any normal man's would. And the more he thought about it, the more jacked up he got.

He rolled over and stuffed his face into the pillow. Maybe he needed a woman. After all, it had been a while. He purposely tried not to be too preoccupied with sex until his own need forced his preoccupation. Then he'd find someone who could take him away from the craziness, even if only for a while. Over the years, he'd made acquaintance with several women in several different cities that would come to him if he made a call. Hell, he was human. On occasion he'd take one to bed, close his eyes and escape. Nothing more expected of him than a quick tumble and a story to tell their friends. Nothing beyond physical satisfaction. No promises. No commitment. Just like he liked it.

When the familiar rush of loneliness filled him, he ignored it, same as always. He couldn't afford the distraction. Any distraction.

Brett stood, parted the curtain again and discovered that Cammie and Bud had almost reached the hotel's entrance. The sun bounced off the reddish highlights in her hair as she tilted her head back and laughed, then discarded her denim jacket. Her clothes were simple—faded jeans that fit maybe a little too well, a plain blue plaid flannel shirt that kept the majority of her body hidden. Like it or not, that fact disappointed him. She wasn't all that tall and she sure as hell couldn't weigh more than one-twenty, which made him wonder how much help she'd be with loading and unloading. Maybe Ms. Carson sported some muscle underneath the baggy shirt, and maybe some other surprises, too.

For some reason, he couldn't tear his gaze away when Bud grabbed her by the waist, then swung her off her feet like someone would a kid. Brett suddenly imagined running his hands through her hair, wrapping his arms around her and holding her tightly against his...

He blew out a tuneless whistle. His head told him, *Hold it right there, Taylor.* His body said something altogether different when his fantasy took flight. A really detailed fantasy. Slick naked flesh, rumpled sheets, uninhibited sex. Slow, hot sex, not a quick roll between concert stops. All night long. He'd do all the things to her that he normally didn't have enough time to do, using his mouth and his hands to play her like his favorite Fender. Yeah, slow, hot sex with...his bus driver?

He had to remember she was an employee, even if she was a damn good-looking one. Anything other than a professional relationship created a dangerous conflict. The road was no place to forge any kind of relationship with a woman, a painful truth he had learned years ago.

He didn't believe in love at first sight, even though he'd sung about it. Lust maybe, but not love. In fact, he wasn't sure he believed in love at all. He did believe in staying ahead of the game, writing good songs, chasing the top spot on the charts. He also believed that everyone eventually left, the way it had always been in his life.

In spite of what he knew to be best—that his new driver would remain off-limits—the images still refused to disappear.

Damn his overactive imagination. Damn his recent celibacy. And damn Bud Parker for bringing another complication into his life.

CHAPTER TWO

SHE'D PASSED THE FIRST TEST—making it to Austin without incident.

Cammie maneuvered the bus into the coliseum's back lot and parked next to one of the two tractor-trailers hauling the equipment. After the band piled out and left for their bus to prepare for the performance, she remained patiently in her seat, watching the road crew unload equipment for the upcoming concert. Pat eventually came on board to socialize with Bud, yet neither man seemed to remember she was there. She felt somewhat awkward and unsure of what to do next.

A few moments later, Pat stood and summoned her to the door. "Come on backstage and watch tonight, Cammie. You won't get many opportunities to do that once Bud leaves. He'll stay and you can be our guest."

"I don't know if that's a good idea." Not with the prospect of angering her obviously temperamental boss hanging over her.

"Go on, Cam," Bud said. "Brett won't mind. You'll get to see what it's like behind the scenes."

She already knew what went on behind the scenes. Perhaps not at this professional level, but her tenure singing backup for a couple of aspiring bands in Nashville during college had exposed her to the life. And most of those experiences hadn't been all that great. Yet she couldn't ignore her curious nature. "Fine," she said as she pulled on her denim jacket. "But I'll only stay for the first set."

After Bud draped an access pass around her neck, Cammie followed Pat to the rear entrance of the venue where a security guard checked the credentials to make sure she wasn't an intruder. Pat then showed her to a stool near the outskirts of the stage where she assumed her perch to observe.

The road crew attended last-minute adjustments while the band members milled around looking well-groomed, unlike their earlier disheveled state of torn jeans and wrinkled shirts. After a time, they took their positions, geared up to go…everyone except Brett Taylor.

Cammie could hear the rumblings of the crowd and smelled the acrid scent of the fog machines as they poured a mist over the stage. The steady voices melded into a cheer when the lights went down. Pat counted off the beat and the group took his lead as the band played an instrumental while the audience clapped in time. But still no star.

Somewhat concerned, Cammie looked around and glanced to her right to find Brett had stopped nearby to take a drink of water from a bottle set out on a small table. He was clean-shaven, wore a blue chambray shirt and slightly faded jeans that looked as if they'd been tailor-made for his body. A man from the crew approached Brett and handed him a guitar, which he flung over his shoulder. He drew in two deep breaths and wiped his forehead with the back of his hand before resettling the black cowboy hat securely over his dark hair.

As the song took on a fevered pitch, the crowd grew more delirious. Then from out of nowhere, a voice boomed, announcing his name. And for Cammie, it finally began to sink in.

I work for Brett Taylor.

Yet she refused to let that fact leave her silly and starstruck. On that thought, she assumed a casual position as Brett started toward the threshold of the stage. But before he answered the call of his myriad fans, he stopped short and caught her gaze. After taking two more steps, he paused again and frowned, seeming as if he didn't quite believe what he'd seen.

Great. Bud had been wrong. Brett wasn't at all pleased over her presence. While he continued to stare at her, she managed a polite nod and braced herself for the possible repercussions. A verbal slap on the wrist. A "get thee back to the bus." An invitation to join the unemployment line. Surprisingly, he only smiled—a cynical one at that—and went about his business.

The star entered the stage like a wild man, with

an energetic leap and a thousand-kilowatt smile. The place grew manic when realization dawned that the performer they'd paid good money to see had finally arrived on scene. In record time, he whipped the hordes into a greater frenzy with a brassy country song, then kept them on a roll with one hit after another until the atmosphere itself became a living entity.

During one number, he wiped his face with a towel and tossed it into the crowd. Cammie had seen the same ploy time and again, always amazed and amused that grown women would fight like alley cats for the privilege of owning a piece of sweat-laden cloth. If she had an entrepreneurial spirit, she could sell his used bath towels on the internet for a mint.

The screams intensified when Brett approached the front of the stage. Bouquets of flowers fell at his feet, sprinkling the floor like a kaleidoscope gone haywire. He did a balancing act while he shook the hands of a few fortunate fans. Cameras flashed at thousands per second, women fanned their faces as if they might swoon. At any given moment, Cammie expected to see bras and panties sailing onto the platform or worse, the front-row cluster of overwrought females pulling him off the stage. Fortunately, neither happened and when it came time for the finale, Cammie was exhausted.

For the first encore Brett took to the stage alone, picked up his acoustic guitar and began to sing with no accompaniment whatsoever. The first ballad spoke of lost love with a woman, the second described a father saying goodbye to his grown-up little girl. Cammie knew them both well, had even sung along to them on the radio. And in those few quiet moments, with the once-delirious audience lulled into total silence, she began to understand why he was such a sensation, why the women loved him. In her opinion, this was the true test of a musician's skill—singing with no other instrumentation, studio mixing equipment or backup vocals. He hit every note with precision, his voice as clear as a summer morning, as reverent as a preacher's prayer.

So engrossed in the sweet strains of Brett's intoxicating music, before Cammie knew it, the band had reentered the stage for the finale. She realized she should leave, but like the crowd, she remained engrossed in the show until the group struck the last chord and took their final bow.

After she shifted off the stool and started toward the exit, again she caught sight of Brett, only this time he didn't notice her at all. He focused his attention on a girl with long blond hair wearing tight jeans and black boots and a face full of makeup most likely designed to mask her youth. As far as Cammie was concerned, she barely looked old enough to drive. Nothing more than a teenager playing at being a woman trying to get close to a star. And worse, she might actually succeed.

Unfortunately, Cammie would have to walk past

the pair in order to leave. She strode forward, chin up, eyes focused straight ahead, determined to ignore them both. But her efforts to make a covert departure were thwarted when Brett called her name.

"Give me a half hour or so," he said before he draped his arm over the girl's shoulders and led her away.

As she left out the heavy metal door, Cammie resigned herself to the fact that she'd have to get used to the delays, the life, the women. At least, this time, she wouldn't suffer the consequences.

"DOES YOUR MAMA KNOW you're here, Caroline?"

"Yes, Brett, she knows."

"And she didn't care that you drove all the way to Austin by yourself?"

She gave him a good eye-rolling and a smirk. "First of all, I'm not by myself. My boyfriend's gone to get the car. Second, I only drove about a mile to get here. I'm going to UT now, remember?"

Actually, Brett didn't remember that at all. His baby cousin should still be in braces and riding a bike, not attending a concert with a boyfriend. "I think Mom might have mentioned that a few months ago. Sometimes it's hard to keep up with what's going on back home."

"Maybe you should try to come home more often."

He wasn't in the mood to be run through the guilt wringer, but it looked to be unavoidable. Feeling suddenly tired, he dropped down into the dressing room's leather chair and pointed at the sofa. "Have a seat."

Caroline perched on the edge of the cushion and studied him straight on. "Aunt Linda really missed seeing you this Christmas. We all did."

He brought out the usual excuses. "I had that Christmas special on TV and then the tour began. It's been pretty crazy. I've tried to convince Mom to move to Nashville to be closer to me, but she won't budge."

She frowned. "Kerrville's her home, Brett. She's not going to leave her friends and the family."

How well he knew that. "Hopefully I'll have a break in a few months and I can come in for a visit."

"Your mom would appreciate that." Caroline remained silent for a few moments, her gaze focused on the coffeemaker on the adjacent counter. "Jana brought Lacey to see Aunt Linda on Christmas Eve."

Just hearing the familiar names sent his heart beating a path into his throat. "Oh, yeah?"

"Yeah. Do you want to see a picture of her?"

Before Brett could respond, much less refuse, Caroline had already retrieved a fancy phone from her pocket, hit a few buttons and then handed it to him. He studied the digital picture displayed on the screen, noting that his mom looked much the same, her black-and-silver hair twisted into her usual long braid, her face showing signs of a hard life as a single mother working as a waitress to raise her son.

And next to her stood the little girl that had been his at one time. Only she wasn't exactly little anymore. She'd grown into a pretty preteen, just like her mom had been way back when they'd gone to school together. But with her blue eyes and dark hair, she looked like him. A lot like him.

The ever-present ache weighted his chest and brought about a strong surge of remorse. He tore his gaze from the photo and handed the phone back to his cousin. "She's really grown up."

Caroline pocketed the cell and smiled. "She's a typical twelve-year-old. Jana said the boys are chasing after her in record numbers."

That didn't exactly surprise Brett, nor did it sit too well with him. But several years ago, he'd lost all control over his daughter's life. "Is Randy good to her?"

Caroline nodded. "He's a real good dad. Strict, but not too strict. Lacey seems to care a lot about him, but that hasn't kept her from asking about you."

That caught Brett totally off guard, though it probably shouldn't. He'd been involved in his child's life before his ex-wife remarried. Before he'd handed his kid over to another man to raise her in order to protect her from the chaos his life had become.

When a rap sounded at the door, Brett welcomed the distraction. "Come in," he called.

A security guard opened the door and cautiously peered inside, like he wasn't sure what he might be interrupting. "Mr. Taylor, there's some guy named

Andrew at the back entrance who says he knows the lady."

Caroline shot to her feet like someone had lit a fire under her backside. "That's my boyfriend. You can send him back."

The guard gave Brett a questioning look. "That okay with you?"

"Yeah." As much as he appreciated seeing his cousin, he was more than ready to get back on the road, away from the reminders of what he'd sacrificed for the sake of his career.

A few seconds later, a tall, lanky guy with sandy hair and a self-conscious smile entered the dressing room, causing Caroline's expression to brighten like a neon billboard.

For the sake of politeness, Brett stood and stuck out his hand for a shake. "Brett Taylor."

The kid looked a little shell-shocked and hesitated before accepting the offer. "Andrew Grimes."

Caroline linked her arm through his and stared up at the guy like he was the only man in the universe. "Andrew's in his first year of law school."

He was glad his cousin had hooked up with a college man who had normal aspirations, not some worthless no-account with a serious case of wanderlust. "Congratulations."

She let go of Andrew long enough to give Brett a hug. "We better get back before they lock me out of my dorm. Be careful, and call Aunt Linda, okay?"

"Okay." And he would, as soon as he had some

distance. His mom wouldn't understand how he could be this close and not pay her a visit. She'd never understood his schedule, even though she'd accepted his obsession with realizing his dream, just like she'd finally accepted that her husband was never coming back.

After the couple left, Brett closed the door behind them and rested his forehead against the facing. At times he hated this life—empty, alone, even with thousands of people worshiping him every night. Even though he had a life many men would kill for. Still, he couldn't help but wonder if the trade-off had been worth it.

CAMMIE MILLED AROUND the bus to explore while Bud dozed on the sofa. After a time, she tiptoed to the refrigerator, grabbed a soda and turned to see three of the band members filing inside.

"Get up, Bud," Pat said as he approached the couch. "We need to leave ASAP because Bull's got a craving for a double cheeseburger."

"Screw you, Pat," Bud growled.

Rusty cleared his throat and nodded toward Cammie. "We forgot there's a lady on board. Guess we'll have to tone down the language."

Cammie leaned back against the kitchen counter and smiled. "I've heard a lot worse. In fact, I'm sure I know some of the rankest jokes this side of the Mason-Dixon. Bud can attest to that. He told them to me."

"Did not," Bud said, straightening to put his boots back on. "She told me."

Typical Bud, teasing her like the big brother she'd always wished for. "Liar."

"You've got to be lying, Bud," Pat said. "I can't believe anyone with eyes like that would even know a dirty joke."

"I resent that," Cammie said. "Just because I'm a woman doesn't mean I can't handle a few off-color jokes now and then. You boys have a lot to learn."

Bull scratched his head. "I can tell."

"Where's Brett?" Rusty asked.

"Still inside the coliseum," Cammie said, not bothering to hide her disdain. "It seems he's tied up with a female fan at the moment. He informed me he needed half an hour to do whatever."

"Don't sound so surprised, Cammie," Bud said as she returned to the living area. "You'll be seeing this every now and then."

Her scorn came out in an acid look aimed at Bud. "Oh, really? I hope he practices safe sex. And I hope he can work jail into his schedule because this particular little blonde groupie looked to be a minor."

"You don't have to worry about Brett," Rusty said. "He's real careful about things. And she's got to be of age. That's the rules."

Rules. How nice. Perhaps she could see a list of the *rules* in case she might be required to screen Brett Taylor's women. That would be a really frigid day in hell. Four weeks could be a very long time if she had to tolerate this kind of behavior. Of course, she didn't expect him to live like a monk, but she'd never approved of indiscriminate sex. And like so many people, she had once held performers in very high esteem. But through painful personal experience she'd discovered they were imperfect, just like everyone else. She'd honestly hoped Brett Taylor was somehow different. Wrong again.

The guys soon left to board the other bus, with the exception of Pat, who dropped down onto the chair opposite the sofa and crossed his legs at the ankles. He gestured toward the space next to Bud. "Take a load off, Cammie, because this could take a while."

She'd rather wait outside, but out of the need to prove she could handle all aspects of life on the road—the good, bad and questionable—she claimed a place on the couch.

"I know what you're thinking about Brett," Pat began. "But this hasn't happened in a real long time. Sometimes a man just needs someone to hold."

Cammie sipped the soda, hoping to alleviate the bitter taste in her mouth. "I'm sure that's true, but I'd think road sex would get old."

"Like I said, it doesn't happen very often," Pat said. "Right, Bud?"

"Right. Brett usually stays to himself while he's touring. He's never been the same since—"

Bud and Pat exchanged a look but remained silent.

She couldn't contain her curiosity. "Since what, Bud?"

"Should I tell her?" Bud asked when Pat failed to speak.

"Might make things easier to understand," Pat said. "As long as she also understands it can't go any farther than this bus."

Could the conversation be more confusing? "You can trust me to keep my mouth shut, so just spill it."

Bud shifted several times in his seat as if the whole subject made him uncomfortable. "Brett was married once a long time ago. They were both young and his wife wasn't too keen on the touring. She pretty much left him high and dry without any warning, right about the time he signed with the record company."

Cammie couldn't mask her surprise. "I've never heard that story."

"Not many people have," Pat said. "His manager's tried hard to keep it under wraps. Brett's a real private person."

Cammie couldn't let it go without one more question. "Did he have a fondness for groupies back when he was married?"

Bud patted her leg. "No, Cam. When Brett started out, Jana was on board the bus every night along with the rest of the band. He never cheated on her."

That would be new and different. Cammie put away her sarcasm for the time being. "You're saying he's never gotten over it?"

Pat rubbed his whiskered jaw. "Not really. The night when we were celebrating his first album going platinum, he had too much to drink and he told me he nearly gave up on his music when Jana left him. Many a man probably would have, but Brett threw his grief into his songs."

That much Cammie could understand. All of it. First, suffering the loss of her parents. Later, being left alone with a trampled heart, compliments of an aspiring singer with a penchant for booze and wild women. Composing songs had proven to be great therapy.

"Most of the time Brett's okay to be around," Bud added. "But those times when he reaches a dead spot in his writing, that's when he gets really hard to live with."

Pat got up to retrieve a beer from the refrigerator and a mangled bag of corn chips from the cabinet. He sat back down and took a swig of the brew, grabbed a few chips, then passed the bag to Cammie. "It's been better since Tim, Brett's manager, convinced him to look for new writers for his material. It's taken the pressure off but he still prefers to write his own songs. And he's real good at it."

"Do you still write?" Bud asked Cammie after taking a generous handful of the snack that she'd declined.

He could have gone all year without mentioning that. "Not lately."

Pat looked at her curiously. "You write songs?"

"I was a music major in college, but songwriting is just a hobby. I've never been that great."

"Don't let this gal fool you, Pat," Bud said. "She's written some good material and she can sing like an angel. She's got as much if not more range than a lot of the female country-music performers today."

Good old Bud, always her champion. "I prefer classical to country music, Bud."

"You write damn good music," Bud said, his words barely discernable over major crunching sounds. "Whatever you want to call it."

A subject change was definitely in order. "So how long has it been since lover boy's been gone?"

Pat consulted his watch. "About fifteen minutes."

Fifteen minutes down, who knew how many more to go? Oh, joy.

A short time later, the door opened and the star strode into the cabin, looking as if he'd lost his best friend. "I'm ready to get on the road, so let's go."

"That didn't take long," Pat said. "But I guess that's what happens when a man does without for too long, then hooks up with a fresh, young thing."

Brett nailed Cammie in place with a scowl. "That fresh, young thing happens to be my cousin."

Bud barked out a laugh. "Kissing cousin?"

"You can kiss my ass, Bud." Brett sent Cammie a surprisingly apologetic look. "Sorry."

"This is ridiculous," Cammie said as she stood to leave. But before she made a quick exit, she turned back to the group and settled her gaze on Brett. "If you're through taking care of all *outstanding* business aside from the shower, I'm going to do a quick check on the bus so we can get out of here before dawn."

Once outside, Cammie breathed in the cool, crisp air and found the change of scenery did her a world of good. Even the smell of diesel was less oppressive than the testosterone parade going on inside.

She walked to the rear of the bus and lifted the hatch to aimlessly examine the inner workings as well as her opinion of Brett Taylor. Maybe he'd been telling the truth—the girl was a cousin. Maybe he was different. Maybe she should check back into reality. Regardless of his apparently devastating divorce, men like Brett Taylor reveled in female adoration and took supreme advantage of it. They could sleep their way across the country without giving it a second thought. They could discard a woman's feelings at the drop of a cowboy hat and—

"Is it going to make it to the next stop?"

The voice was as deep and clear as the night sky and held a touch of amusement. She looked up at the tall figure silhouetted against the halogen guard light to see the man she'd just burned in effigy hovering over her. She turned back to the engine and randomly tugged at a wire. "Considering the low mileage on this monster, I imagine it will make the trip with no problem. At least I hope so. My fragile little female feet might not be able to handle walking."

"I don't think anyone would consider you fragile, especially with you hunkered down in front of an engine."

Cammie straightened, faced him and fanned away a persistent moth. If only she could dismiss him as easily. "Obviously you think I have fragile ears."

"We're just trying to clean it up a little." Brett rubbed his jaw and studied her a long moment. "By the way, Bud just told me you sing."

She rolled her eyes. "I might have to kill him."

"Why?"

"Because I haven't sung in years. Wish he'd let it go."

"But he says you're good."

"Bud's biased."

"I kind of gathered that." He took off his hat and forked a hand through his dark hair. "What's the deal with you and Bud? You two seem pretty close."

Cammie blew out a frustrated breath. "He's like a brother to me. Before he came to work for you, he was a driver for my grandfather's charter business. He's known me since I was in junior high."

He settled the hat back on his head and sent her a cynical smile. "If you say so."

"I say so, and I need to finish up here." She crouched down to check the oil, hoping he'd take the hint and go away.

"That's the biggest dipstick I've ever seen," he said as he continued to loom over her. "Except for maybe Bull."

Cammie couldn't help but smile even though she

really didn't want to encourage him. After shoving the metal rod back in place, she stood and slammed down the hatch, then turned back to him. "All through and ready to go. Unless you're expecting another *cousin*."

His grin deepened. "Nope. Just me, you and the boys."

Either she was imagining things, or he'd somehow moved closer. She leaned back against the bus, feeling more than a little crowded and very conscious of his charisma.

He surveyed her face with eyes that looked incandescent, even in the dim light. "I take it you didn't like what you saw backstage."

A definite understatement. "It's really none of my business what you do in your spare time."

"But you don't approve."

He was too close for her comfort, but she couldn't move without bumping into him. "What I think about your exploits shouldn't matter to you."

"It does."

She raised an eyebrow. "Why?"

"I just think since we're going to be spending a lot of time together, we should have an understanding about some things."

"Look, if you're waiting for me to say I approve of indiscriminate sex, then you'll be standing here all night."

"Sometimes it's part of the life."

"It's a choice. And men who choose it are on the bottom of my list."

Brett took a step back and frowned. "Guess I'm treading on shaky ground here. What was his name?"

She feared Bud had revealed more than just her singing abilities. "Excuse me?"

"The man who stomped on your heart…what's his name?"

"What makes you think this has to do with some man?"

He had the gall to grin. "I can spot a wounded female from a mile away."

"I'm sure you can since you've probably left casualties all over the country."

His amused look faded into a solemn expression. "They always know going in that it's only for an hour or so, not forever."

How well she knew that concept. And how crass for him to admit it. "Do you include an autograph with your hour of undivided attention?"

He narrowed his eyes and nailed her with one heck of a smoldering look. "You don't want my autograph, do you, Camille?"

Brett Taylor was the worst kind of danger, and she wouldn't fall into that trap again. She moved around him and grabbed the rag she'd tossed on the ground before facing him again. "You sign my check. That's the only autograph I need."

"So you're saying money's all you need? I've learned from experience money isn't everything."

"I guess having what you have, you wouldn't understand what it's like to do without."

"Without what? Money?" He stared off into space as he spoke. "At times I'd gladly buy a real friend. Someone to talk to who doesn't want something from me in return. That doesn't happen too often in this business." When he returned his gaze to hers, his eyes reflected a sadness that matched his tone. "There's all kinds of doing without, most of which has nothing to do with money or sex."

She pushed her hair back from her face and tucked it behind her ears. "I didn't mean to offend you."

"No offense taken," he said. "I do choose to make a living this way, good or bad. And to set the record straight, that girl *was* my cousin. She's going to college here in Austin and dropped by to introduce me to her boyfriend. I have her phone number if you want to call and confirm it."

For the life of her, Cammie didn't understand why he even cared what she thought. Better still, why would she choose to believe him? For some reason, she did. "Fine. I'm sorry I assumed the worst."

"Apology accepted." An uneasy silence hung over them for a few moments before he pointed to her cheek. "You have some grease right there."

Her hand immediately swiped at the place he'd indicated. "Did I get it?"

"No. You're just making it worse."

As Brett reached out and rubbed the smudge with a callused thumb, Cammie tried to look away, but couldn't. He'd somehow captured her total attention with those incredible blue eyes and held her there like a captive animal. Even after he'd dropped his hand, he continued to caress her with a look as deliberate as his touch.

The sound of the opening door brought Cammie out of the momentary stupor. "Thanks," she muttered, and quickly put some much-needed distance between them, as if they'd been doing something wrong.

"Everything okay out here?" Bud asked as he rounded the bus.

She sent Brett an anxious glance and hoped she could steady her voice. "Yeah, everything's fine."

"Nice talking to you, Cammie," Brett said before he started away. "See you in the morning."

After Brett disappeared out of sight, Bud sent Cammie a serious scowl. "What's going on?"

Cammie gulped down a good dose of guilt. "Nothing's going on."

"With Brett, it's never nothing. What did he want?"

"To check out his employee." And that sounded completely suspect.

"That's what I was afraid of," Bud said. "Just keep in mind that he has one hell of a way with women."

"He wanted to see if I know my job. That's all."

Bud laughed. "Don't believe that for a minute.

When you left to come out here, he said you had to be the prettiest bus driver in all the music industry."

She could very well be the only female driver in the industry. "Oh, please. When are men going to learn to respect women for something other than looks?"

"Sorry, Cam, but you just can't take your looks for granted. They kind of slap people in the face when you enter a room, especially men. Brett's only human and he's bound to notice, but at least he's not a lowlife like that Mark Jensen."

Cammie wiped the dirt on her palms off onto her jeans, yet she couldn't wipe away the memories. "Do you think I'll run into Mark on the road?" she asked quietly.

Bud rubbed his palm over his neck and lowered his eyes. "It could happen."

She suspected he wasn't being completely forthcoming. "Could or will, Bud?"

"He's scheduled to perform in Fort Worth, so I guess it's possible you'll run into him. Can you handle that?"

"Why, of course," she said cheerfully, but not too convincingly. Coming in contact with Mark Jensen again was the last thing she needed in her life right now.

Cammie rarely thought about him, at least not fondly. He only crossed her mind when she'd seen some article heralding his success. Still, she wondered, if things had worked out, would she be touring with him now? Probably not. Mark didn't have the capacity to be faithful to one woman. If by chance she did happen to run into him, she'd face it when the time came, knowing he'd done her a favor by setting her free.

Pushing the unpleasant thoughts aside, she started toward the entrance. "Time to go, Bud. We've got to get on the road before dawn or we'll be fighting rush-hour traffic."

Bud grabbed her arm, preventing her from going inside. "Listen to me for a minute. Brett's a real good guy, but he's lived so long in this atmosphere, he doesn't know any other way. I don't want you to be caught up in another bad relationship."

Neither did she. "Do you honestly think I'm that foolish?"

"I'm just saying you need to be careful."

"I will," she said. "Nothing Brett Taylor could say or do will make me forget what I want out of life, and it's not getting involved with another high-strung singer."

Bud grinned. "That's the spirit, Cammie. And who knows, by the time I get back, maybe you'll have him whipped into shape."

An hour later, with thoughts of Brett Taylor weighing heavily on her mind, Cammie drove out of the lot hoping she hadn't made a terrible mistake.

CHAPTER THREE

BRETT LISTENED TO the steady roar of the engine, palms resting on his chest as he contemplated whether or not to get out of bed. From the look of the diffused light coming into the shaded window, he assumed it was probably early morning. He was too keyed up to rest, too frustrated to settle down. And when the phone began to ring, he decided he was too damn tired to talk to his mother.

He didn't even have to check the cell to know it was her. Only a few people had his private number. Only one of them got up with the chickens. As much as he wanted to ignore the call, putting off the conversation only delayed the inevitable lecture.

Brett fumbled for the phone, sat up on the edge of the bed and braced for the fallout from his many sins. "Hey, Mom."

"Don't you 'hey' me, Bobby Brett Taylor."

"What did I do now?" Like he didn't already know what he'd done.

"I can't believe you got so close to home and you didn't bother to stop by."

He should've known his cousin would've let the

cat out of the bag. "First of all, we got into San Antonio midafternoon. Since I had some songs to rehearse and a show to perform, that would mean by the time I made it to Kerrville, I would've had all of fifteen minutes to visit."

"That's fifteen minutes more than you've given your family in months."

Here we go again. "I'm sorry. I'll have some time at the end of the summer to come home. Or you could come to Nashville and see me."

"Who's going to take care of the ranch and the house?"

As usual, no good deed went unpunished. "You've got plenty of people to look after the horses and the house."

"I don't want to impose on them."

No surprise there. "How's everyone doing?"

"Caroline didn't catch you up?"

"We didn't talk that long."

"But she did show you the pictures from Christmas."

Obviously his cousin had set the gossip line on fire. "She showed me one picture." And that photo had disturbed his sleep the past three nights, along with the guilt that had accompanied it.

"She's asking more and more about you, honey."

He didn't have the energy to deal with that now. "Jana will handle it. She always has."

"Lacey's still your daughter, Brett."

"She thinks of Randy as her dad now. At least

that's what Jana's been saying the past seven years, and she's probably right." A fact that still wounded him to the core, even if he'd been partially responsible through his absence.

"True, he's been there for her," his mom continued after a slight pause. "But she's still legally yours, and she knows that. It's time for you to decide whether to try to rebuild a relationship with her, or let her go and sign away your rights so Randy can adopt her."

He couldn't do that even though he probably should. Maybe he hoped someday he might be in a better place where he could reconnect with her. Maybe someday she'd seek him out and want to have a relationship with him. Regardless, he wasn't ready to give her up completely. "Look, Mom, I've barely had any sleep and I have to perform again in a few hours. I can't think clearly right now, much less make any serious decisions."

"Guess some things never change," she said. "But someday soon, you're going to have to decide for your daughter's sake. She deserves that much from you."

She deserved better than him. "I'll take care of it, Mom." He wasn't sure how, but he'd figure it out later. "And hopefully I'll see you later this summer when I have a break."

"That would be real nice, son, but I'm not going to hold my breath."

After his mom hung up, Brett tried to go back

to sleep, but sleep wouldn't come. Time to take a shower and face the day. And his bus driver.

EARLY MORNING WAS Cammie's favorite time of day, when she could absorb the beauty of the passing countryside in the moments before the sun began to rise. Right then a silvery mist lingered over the landscape, giving the Texas terrain an almost heavenly quality. Considering she'd been driving for a good five hours, with two more to go, she should be exhausted. But she didn't feel the least bit tired. In fact, she experienced a strong since of serenity and calm—

The rasp of the curtain sliding open behind Cammie startled her so badly she almost jumped out of her skin and into the left lane. Even more surprising, Brett dropped down in the seat to her right. Since the night they'd left Austin, he'd barely said two words to her. And now here he was, sitting next to her and acting as if he'd never played the part of phantom passenger.

"Where are we heading?" Brett asked as he propped his bare feet on the dash.

Nice toes—her first thought. *Watch the road*— her second. "Fort Worth."

"I know, but what venue?"

She sent him a quick glance before turning her attention back to the highway. "Do you really have that much trouble keeping up with the schedule?"

"Yeah, I do. One day melts into the next until the

weeks become one big blur. It's your job to tell me when we get there and the boys let me know when it's time for me to go on."

Obviously he could use a copy of the schedule Bud had given her. "At the moment, we're just this side of Waco, which means we have about two hours before we arrive at some giant racetrack north of Fort Worth where you're scheduled to perform at approximately 1:00 p.m. to kick off a multi-act concert before a hundred thousand or so fanatical fans."

"Okay. That's probably more detail than I need to know."

"Sorry," she said. "I'm a stickler for detail."

"No kidding."

She glanced his way to catch his grin. "What's so funny?"

"Nothing. It's kind of weird having you here instead of Bud. No offense."

"None taken," she said.

"By the way, where is Bud?"

"In the other bus on his way to the airport."

"I thought he was going to Oklahoma before he headed back home."

"That was the plan before Bud's baby girl got impatient and Jeanie went into labor about thirty minutes ago." She sighed. "You know, it's hard for me to imagine Bud raising a daughter. Actually, it's hard to imagine him being a dad, although he'll probably be a good one."

"I'm sure he will."

Cammie took another quick look to see his smile had faded as he stared out the windshield. After a sudden span of silence, she welcomed the passing car full of coeds hanging out the windows and waving madly. "Looks like you've been spotted by some fans," she said.

"It happens now and then. It's like they think I'm going to pull over or something. If they saw me now they'd probably have a change of heart."

True, he hadn't shaved and his hair was mussed, but Cammie found something appealing in Brett's disheveled state. "You could probably come out wearing rags and not shave for a week and it wouldn't matter."

"You think so?"

Cammie laughed. Surely he was kidding. "I know so."

He looked at her with a sideways glance. "You could always tell when Bud didn't get enough sleep. His eyes got real bloodshot and he grumbled a lot. But not you. You look like you've had eight hours and just stepped out of the beauty parlor."

She fidgeted with the radio, more out of self-consciousness than necessity. "Thank you, I guess, but I wouldn't go quite that far. I'm used to crazy hours. I don't require much sleep. Never have."

Cammie felt a little twinge of disappointment when Brett slid out of the seat and started to the back of the bus. So much for a decent conversation.

Then, without turning around, he asked, "Can I get you something to drink?"

She looked back at him from the overhead mirror. "Yeah, I'd like that," she said, almost too enthusiastically. "Orange juice would be good."

After a time, Brett brought back a large white tumbler and set it into the drink caddy mounted on the dash. "Thanks," Cammie said, looking into his crystal-blue eyes that seemed full of amusement.

Brett reclaimed his seat. "Bud told me you used to sing backup in a band."

She didn't have the energy or the want-to to travel down memory lane. "Yes, I sang backup in a couple of bands on the Nashville club circuit. The money helped put me through college."

"That wouldn't be the real reason you took this job, would it?"

Cammie's face flushed from anger. Brett Taylor had basically accused her of hidden motives. The thought never crossed her mind to latch on to some superstar to establish a career. "That is an absolute untruth," she said through clenched teeth.

"Sorry. I didn't mean to tread on your feelings—"

"Let's just get this straight, shall we? If you think I have any other reason for sitting *temporarily* in this seat aside from doing a favor for a friend, you're wrong."

Brett came to his feet and raised both hands, palms forward. "Beg your pardon. I won't bring it up again." He quickly turned on his heels and walked away.

Cammie's shoulders slumped forward, her neck throbbed with tension. She was tired, but that was no excuse for her abrasive attitude. She'd truly wanted to know him better, and now she'd insulted him.

But singing was a subject she didn't often broach. Music only reminded her of Mark Jensen and their debacle of a relationship. Recollections of having to leave college, dashed hopes of becoming a teacher and passing on to children the only love in her life she could still count on. Regardless of the harsh memories, the biting resentment, she should learn not to take it out on other people. Especially her boss.

THEY ARRIVED AT FORT WORTH five hours before Brett was scheduled to share the stage during the day-long spring music festival with some of country music's finest. After the star left to join the band for a quick rehearsal, Cammie watched several buses bearing the names of notable singers pull into the lot. She should be excited and totally thrilled by her surroundings, but she'd been feeling a little down, maybe even a little homesick, even though she refused to give in to those emotions. Confronting Brett hadn't exactly helped her despondency, particularly when she considered she still had a month to go before she had to relinquish her duties to Bud. She really needed a good, long nap. The world would look much better then.

After a quick shower, Cammie stretched out on the berth and immediately fell asleep, only to be awakened by the sound of the door closing to Brett's stateroom. She hauled herself out of bed and immediately went to the refrigerator to take inventory. Three beers, one cola, a jar of picante sauce, a tub of cream cheese and one half-eaten sub sandwich. Slim pickings.

She tucked the cream cheese container under her chin, grabbed the soda, then rummaged through the kitchen cabinet and pulled out a box of crackers. The limited fare would have to do for now, or at least until she gathered enough energy to explore the area for some real food.

Cammie sat down at the dining table and began to spread the crackers with cheese when Pat entered, well dressed and good-smelling. "You handsome rascal. I'm surprised you made it all the way to the bus without getting assaulted."

His grin traveled all the way to his kind eyes. "You're great for an old guy's ego, Cammie. Now how much do I owe you for that one?"

She bit into the stale cracker and took a long drink to wash it down. "Not a thing. I meant every word."

Pat settled onto the couch with a skeptical grin and picked up the guitar laid out on the sofa. He began to sing a classic country love song, lifting Cammie's sullen mood with the melodic strains.

She only intended to watch, but as if the tune had molded into a chisel bent on tapping into her soul, she was unable to stop herself. Before she knew it, she'd opened her mouth to join him in a duet. Pat looked at her with amazement when she hit the first note, but never broke stride with the lyrics.

Once they ended the final chorus, Pat shook his head. "Honey, Bud said you were good, but he didn't say you were that good. You put your heart and soul into that song."

The sudden rush of memories brought about Cammie's sigh. "It was one of my mother's favorites. She used to sing along with it on the radio."

Pat's expression turned serious. "Bud mentioned the bus accident that took your parents. I'm real sorry about that."

She shrugged around the sadness. "It happened a long time ago, when I was eight. But that's the funny thing about music. Just when you think the memories have faded out of sight, you only have to hear a certain song, and it brings everything back." The good and the bad.

"Yep, you're right about that." He began to strum the guitar again. "Do you know this one?"

Cammie smiled. "Does the sun rise in the east?"

As she joined Pat again in singing another classic country hit, she realized she'd lied to Brett last night. She couldn't deny that she still deeply cared about music, but she didn't plan for it to be a major part of her life again. That would simply be too painful.

Not long after the song ended, Cammie looked up to find Brett standing in the kitchen, arms crossed over his chest, his shirt unbuttoned, hair wet, feet bare, one hip cocked against the sink.

He hesitated for another moment, then stepped forward. "What the hell was that?" he asked.

"I didn't think I was that bad," Pat answered.

Brett caught Cammie's gaze. "Was that you singing?"

"Yeah, that was me," she said as she came to her feet, fighting the urge to crawl under the table. She could feel heat radiating from her cheeks, mortified that he had actually caught her in the act.

"Try to be gentle, Brett," Pat said, seeming to sense Cammie's self-consciousness. "We have fragile egos."

"That was good" was all Brett managed before retiring back to his room.

Pat put down the guitar and stood. "You should be flattered, Cammie. He never pays too many compliments."

"Unfortunately, he's convinced I'm looking for my big break, which couldn't be farther from the truth. Guess I just got carried away."

He patted her back. "Once music's in your blood, you can't escape it. That's why an old goat like me is still going at it like he's still some young buck like Brett."

Cammie smiled. "You're not old. You sound great."

"I ain't getting any younger," he said as he headed for the exit. Before he left, he paused and turned to her again. "Just a few words of advice from someone who's been around the block a time or twelve. Don't let life pass you by without getting what you want, Cammie. Grab those dreams and let 'em take you where they will. Before you're past your prime and it's too late."

Grab some dreams.

It suddenly occurred to her she didn't really have any dreams. She didn't believe in forever relationships, or in fate falling into your lap, at least in most cases. She didn't believe she was destined to do great things, or to find great love. One day at a time seemed appropriate for now, the only option she had at the moment. Dreams only led to disappointment.

Cammie glanced at her watch to find it was almost showtime and Brett clearly wasn't close to being ready to perform. But he had shown her a side of himself she hadn't seen before, and couldn't seem to forget.

Ridiculous. It wasn't as if he'd walked in naked, but it was the next best thing. She had tried not to notice the light shading of hair on his sternum or his ridged abdomen that sported some kind of tattoo. She certainly hadn't intended to glimpse his zipped but not buttoned fly. And she had to admit he looked incredibly sexy with wet hair.

Best to concentrate on something else besides

those images. Anything else. She dropped down on the couch, turned on the TV with the remote and surfed through the channels. Unfortunately, all she found were sitcom reruns, an ancient Western and a televangelist with his very own 900 number urging all sinners to call. Then there was the buxom blonde and burly lifeguard lying on a beach in the clutches of passion—definitely not advisable to watch.

Then something else called to her. She switched off the television, walked to the berth reserved for her stay and pulled a bag from the cabinet underneath. She took out a ringed binder, its black cover once textured now worn smooth. The notebook had been many a mile with her and held several compositions she'd been working on over the years, none completely finished.

She turned to the latest page—her most recent endeavor—a song she'd started in her head while driving a busload of elderly women and men to a tour of Graceland. The lyrics jolted not only her mind but her heart. Although the title inferred happiness, it was about the pain of loss and the search for love.

The melody frequently played in her head, calling to her to be put down on paper. Again forgetting she wasn't exactly alone, she softly sang the chorus.

"'Seeing you in my dreams most every day is the price I've had to pay for loving you. Someday I'll reach my destiny and I'll no longer find thoughts of you still burdening my mind. That's when I'll be on the road to getting over you....'"

She quickly clamped her mouth shut when she sensed his presence. No doubt Brett believed she'd meant for him to hear her sing.

Cammie slammed the binder closed but failed to raise her eyes from the notebook. "I didn't know you were there."

"You don't have to stop on my account," he said quietly. "That was real pretty, ma'am."

"It's mediocre at best," she said, still not brave enough to venture a look at him in case he was in a state of undress.

"Mediocre? Anyone who sings like you doesn't come close to mediocrity." He sat down beside her on the tiny bed, leaned forward and rested his elbows on his knees, his hands laced together. "And about earlier today, I didn't mean anything by what I said about you trying to be discovered. I was kidding. Bud told me you had a sense of humor."

"I do. Most of the time." She ventured a glance and a weak smile. He was already dressed in a navy blue neatly pressed shirt and blue jeans, his trademark black hat resting brim-up between them. "I'm a little touchy when it comes to music. Sorry I jumped down your throat."

"You're not the first and you won't be the last." He pointed to the binder. "Are those songs?"

"Yeah. My decrepit book of dreams."

Brett smiled so gently it took her aback. "When I have a chance, will you let me look at those?"

"Take my word for it, you aren't missing anything."

"Why don't you let me decide?"

She studied the front of the binder to avoid his scrutiny. Then he touched her.

It was no more significant than a lift of her chin so she would again meet his eyes. But when he dropped his fingertips, the area tingled with the memory of that simple gesture.

"I don't know why, but for some reason you don't understand your talent," Brett said. "Now, it's not my place to say what you should or shouldn't do, but I'd continue to work real hard on that last song. It's got *hit* written all over it."

Cammie looked at him with doubt, just a bit afraid of her sudden awareness of him, every little nuance, including his aftershave. "You don't have to humor me, Brett."

He grinned, exposing perfect white teeth. "That's the first time you've called me by my name, Cammie. And now that we've been properly introduced, I'll go to work." He pushed off the bed, put on the hat and adjusted it low on his brow. "You'll still be here when I get back?"

An odd question. "Of course. Nothing better to do."

"I don't know. A girl as pretty as you just might run off with one of my fellow performers. Mark Jensen's bus is parked on the other side of the band's."

Cammie's heart grew stone cold at the mention

of his name. Bud had warned her this would happen, but she needed more time to prepare, to gather some courage. If she was lucky, they'd leave before Mark realized she was there.

"Really?" Her voice sounded hoarse and tentative.

Brett frowned. "You okay, Cammie?"

"I'm fine."

He walked toward the door and paused to face her again. "Are you sure? You look a little rattled. But I guess Mark Jensen's been known to have that effect on the ladies."

Talk about the pot calling the kettle black. If he only knew what she really thought of Mark Jensen. "You're going to be late, Mr. Taylor. If you don't leave, there might be some rumors started about us."

"I can think of worse things than that." He smiled and tipped his hat.

So could Cammie—turning the rumors into reality.

A sudden image of Brett kissing her played out in her mind. How foolish to imagine something so absurd. He wouldn't be interested in a woman who drove buses and had reached a total stalemate in her life. And she wouldn't be interested in a singer who had women falling all over him every day of the week.

She'd already had enough bad experiences with one talent too many. It would take a lot more than a little innuendo from a certified living legend to lead her to believe Brett Taylor would be any different.

"DON'T LOOK NOW, but here comes trouble."

In response to Pat's comment, Brett glanced toward the edge of the white tent set up behind the outdoor stage. Yeah, trouble was heading their way in the form of Mark Jensen, an up-and-coming singer with a huge ego to match his big mouth. He wore a sleeveless T-shirt revealing a roadmap of tattoos snaking up both arms, a camouflage baseball cap and a cocky expression as he arrived at the semicircle of chairs where the band had gathered after the concert.

"Great show, Taylor." Jensen surprisingly offered his hand.

Brett reluctantly accepted the handshake, but he damn sure wasn't going to stand. "Thanks. Didn't see yours." Intentional on his part.

"It turned out pretty good," he said. "Oh, and I also wanted to say I'm sorry I knocked you off the top spot with my number one."

So much for courtesy. "Well, after hanging in there for seven weeks, it was bound to happen."

"We could go celebrate with a cold one in my new bus."

Brett figured from the look of the jerk's glassy eyes, he'd already had a few too many cold ones. "No, thanks. We're going to be heading out shortly."

Jenson pulled up a canvas chair and sat without an invitation. "You don't know what you're missing. My rig's custom, right down to the surround sound. It's pretty sweet."

"Brett's got that setup, too," Rusty chimed in. "But I bet he has one thing you don't have."

Mark looked skeptical. "I doubt that."

"Do you have a good-lookin' female bus driver?" Bull asked.

Jensen frowned. "No way that's the truth."

Rusty grinned. "Yeah, way. And she can sing, too."

The whole conversation gave Brett an uneasy feeling. "Drop it, guys."

"Brett's right," Pat joined in. "Cammie's a professional and she should be treated like one."

That seemed to get Jensen's complete attention. "Cammie?"

"Short for Camille," Bull said.

Jensen rubbed his scruffy chin. "She sounds damn interesting. Might have to check her out in case you're pullin' my leg."

Brett had an urge to knock the smirk off the bastard's face. "Leave her alone, Jensen."

When Mark grinned, pushed out of the chair and headed toward the parking lot, Brett came to his feet, intent on following him.

"Sit back down, Brett," Pat said. "If you don't, then you're headin' for a fight. You bruise your knuckles, you can't play. You break your nose, you ain't gonna be as pretty."

He never looked for a fight, but sometimes they found him, anyway. "I don't trust that guy, and I'm going to make sure he doesn't mess with Cammie."

Bull laughed. "Cammie can take care of herself, Brett. And she'll be real pissed off if you charge in there to defend her honor."

"I doubt she'll even open the door to him," Rusty said. "In fact, when I went to ask her if she wanted to join us, she was sound asleep."

Brett realized they had a point. Cammie was probably still sleeping, and she could put Jensen in his place with just a look if she wasn't. Besides, he didn't want to suffer her wrath if he made a misstep in the macho department. For those reasons, he reclaimed the chair. He'd give it five minutes, and then he'd go check on her, even if it made her mad.

CHAPTER FOUR

CAMMIE WOKE UP mad as a hornet, thanks to some heavy-duty knocking that nearly startled her out of the bunk. She made her way to the cab in a fog and opened the door, expecting to find Brett waiting to gain entry. She couldn't be more wrong. The man appearing at the bottom of the steps would send some women into the kind of hysterics reserved for the naive starstruck. But she knew what resided behind the disarming smile and dark green eyes. Those attributes only served as a shell for the arrogant singer who had an affinity for booze and—as he'd termed it—broads.

"Hey, darlin'."

At the sound of the familiar and unwelcome endearment, Cammie's frame went as rigid as the gearshift. "What are you doing here, Mark?"

He scaled one step and tried on his patent grin. "Come on, Cammie. That's no way to greet your boyfriend."

"Ex-boyfriend." Heavy emphasis on ex.

Without the slightest hesitation, he scaled the second step and entered the bus. "Just thought we'd have a little visit for old times' sake."

She had no desire to repeat a past she'd vowed to forget. "I have nothing to say to you, so please leave."

Blatantly ignoring Cammie's request, Mark brushed past her, walked into the living area and sat on the sofa, as if he had a right to be there.

He sized up the area a few moments before turning his gaze back to her. "Not too bad, but it's not as good as my rig."

Arrogant jackass. "Then I suggest you return to your rig and let me get this rig ready to roll."

Mark removed his cap, set it aside on the sofa and forked a hand through his gold-blond hair. "No need to rush, darlin.' Your boss is havin' a little party in the hospitality tent with his band. That gives us plenty of time to talk, or whatever else we might want to do."

Cammie wanted to scream from frustration. "Again, I don't care to talk to you, and 'whatever' is definitely out of the question."

The smile disappeared and his expression turned stone cold. "Still a little prissy, aren't you? Always just a little bit too good for me."

Obviously his insecurities still existed, masked by his overinflated ego. "No, Mark, I'm a lot too good for you. So why don't you run along and grab a groupie."

He reached up, caught her arm and dragged her

down beside him. She smelled the overpowering scent of whiskey as he placed his lips to her ear. "Why don't we take up where we left off?"

Cammie shifted all the way to the end of the couch, putting some much-needed distance between them. "Not on your life."

He turned and faked a pout. "Now, you don't mean that."

"Oh, yes, I do."

"Don't you think you at least owe me an explanation as to why you ran out on me without even giving me a reason?"

She tapped her chin and pretended to think. "Let's see. I believe her name was Sandy, or maybe it was Sheila. Of course, we can't forget Bethany and that tall, skinny blonde whose name escapes me. I believe that's enough reasons, don't you?"

He streamed a fingertip down her arm. "Well, sweetheart, since you weren't putting out, I had to find someone who would."

And she had no regrets that she hadn't let the relationship go that far. "I wasn't about to sleep with you after learning I'd have to take a number."

"Those girls didn't mean anything to me, Cam," he said.

She wanted to laugh. "You're a creative person, Mark. Surely you can come up with a more original line. Better still, let's just pretend we never happened. Now if you'll excuse me, I have things to do."

She glanced toward the hall and decided that

going into the bathroom would be the best move.
Even if he didn't immediately depart, he'd probably grow impatient and finally take the hint, or get
tossed out by one of the guys. At least that's what
she hoped would happen.

But as she stood, he again grabbed her hand and
pulled her back down, this time into his arms. "I'm
not done with you yet, Camille."

Cammie felt trapped and anxious. He'd never
been violent, at least not with her, but when he drank
excessively, he tended to become easily agitated.
Only one of the many reasons she'd broken off their
relationship. "You're hurting me, Mark." Her voice
sounded tentative, shaky, and she hated that.

"I won't hurt you, baby. I'll make you feel real
good."

Before she could wrest out of his grasp, he tried
to kiss her. She had enough wherewithal to clamp
her mouth shut and turn her face away. "I mean it,
Mark. Leave now, or you'll wish you had."

"I'm not leaving until I get what I came here for,"
he said. "What you wouldn't let me have when we
were together."

Fear prompted her fight-or-flight response when
he began to work the buttons of her shirt. She managed to shove his hands away, at least for the time
being. "I said no, and I mean no."

He pushed her back on the couch and hovered
over her, looking larger and more menacing than

she remembered. "Come on, darlin'. You know you want it as bad as I do."

Anger kicked in along with a spurt of adrenaline. She would not allow this to happen. He'd have to knock her senseless before she'd let him touch her again.

Cammie bit down hard on Mark's shoulder the minute he moved on top of her, and when she lifted her knee and hit the intended target, he slapped her face with the back of his hand, sending a pain shooting all the way to the top of her head.

"Get off her!"

Cammie felt the pressure of Mark's body lift away right before she saw Brett backing Mark up against the refrigerator, one arm pressed against Mark's throat.

"What in the hell do you think you're doing, you son of a bitch?" Brett hissed.

"I know her, Taylor." He looked back at Cammie with a provocative grin. "Real well."

When Brett glanced over his shoulder, looking for confirmation, Cammie had no choice but to tell him the truth. "We *knew* each other, but that was a long time ago, and he's not welcome in my life anymore."

Brett turned back to Mark. "Do you want me to call the police, Cammie?"

Did she? No. She couldn't afford to invite a scandal into Brett's life and end the job before it had barely started. "Not this time, as long as he promises to never come near me again."

"You heard the lady," Brett said. "The next time you pull a stunt like this, I'll turn what's left of you over to the law. Understood?"

When Mark grumbled a halfhearted acknowledgment, Brett released him and shoved him toward the door. "Now get the hell out of here and don't ever come back again."

Mark picked up his cap from the floor, slapped it across his thigh and gave Cammie a suggestive wink. "Later, darlin'."

Once he was gone, Cammie collapsed against the cushions and released a ragged breath. The tears she'd been determined to keep at bay rolled down her cheeks, regardless of her determination to stop them.

Brett sat beside her and surveyed her face. "Did he hurt you?"

With great effort, she swallowed a sob. "It's nothing."

"He slapped you. I don't consider that nothing."

After swiping at the latent tears, she made an effort to smooth her tousled hair. "I don't want to talk about it."

He softly touched the tender area on her cheek left by Mark's hand. "I don't know a hell of a lot about Jensen, but I don't like what I saw just now. Do you really know him?"

"Yeah, I know him."

"How well?"

Cammie shot off the couch and walked to the kitchen sink. "Well enough to steer clear of him."

"And you let him in here?"

"He didn't give me much choice." She drew some water into a plastic cup, took a quick drink and dumped the rest into the sink. Then she turned and leaned back against the counter. "I knew him back in Nashville when he was playing the club circuit."

Brett stood but remained planted in the same spot. He looked as if he wanted to say something but stayed silent.

"Anyway," Cammie continued, "I haven't seen him in about four years. I was afraid I might run into him while we were on the road, but I didn't expect it quite this soon. He's always been a drinker, and aggressive when he drinks, when it comes to fighting. But I've never seen him act that way before."

Brett pulled a bandanna from his back pocket and handed it to her. "He might have more than booze on board."

She wiped the moisture from beneath her eyes. "What do you mean?"

He shrugged. "He could be on speed or sleeping pills or painkillers. Whatever he thinks he needs to get by in this atmosphere. It happens."

"But not with you?"

He sighed. "I used to drink to cope when I first started out, but Pat set me straight before it got too out of hand. I know my limits, and that's a beer every now and then. No hard stuff, and no more than two."

She suspected his drinking resulted from his divorce. Not that she dared to seek confirmation. "I'm happy for you, and sad for Mark if that's what he's doing. He's not a bad guy, but he does have a sense of entitlement. He always has."

Brett took off his hat and tossed it onto the dining table. "Whatever's going on with him, I'm just real sorry this happened to you."

"It wasn't your fault, Brett. It's mine for opening the door to him."

He lowered his eyes. "It's the band's fault he knows you're here."

"How's that?" she asked, although she had her suspicions.

"The guys were braggin' about you when Mark stopped by the hospitality tent," he said. "We didn't know he knew you and he never even let on. He just smiled and said he'd catch us later." Brett raised his gaze to hers, his blue eyes full of remorse. "I swear, Cammie, if I'd known about the two of you, I would've never let him get near you."

Unsure how to respond to the revelation without sounding ungrateful, Cammie pushed past Brett and straightened the throw pillows that had found their way to the floor during Mark's sick attempts at seduction. "Are the guys on their way?"

"Yeah. We've got a crew coming in to service the buses while we have dinner. Then we'll come back here and move the buses to the hotel. I'll bunk with Pat and you can have my room."

"That won't be necessary," she said. "I can sleep on the bus."

"It's already been arranged, so I don't want any argument. You could use a good night's sleep on a regular bed before we hit the road again. It's going to be a long haul for the next couple of weeks."

The thought of sleeping on a full-size mattress did sound appealing. "Thanks. I appreciate it."

The sound of familiar voices drifted through the door as the band members filed in, looking more than a little concerned. "What in the hell happened between you and Jensen?" Bull asked when they moved into the living area.

Brett sent a brief glance in Cammie's direction. "He's drunk and he got out of hand."

"He says you bit the hell out of him, Cammie," Rusty added. "My question is, what did he do to warrant that?"

When Cammie looked away, everyone went completely silent.

"He didn't hurt you, did he?" Pat asked.

"I handled it," Brett answered. "Cammie's okay now and I don't think she wants to talk about it."

Rusty stepped forward, hands balled into fists at his side. "I'll kill the son of a bitch if he ever lays a hand on you again. That goes for all of us."

Cammie drew a deep breath and exhaled slowly.

"Thanks, but I don't think we'll have to worry about him anymore. Brett set him straight."

Pat laid a gentle hand on her shoulder. "Since Brett seems to have everything under control, we're going to go get cleaned up now and we'll meet you both outside in a bit."

Brett checked his watch. "The limo should be here in about thirty minutes."

Limo? "Sounds great," she said. "That should be enough time to get my stuff together." She needed to get herself together.

When Brett retired to his stateroom to shower, and the guys left, Cammie opened the small closet that contained the few items of clothing she'd brought with her, basics consisting of comfortable jeans, shorts and T-shirts. But for some reason she wanted something a little dressy. She pulled out a pair of her better jeans and a red silk sleeveless blouse, then retrieved her black leather jacket.

She smiled when she remembered what her grandfather had called the outfit. "Biker duds" came out of his mouth the first time she'd worn it. Then he admitted it turned too many of the drivers' heads and forbade her to work in it.

Well, tonight she wasn't working. She was going out to dinner with friends and she was going looking like a woman, not a long-haul truck driver.

After Cammie dressed and applied some makeup, she called for Brett. When he didn't respond, she grabbed her purse and headed out the door. Dusk had settled onto the dusty grounds, the March evening relatively cool for Texas. She spotted her escorts among several of the road crew assembled at the rear of the band's bus.

She faked a smile as she joined the group, determined not to let the harrowing experience dampen her spirits. "I'm ready."

When she failed to receive a response, for a moment she worried she'd forgotten some vital article of clothing.

"Close your mouth, Jeremy," Pat said.

Bull let out a whistle and Rusty let out his breath.

"What's wrong?" she asked.

Brett gave her a slow once-over and an even slower smile. "You're wearing leather."

Nothing like stating the obvious. "Haven't you ever seen a girl in leather before?"

"Yeah, Cammie," Pat replied. "We've seen lots of girls in leather. Leather pants, leather boots, all kinds. We just haven't seen you in leather. And it does become you."

Rusty slapped a palm to his forehead. "Damn. My wife drove in from Lubbock today with Bull's girlfriend and they're meeting us at the restaurant. I don't know how to explain you to her."

"What about me?" Bull asked. "Bonnie's the jealous type and she has one hell of an imagination."

Cammie certainly didn't want to get off on the wrong foot with their significant others. "I'll change."

"You don't have to," Brett said. "I'll tell them you're with me."

"Good thinking," Pat added. "But why can't we tell them she's with me?"

Brett slapped Pat on the back. "Because they'd never believe it."

Cammie came up with a more logical plan. "How about we tell them the truth?"

Pat shook his head. "We'll ease them into it gently, after they get to know you. A woman on board a bus, even if she's driving, could be a cause for concern for wives and girlfriends."

On some level, Cammie understood that issue when it came to this way of life. On the other, she wasn't the kind to tread on another woman's territory. Hopefully she could convince them of that.

After they climbed into the awaiting limo, Cammie squeezed into the seat between Pat and Brett. No one said much as they made their way to the historical Fort Worth Stockyards. When Pat poured himself a shot of whiskey from the onboard bar, then leaned back against the headrest, Cammie noticed he looked exhausted. The schedule would do that to anyone, even those much younger than the band's senior member.

"Hate black limos," Pat said, shattering the quiet. "Reminds me of a funeral."

Brett came back with, "My mistake. Next time we'll get white. Will that keep you from bitchin'?"

"Hell, no. White limos remind me of weddings, just about the same thing as a funeral."

The other band members continued to silently stare out the window, as if they didn't have the energy to comment. Cammie recognized the "coming down" phase common after a performance. But past experience had taught her it didn't take much to recharge a man's batteries. Especially a walking testament to testosterone like Brett.

She was extremely aware of him at the moment, and uncomfortable over his nearness. Yet when his hand inadvertently brushed hers, she found herself wishing he'd leave it. She wrote off the feelings to gratitude. After all, he'd gotten her out of a jam. Only gratitude.

When Pat announced, "We're here," Cammie glanced out the window. The limousine slowly passed by a stucco restaurant where a line of waiting patrons snaked around the building. The driver stopped the car near the back alley, well beyond the entrance, most likely to avoid calling too much attention to their arrival. The group exited the limo and entered a patio that reportedly led to the private quarters reserved for the group. Brett lowered his head as they strode through the crowded dining room. Most of the people didn't bother to look up from their food long enough to notice the group, but Cammie noticed several who obviously recognized him—or at least that he was *somebody*—indicated by fingerpointing and subtle whispers.

Nevertheless, they managed to sneak by with very little attention as they entered the secluded dining room. The man that approached them first was as wide as he was tall, an unlit cigar butt protruding from the corner of his mouth. "Brett, my boy, how are you doing?"

"Can't complain, Tim," Brett said as he shook the man's offered hand.

Brett gestured toward Cammie. "This is Cammie, Bud's temporary replacement. Cammie, this is my manager, Tim Braker."

"Good to know you, Cammie." His eyes crinkled at the corners when he smiled as he took her hand and patted it. "My, my. Brett's description of you was pretty accurate, but it certainly didn't do you justice."

Cammie felt her face flush. "Thank you," she murmured.

"Let's eat," Brett said, tugging at his collar.

Brett pulled out the chair next to his for Cammie, then introduced her to Bull's girlfriend, Bonnie, with a petite stature and short brown hair, and Karen, Rusty's wife, whose long auburn tresses nearly matched her husband's. They both seemed very personable and happy to meet her, at least for the moment.

The informal atmosphere and lively conversation was as satisfying as the spicy fajitas and tart margaritas that came to the table in endless quantities. Cammie settled for a soda and ate sparingly while the guys, in typical male unmannerly fashion, dug in like it was their first meal in days or their last on earth. After the food had been cleared, the men gathered in the corner of the room to talk business, while Karen and Bonnie claimed the two chairs opposite Cammie.

"So, Cammie, have you been on Brett's bus yet?" Karen asked.

Let the inquisition begin. "Yes, I have."

"You poor thing," Bonnie said. "When anyone sees a woman within a hundred yards, they think maid service has arrived."

"So far that hasn't been a problem." And it wouldn't be if she had any say in the matter.

Bonnie folded her hands on the table. "When did you meet Brett?"

"Not long ago."

"Did you meet him at a concert?" Karen asked.

She could see where this was heading, and she saw no reason to go there. "Look, just to set the record straight, I'm Bud's replacement driver. The guys were worried that you might be concerned since I'm a woman. But rest assured, my only intent is to provide a ride for Brett." Surely she hadn't just said that. "I meant, I'm a professional driver. I can even drive with my foot in my mouth."

The women exchanged a look, then fortunately laughed. If Cammie could run out of the room without being too obvious, she would.

"I guess I can understand the guys' concerns," Bonnie said. "If I hadn't met you, I might have had my reservations. But you don't seem like the predator type."

Cammie smiled with relief. "Thanks. I just couldn't go on pretending I'm one of Brett Taylor's girlfriends, according to the plan."

"What a horrible thing to imagine," Karen said. "But if you ask me, Brett definitely appeared to be enjoying the make-believe. He couldn't seem to take his eyes off you during dinner."

She couldn't exactly dispute Karen's observations. She had noticed a few glances now and then. "Brett was just trying to help out his friends," she said. "There's nothing else to it."

"We'll see," Bonnie added. "We might trust our boys, but Brett's another story. Never underestimate his power over women."

Nor should anyone underestimate her self-control. "I can handle him for a couple of months."

Karen leaned over and patted her hand. "You just keep telling yourself that and you'll be fine."

When her phone began to chime, Cammie fished the cell from her purse and saw Bud's name on the incoming text. She opened it to find a photograph of a tiny, round-faced newborn wearing a pink knit cap, her tiny fist balled against her chest like a miniature prizefighter. And below that, a simple, poignant message.

Meet Emma Jane Parker. I hope she does the name proud.

Cammie's hand immediately went to her mouth to cover the slight gasp, earning her concerned looks from her companions.

"Is something wrong?" Karen asked.

"Not at all," she said as she turned the phone around for the girls to view the photo. "Bud's got a new baby girl, and he named her after my grandmother."

Both Karen and Bonnie spent a few minutes mooning over the picture before Karen took the phone over for the guys' inspection. And as usual, they had to endure the male "all babies look alike" comments. Yet Brett never even afforded the photo a passing glance before he turned his back on the crowd.

When Karen returned with the phone, Cammie decided to ask about her boss's suspect behavior. "Does Brett have an aversion to kids? He wouldn't even look at the baby's picture."

"Should we tell her?" Bonnie asked Karen.

"As long as she keeps it to herself," Karen said.

Cammie geared up for yet another major revelation. "Tell me what?"

"Brett has a daughter," Bonnie said.

Clearly she'd only scratched the surface of the star's secrets. "Bud and Pat mentioned he'd been married, but they didn't say anything about a daughter."

Karen sighed. "It's been kept quiet to keep her out of the limelight. Unfortunately, he hasn't seen her in several years."

Cammie couldn't fathom a parent not having a relationship with their child. Not when she'd lost both her parents through a sad twist of fate. "And he's okay with that?"

"His wife has full custody and she hasn't made it easy on him," Bonnie said. "Or at least that's what Doug told me."

When Karen cleared her throat, Cammie glanced back to see Rusty stumbling toward the table. He came up behind his wife and leaned to kiss her cheek. "Is my girl ready to go?"

Karen rolled her eyes as she stood. "Three shots of tequila and you're out, as usual. No more liquor for you, mister."

"I can handle my tequila, wife." Rusty turned around and immediately tripped over the leg of a chair.

"It's been nice meeting you, Cammie," Karen said as she attempted to steady her husband. "I'm flying into California next month. I'll see you then."

Bonnie stood and pushed her chair under the table. "I need to go, too. I'll round up Doug so we can put an end to this party. I'm sure you'd like to get some rest."

She wasn't sure she would rest considering the

disturbing discovery. "It's been great meeting you, too. I hope to see you again before I head home."

After a round of goodbyes, Cammie followed Brett, Pat and Jeremy into the awaiting limo for the somewhat silent return trip. When they arrived back at the bus, Brett announced he was going to accompany her to the hotel.

"That's not necessary," Cammie said as the limo came to a stop. "I can find my way there."

"Now, Cammie," Pat began in a fatherly tone, "Dennis has already gone and we'd feel a whole lot better if someone went with you, especially after what happened with Jensen."

She had to admit that seemed like a good plan. "All right, if you insist."

When they arrived at the bus's entrance, Cammie immediately spotted the folded note taped to the door. She yanked the paper down before Brett beat her to it.

We got off to a bad start tonight, but I'll be back to finish it. Mark

Thoroughly disgusted, she crumpled the paper into a tiny ball, stuffed it into her pocket and hurried inside the bus to take her place behind the wheel.

Brett followed behind her and claimed the passenger seat. "Is it from Jensen?"

"Yes."

"What did it say?"

Did she dare tell him? Yes, she should. From this point forward, she intended to keep him informed of Mark's plans. "He said he's coming back to finish what he's started."

Brett scowled. "He better not be serious unless he's in the mood for an ass-whoopin'."

Cammie started the bus and internally cringed over Mark's threat. "Who knows what he'll do? Come to think of it, I never really knew him at all."

"Do you want to talk about it?"

She shifted until she faced Brett. "Not really. There's not a whole lot left to say."

"Fine, but if you ever want to talk, I'm here."

What she really wanted to do was forget the ugly episode. Forget Mark, period. Forget she'd been mistaken to think he was out of her life.

She left the seat to retrieve her overnight bag from the small overhead bin and prepared to gather a few things. Brett showed up a few seconds later and leaned a shoulder against the divider, watching her cram clothing from the drawer underneath her berth into the tote with the force of a jackhammer into cement.

She stopped her reckless packing long enough to look at him straight on. "Maybe I should reconsider working for you. Mark could cause a lot of trouble."

He picked up a pink bra that had fallen to the floor and handed it to her. She tried not to meet his gaze, but she knew he was smiling when she quickly stuffed it into the case.

"We won't be running into him that often," he said. "Besides, he sounds pretty determined. If he really wants to find you, he won't stop until he does. You might as well be running around the country with five guys looking after you."

Cammie smiled in spite of her melancholy mood. "I guess you're right."

She headed into the bathroom, slipped a few toiletries into the bag, and when she returned, she found Brett still rooted in the same spot. "All through here," she said. "Feel free to pack while the bus warms up. I'll wait until you're finished."

"Good idea." He started toward his stateroom and when they tried to pass each other, they moved in the same direction twice. Cammie finally turned to one side and made a sweeping gesture toward his room. "Go ahead."

Brett grinned, showing his smile to full advantage. "Thought for a minute there we might dance."

Cammie couldn't help but smile back. His eyes sparkled with sheer amusement. Gorgeous blue, blue eyes. She truly wanted to see what was behind those eyes, but there was nothing transparent about them except the color. She suspected she'd never know the real man behind the star, even if she had learned a little more about his past tonight.

He started down the corridor but stopped midway to face her again. "I'm glad you're here, Cammie."

She felt as if she'd just won a commendation. "Thanks."

When she drove into the hotel's rear parking lot a few moments later, Brett surprised her by asking if she wanted to have a nightcap with him in the bar. She surprised herself by agreeing, putting on the brakes a little harder than intended when the word *Yes* leaped out of her mouth like a jackrabbit. She hadn't given the request a second thought until it was too late to reconsider.

He slipped out of his seat and stepped into the living area without a comment about her nearly throwing them through the windshield. She tapped her forehead against the steering wheel, hoping to bang some sense into her foolish brain.

"First, my disguise," Brett said from behind her. She joined him at the sofa, wondering if he would don a fake nose or beard.

Instead, he removed his cowboy hat, placing it meticulously on the sofa, upturned so as not to flatten the brim. Then he walked to his room and, instead of a mask, came back carrying a folded T-shirt. He stripped off his tailored shirt and tossed it onto the couch next to his hat. Now bare from the waist up, he took his time unfolding the replacement. All too aware of his state of undress, Cammie couldn't help but stare. Biceps and triceps and six-packs. Oh, my.

She centered her attention on the raven tattoo that looked exactly like the one on the bus, only this one spanned his right side and its wing dipped into his waistband. But she didn't get to inspect it for long before he pulled the tee over his head. Why was he doing this to her? Maybe his actions were some sort of a trial run, a test to see how well she could hold up under pressure. She was flunking the test.

After she felt she could speak without sounding like a boy in the midst of puberty, she pointed to the silkscreen bull rider on the front of his shirt. "Have you ever done that?"

Brett flipped open his belt buckle and, at the same time, her heart rolled in her chest like an accomplished gymnast. "I climbed on a bull's back a few times when I was young and stupid. In fact, I got the raven tattoo in honor of the first bull I stayed on for the required eight seconds. He was mean and black and named Raven."

She prayed he hadn't noticed how unwound she was at the moment, then inwardly scolded herself for believing he was about to make some flagrant pass—and mentally chided herself for realizing she wouldn't mind if he did.

When she heard the rasp of his zipper, her face heated up. But she wasn't so mortified that she avoided watching him tuck in his shirt.

"Anyway, I ran the rodeo circuit for several years," he said as if he hadn't noticed her morbid fascination. "But I ended up choosing something a little less dangerous than bull riding."

Cammie bit the inside of her mouth in an attempt to concentrate on the exchange as he redid his belt. "You chased rodeo queens?"

He grinned. "Mostly I chased cows. I was a calf roper. That's where I got this." He pointed to the silver oval on his belt. "My lucky buckle."

Cammie took a quick glance at the buckle, then clucked disapprovingly. "A cruel sport."

Brett shrugged and splayed one large hand in front of her face. "The livestock always fared better than I did. I got this little souvenir from a rope burn. Almost lost a couple fingers."

She studied the wide scar that spread across the length of his right palm and snaked between his thumb and forefinger. She also noted a few calluses, trademarks of a guitar player. Then, as if her body had developed its own will, she reached out and slowly ran her fingertip over the raised flesh, tracing the wound's path.

Cammie looked into his eyes, as if she'd become someone else—someone totally disconnected from her physical self. Brett seemed just as shocked by her gesture, but he didn't take his hand away.

As far as she knew, there was no correlation between touching a man's scar and a woman's mouth going completely dry. But at the moment she felt parched, her tongue as scratchy as a cat's. She rejoined with reality, swallowed hard. "Impressive, but you'll get no sympathy from me."

He smiled and dropped his hand. "Should've known you'd feel that way."

Cammie shifted her weight from one foot to the

other. "So whatever possessed you to ride a bull the first time?"

"Someone dared me."

"Do you still do things on a dare?" Her tone was provocative, so much so she wanted to rip her scratchy cat's tongue clean out of her mouth for being so obvious. For heaven's sake, she was flirting like an adolescent. She didn't believe in playing games, just tell-it-like-it-is honesty. She didn't flirt. Or she hadn't in quite some time.

He gave her a half smile. "Did you have a dare in mind?"

Cammie's chest tightened, her pulse skittered. "I like to know what motivates people."

Brett dropped down in the chair before her, leaned back and laced his fingers behind his head, looking one-hundred-percent-all-American-and-proud-of-it cowboy. "I'm all yours, Camille. Tell me what you want to know and then I'll tell you what motivates me."

The only thing she wanted to know right now was how he'd managed to reduce her to absolute feminine frailty by exposing his chest and presenting a wound for her inspection.

Mark's ability to entice a woman involved mostly verbal coaxing. He'd worn her down with pretty words. Brett was a man of few words and, she suspected, many unspoken talents. She'd never believed that someone could radiate sensuality like a full-blast furnace with only a look, but he could. Gentle persuasion came to mind. Not forceful, not over-bearing and loud, like Mark.

Now, why would she keep comparing him to Mark? She shouldn't be comparing him to anyone. She shouldn't be standing there, about to throw her-self into a situation that could lead to the most in-advisable move she'd ever made.

As Cammie nervously toyed with the buttons on her jacket, Brett visually followed the movement. "I'm not normally so nosy," she added. "Really, you don't have to answer all my questions. I'm sure you get tired of answering questions."

"Do you, Cammie?" His voice was pleasantly toxic.

"Do I what?" Her voice was unnaturally high.

Brett leaned forward and rested his arms on his thighs. "Do things on a dare. Do you ever take chances, Camille Carson?"

"When I turned eighteen, I got a tattoo." Lord, she'd lost her mind. But she didn't want him to think she was a total loser.

"Where and what?" he asked.

"It's a rose and it's in a place no one can see." If he asked to see it, she'd come totally unglued.

He only smiled. "Interesting."

She had the strongest urge to lean over and place her hands atop his arms. "Anyway, I'm pretty much over my daredevil days."

Brett stood and brushed a fingertip across her

cheek. "Too bad." He pulled the baseball cap low over his eyes. "I'm ready if you are."

"As ready as I'll ever be," she said, although she wasn't sure she was ready to spend more time with a tempting man like Brett.

CHAPTER FIVE

THEY LEFT THEIR BAGS with the clerk at the front desk, picked up their keys and headed for the hotel lounge. Cammie followed Brett to a remote table in the corner, although the place was virtually deserted, with the exception of two businessmen at the bar watching some sports show.

Not long after they were seated, a pretty waitress with long curly blond hair arrived to take their order. But before the woman could speak, awareness dawned in her expression. "Are you that country star Brett Taylor?"

"Could be." He turned his attention to Cammie. "Is beer okay with you?"

Not exactly her favorite, but she wasn't going to refuse as long as he picked up the tab. "Sure."

As if she hadn't registered the request, the waitress thrust a napkin at Brett. "Can you autograph this?"

When Brett smiled, she dropped her tray, spare change and all, onto the table. "Sure," he said as he helped her gather a few random coins before they rolled onto the floor. "What's your name?"

For a moment she didn't seem to know the answer to that question. "It's Heather."

As he scribbled on the napkin, Cammie tried not to look, just in case he might be sending a personal note, such as "I want your body, meet me in my room." Instead, she watched the woman's face while she watched Brett.

A ridiculous bite of jealousy latched on to Cammie as she considered Brett's message. If Brett said—or wrote—the word, this girl would be all over him in a nanosecond. And it would probably take him less time to respond.

When Brett handed the waitress the napkin, hapless Heather stood for a long moment and stared at the paper.

Oh, for heaven's sake. "Could we have our drinks now?" Cammie reminded the woman in a tone that was falsely sweet.

The waitress finally came to. "Oh...sure."

After Heather wandered away, Cammie shook her head. "This must happen all the time."

Brett sighed. "Yeah, but I don't mind. Fans keep me in business."

"But don't you get a little tired of it? I mean, you probably can't even go into a convenience store without creating a scene."

"If it gets to be too much of a hassle, or I get to feeling just a little bit superior, I remember when I bought my one meal a day in a convenience store."

She rested her bent elbow on the table and supported her jaw with her palm. "So what did you write to Heather, if you don't mind me asking?"

"The usual," he said. "'To Heather, good luck, Brett Taylor.'"

"That's all? No invitation?"

His smile faded into a frown. "If you're asking if I gave her my room number, nope."

"Why not?"

"I don't remember it." He sat back in the seat and flashed his deadly grin. "In all honesty, she's not my type."

"What is your type?" Cammie couldn't believe she was actually asking such inane questions. Questions that could lead him to believe she was really interested in what he wanted in a woman.

His smile disappeared again, but that didn't take away from his gorgeous face. "You first. What's your type?"

Luckily the drinks arrived before she sputtered some stupid answer.

As soon as Heather retreated, Cammie took a quick sip before turning the topic back on him. "Is the trade-off worth it, not having any real privacy?"

He shrugged. "I swore if I ever got here, I'd never complain. But some days I'd just like to be home cleaning stalls and riding horses. I don't get a chance to do that often enough."

"Where is home exactly?" she asked.

"I have a ranch outside of Nashville," he said.

"But I grew up right here in Texas in the Hill Country. What about you?"

She took another sip. "I'm a die-hard Tennessee girl. I grew up in Memphis and, sadly, I still live in the same house with my grandparents. It's next to their charter business."

"What about your folks?"

She shifted in her seat from discomfort. "My dad and mom were both involved in the business. They always traveled together and traded off driving duties. Then one December, they were on their way to Pigeon Forge with a group of seniors when an eighteen-wheeler jackknifed right in front of them. They were both killed instantly, along with two of the passengers."

"That must've been tough for you." He looked and sounded sincerely sympathetic.

"I was only eight years old at the time," she said. "It was just a terrible, unavoidable accident."

He stared off into space for a few moments before turning his attention back to her. "My dad died before I ever really had the chance to know him."

Her heart ached over the regret in his tone. "I'm sorry, Brett."

"Don't be," he said. "He did it to himself. He was a frustrated musician who had a fondness for booze and not enough drive to succeed. He left my mom when I was twelve and he never came around much after that. For a long time I resented him. Now I'm just sorry I never had the chance to ask him why he left."

Cammie couldn't help but wonder how he could virtually do the same thing to his own daughter, yet she didn't dare ask. "That's really a shame. At least I have good memories of my mom and dad. Knowing I had two parents who were totally devoted to each other helped lessen the sense of loss, although it never really goes away, I guess."

Brett sat silently for a few moments before he downed most of the beer. "Do you want to dance?"

Did she? "It's been a while."

He came to his feet. "It's just like riding a bicycle and making love. Once you've done it, you don't forget how."

The making-love comment totally flustered her. "Yes, but I—"

Before Cammie could issue a protest about being tired, or hand him a thousand other lame excuses, Brett was already taking her hand to help her off the high-backed chair.

Once they reached the small wooden dance floor, he put his arms around her and gently tugged her close. The bluesy instrumental made for a perfect lucky-belt-buckle-polishing slow dance. And this was exactly what she'd sworn would never happen again—finding herself in the arms of another entertainer. She didn't want to touch him or have him touch her, yet she very much enjoyed the way he pressed his hand into the small of her back, and the gentle smile he gave her when she finally looked up at him. But the peculiar way she felt at the moment, somewhat light-headed and very warm in a nice way, worried her the most.

She'd only had two sips of beer, but it was as if she'd consumed the entire keg. She felt clumsy and her pulse raced, her limbs tingled. She was perspiring, although she couldn't claim it was the room temperature because she'd been fine at the table. Of course, it had to be the alcohol. Had to be. Why else would she rest her cheek against his chest?

It certainly couldn't be the dance. After all, it wasn't like she hadn't danced before. In fact, she'd danced with plenty of men. All shapes and sizes, all with varying degrees of proficiency. But the way this particular man held her, moved against her, she would have to rank his ability higher than most.

If she could find the courage to admit it to herself, the greatest contributing factor to her current discomfort would have to be Brett.

When he lowered his hands until they rested just below her waist, she sighed against his shoulder.

"Cammie?"

"Huh?"

"Are you still awake?"

Oh, yes. All of her. "Am I dancing like I'm asleep?" she questioned as she made contact with those silvery-blue eyes that caught the reflection of the revolving globe above them.

"No," he said, looking all too serious. "I was just

thinking you haven't had much sleep. I'm being self-ish by keeping you up this late when you have to drive tomorrow."

Sleep was the last thing on Cammie's mind. She'd probably regret it later, but she chose to participate in this game of chance tonight. "I'll live."

"You know something," Brett said, his somber demeanor suddenly replaced with the same sexy expression she'd seen earlier, the one that managed to rob her of all coherent thought. "Your eyes are so dark, almost black." He pushed her hair back from her shoulder. "Real pretty. Kind of mysterious."

She felt suddenly self-conscious. "I bet you say that to all your bus drivers."

"Hell, Bud never looked at me the way you do."

How was she looking at him? Like some love-sick girl? Like Heather? "I'm not sure I know what you mean."

"Maybe I should rephrase this. It's how you see me. Today you've pretty much treated me like I'm just a person, not someone you have to cater to or an employer. Like I'm nobody special, just a man. I can't even remember the last time I talked about my rodeo days. I appreciate having a normal conversation."

She experienced a strong sense of relief. "I can relate to your wanting to have some normality in your life."

"I mean, you really listen to me, Cammie. Most people talk, but they never really listen." He surveyed her face, from forehead to chin, before his gaze came to rest on her lips. "You have a beautiful mouth."

An inner voice called to her to steer clear, to stop before she lost control of her common sense. She dropped her arms from around him and took a step back. "It's really hot in here. Maybe we should sit down."

"Take off your jacket."

Oddly Cammie had forgotten she was wearing it. She forgot everything when Brett slowly unzipped the front closure, helped her out of the leather jacket, then tossed it aside on a nearby table.

When she moved back into his arms, she didn't feel any less warm. Just the opposite. Maybe it was the top's flimsy fabric that made her more aware of his body against hers. Maybe it was the fact his hands had roved to her hips. Or maybe the undeniable, and inadvisable, electricity flowing between them had only intensified.

Brett pulled her arms away from his waist and placed them around his neck, then slid his hands slowly down her sides and past her waist until he was again resting his hands on her hips. She automatically shivered.

"Are you cold now?" he whispered.

"No."

He pulled her closer, anyway. "Do you still want to sit down?"

Fall down was more like it. This whole scenario

was dangerous, but she couldn't stop it any more than she could divert a runaway train with her bare hands.

"You don't have to be afraid of me, Cammie." His face was so close she could feel the warmth of his breath trailing over her cheek.

"I'm not." But she was. Not afraid of him, but afraid of the feelings he stirred inside her. Feelings she had no business entertaining as his employee. As a woman. Somehow he had drawn out long-dormant needs she'd tried hard to ignore.

As the music continued, Brett softly brushed his lips over her cheek, then rested them against her temple. He gently stroked her back, up and down in a slow, sultry rhythm. After a time, he pulled back and studied her eyes, then slowly, slowly lowered his mouth....

Fortunately, the song ended before the inevitable happened, forcing Cammie out of her stupor. When the disc jockey thanked everyone for coming, she didn't know whether to be relieved or disappointed. Maybe a little of both.

Brett hesitantly released her and handed her the discarded jacket. "Let's go before they turn on the houselights."

Cammie was still in a trance when they entered the glass elevator, the nagging cautions running through her head at breakneck speed.

Never underestimate his power....

The trance finally lifted when they made it to the room.

"Here you are, ma'am," Brett said as he offered her the key.

She took the card from him, deliberately avoiding all contact. "Thanks."

"I'm right next door if you need me."

"Okay."

"See you in the morning."

"Yeah," she said. "In the morning."

While Brett looked on, Cammie turned and slipped the card into the slot to unlock the door, without success. She tried two more times, hoping to see an illuminated green light, but to no avail. Locks never, ever stumped her. She was normally sure-handed with nerves of steel. Normally. But this wasn't a normal circumstance.

Brett moved in closer, she presumed to assist in opening the door. Then suddenly his hand was on her waist and the other in her hair, stroking lightly, playing freely. He pushed her hair to one side, and when he brushed his lips over the back of her neck, it appeared the door might have to wait.

He took her by the shoulders and turned her to face him, almost in slow motion, it seemed. She clutched her bag close to her chest as if trying to create a barrier from the man with mesmerizing eyes standing before her. But she didn't move. She simply didn't want to.

Brett slowly lowered his head and lightly touched

his lips to hers once, twice. Cammie feared she might have actually gasped, but if she had, he'd silenced her when he delivered a solid, much less tentative kiss.

He'd had a lot of practice kissing—Cammie's first thought. She should tell him to back off—her second. Yet the kiss wasn't intrusive, but it wasn't restrained, either.

He slid his hand inside her jacket and circled her rib cage, his thumbs resting just below her breasts. She briefly wondered how many women had fallen under the spell of his kiss. And then she thought of Mark.

Cammie pulled away and picked up the bag that had somehow fallen to the floor. "I'm sorry," she muttered.

"For what?" Brett asked, looking confused.

"For letting that happen," she said on a wave of unexplained anger. Anger directed more at herself than at him. "I'm sorry if I gave you the impression that I'm one of your good-time girls."

He tipped her chin, forcing her to look at him. "I'd never think that, Cammie. And after what happened with you and Mark earlier, I probably shouldn't have done it."

She probably shouldn't have put herself in this predicament. "Look, you didn't force yourself on me, and I didn't have to participate. But I do work for you and that's reason enough not to let this go any further."

"Yeah," he said. "You're right."

She fumbled with the key for a few moments before she steadied her hand long enough to finally figure out the correct way to insert the card. When she gained entry, she turned to see Brett was still standing there, looking as if he had something more to say. If she had any sense whatsoever, she would run into the shelter of her room before she did something else they might regret—like invite him inside.

Then he smiled, but only slightly. "Night, Cammie."

"Night."

Cammie rushed inside, closed the door and leaned back against it while she gave herself a major scolding.

In a matter of hours, she'd confronted her ex-boyfriend and kissed her boss. She could probably rest assured she wouldn't have to encounter Mark in the near future. On the other hand, she wouldn't be able to avoid Brett at all in the upcoming weeks. Sad thing was, avoiding him was the last thing she wanted to do.

BRETT LINGERED FOR a few more moments outside the closed door, considering the possibilities if he knocked and she invited him to come in. He highly doubted it would happen, and that was probably wise. But he didn't always heed wisdom.

A man wearing a white undershirt and pink plaid Bermuda shorts passed by carrying an ice bucket.

Without even so much as a glance in his direction, Brett continued to hang around, steeped in indecision, until the clink of ice cubes from the nearby machine drew him from his musings.

He eventually paid attention to the warning bells going off in his head, picked up his bag and started slowly down the hall. First rule of the road: don't get involved with an employee of the opposite sex. It only spells trouble. Second rule. His rule. Don't get seriously involved with any woman. It only invited heartache.

Caution didn't stop him from thinking about Cammie as he strode to his room. He recalled how she'd felt in his arms, the way she'd said his name—in a kind of breathy voice. He felt a twinge in his gut when he thought about dancing with her. He felt another twinge a lot lower when he remembered kissing her.

Hell, no, she wasn't a groupie. Didn't look like a groupie and didn't kiss like one, either. Camille Carson kissed like a woman—a woman who knew what she was doing. She wasn't some young thing seeking a quick screw with a star. She could actually hold a conversation without batting her eyelashes or wetting her lips. Problem was, he still wanted to know her better. A lot better. Every sweet inch of her, and that sent his imagination straight into overdrive.

After Brett unlocked the door and stepped inside the room, another image of Cammie flashed in his mind—when she'd taken off her jacket while they were dancing. To that point, he'd only seen her in formless shirts. Then, in a matter of moments, he'd seen firsthand what she'd done well to keep hidden. He rubbed a palm over his face as if he could make the images disappear. All he needed was a good night's sleep to take care of it. That, and the Bermuda shorts guy's bucket of ice down the front of his jeans.

He sucked in a deep breath, then walked quietly into the room, hoping like hell his roommate was already asleep. No such luck.

He found Pat stretched out on the sofa wearing a white T-shirt, baggy blue boxers and a suspicious expression. "Where've you been, son?"

Brett fell back onto the adjacent bed. "Like it's any of your business, which it isn't, I was in the bar having a beer."

"You didn't hook up with that gal you always call when we're up this way? What's her name?"

"Jennifer." He hadn't even thought to call her, thanks to his bus driver. "I was having a drink with Cammie. We were just talking." And that admission could damn sure cost him.

Pat swung his bare legs over the edge of the sofa, sat up and stared at him. "Are you sure that's all you wanted from Cammie, just some friendly conversation?"

Brett grabbed a pillow and flung it in the direction of his mentor. "Shut up, Pat."

"Struck a nerve, did I?"

"Hell, no."

"Hell, yes, I did. I hope you don't expect us to vacate the bus every now and then so you can have your way with her."

Pat's suggestion came to life in Brett's mind, materializing into one heck of a fantasy that had to do with Cammie sprawled out on her berth, naked. Cammie driving the bus with his hands all over her. Cammie in the shower with him… "She's an employee and that means hands off."

"Good, 'cause I won't be party to you using that little gal."

He had no intention of doing that to Cammie. "Fine. Now that we have that settled, I'm going to turn in."

Brett retired to the bathroom, stripped off his jeans and shirt, brushed his teeth and spent a good twenty minutes washing his face in an effort to wash away the persistent fantasies. It didn't work. Not in the least. He returned to the room and crawled under the covers before Pat could discover just exactly what Camille Carson was doing to him.

UNABLE TO SLEEP PAST DAWN, Cammie was ready and waiting in the bus by the time the band members headed into the parking lot at seven-thirty. She watched out the windshield as Rusty and Bull said goodbye to their girls, then quickly stepped onto the other bus with Jeremy, who looked hung-over and miserable.

Unfortunately, the vehicles weren't well concealed. Dennis attempted to run a group of fans crowded around the entrance of Brett's bus, but without much success. Cammie climbed out of the cab, bulldozed through the mob of young, delirious females and did a routine check of the tires. Before she could reenter the bus, one fresh-faced teenager grabbed her by the arm, halting her progress. "Do you drive *his* bus?"

She immediately regretted she hadn't hurried. "Yes."

"You mean you get to see him every day?"

Nothing like good old hero worship. "Every day, and he puts his pants on just like everyone else." As soon as the words left her mouth, she wanted the parking lot to open up and swallow her whole. She'd sounded as if she'd seen him take his pants off.

The remembrance of Brett changing clothes the day before invaded her thoughts. The recollection caused her face to heat, from forehead to chin. Yet the probable blush went unnoticed as the crowd's attention now turned from her to the star in question as he approached.

The overwrought masses converged, thrusting pens in Brett's face and impeding his progress as he stopped to hand out a few autographs. His jaw was blanketed by a shading of whiskers, his hair shower-damp, and he wore a faded black T-shirt and equally faded jeans, proving to Cammie that no one cared about his disheveled state. She definitely noticed his sex appeal, and so did the other twenty or so young women stumbling over themselves, trying to touch him. And he smiled as if he didn't mind the attention in the least.

Then reality suddenly dawned. She had actually let the notorious womanizer—the object of desire to all these females—kiss her. And worse, she'd welcomed it. Unlike Mark's forceful ways, Brett's kiss had been gentle, the impressions remarkable. So remarkable she'd had trouble sleeping.

Cammie shoved the thoughts out of her mind. Regardless of how he'd made her feel, she wasn't one of his playthings and never would be.

Brett attempted to move toward the bus, inadvertently carrying several fans with him despite two beefy crew members' efforts to hold them back. By the time he worked his way to the door, several other tourists had arrived on scene to investigate the commotion.

Instead of retiring to the safety of the bus, Brett walked to Cammie where she stood near the door, put his arm around her and brushed a kiss over her lips. "Ready to roll, sweetheart?"

Cammie could only stare at him, flabbergasted. Brett then took her hand and led her—more like dragged her—to the entrance. He scaled the steps ahead of her while the crowd chanted his name.

Still dazed, Cammie squeezed past him and dropped into the seat. "Thanks a lot, Brett."

"I was just trying to discourage them so we could make a quick getaway."

Cammie's irritation bubbled to the surface, both from lack of sleep and wisdom. Truth was, she'd gone right along with the ruse. "I don't like being used as a decoy to divert a bunch of groveling pre-pubescent girls."

"They're harmless."

She started the bus and shifted to face him. "How can you be so blasé about this? Some of those girls couldn't have been more than sixteen, if that. Someone less scrupulous might have taken advantage of their admiration."

He propped an elbow on the back of the seat. "I'm not Mark Jensen, Cammie."

"I know that, but I expect you to be more appalled since you have a daughter...." Her words floated away the moment she realized she'd said too much.

His expression turned steely, unforgiving. "How do you know that?"

She lowered her eyes before bringing her gaze back to his. "I heard someone talking about it at dinner last night. And I knew about your divorce the first night I came on board. But you can trust me not to say anything."

"You already have."

How could she answer that? "I'm really, really sorry."

His narrowed eyes told her he didn't accept the

apology. "Pat said they'll need another half hour before we head out."

With that, Brett headed down the corridor, leaving Cammie feeling stunned and ashamed. Just because he'd rescued her from the clutches of a crazed ex-boyfriend, said she had talent and turned out to be one heck of a kisser, that didn't give her the right to comment on his personal life. He was still her boss, which meant she had to attempt to make amends, or find herself on the next plane back to Memphis.

After waiting a good ten minutes, she slid out of the seat, convened some courage and knocked on Brett's stateroom door.

"Yeah," he called.

"Mind if I come in?"

"Suit yourself."

For the very first time, she stepped inside the inner sanctum. The area was surprisingly orderly, well-appointed and very masculine with its brown-and-black decor. A set of weights sat at the end of the bed on the beige-carpeted floor, along with a pair of cross-trainers. Several platinum and gold albums that spanned his amazing career covered the walls. When she recognized most of the titles, the enormity of his fame made the atmosphere seem surreal.

The room held numerous other conveniences—another sound system, another high-tech TV, another bed much bigger than hers where Brett had stretched out and stripped down to a pair of navy boxers. No shoes, no shirt, ready to service any will-ing woman.

He held some sort of entertainment magazine in both hands, the title Cammie failed to see when she caught sight of his bare torso. In fact, she lost sight of everything right then but his body. And this time she took a good, long look, from the curve of his bicep to his tattoo to the dip of his navel. And below that… Happy trails to her.

Then came the magazine now open in his lap. Unfortunately, she didn't stop—couldn't stop—the visual trek as she followed the path from his hair-covered thighs down to his bare feet.

The expedition only took a few seconds, but the terrain had been more fascinating than any scenery she'd encountered so far. By the time her gaze trav-eled back to his face, she realized he'd been watch-ing her blatantly studying him.

He pinned her in place with those deadly blue eyes and a half-formed smile. "Need something?"

She needed to keep her eyes to herself. "I think we need to talk."

"About?"

"I just wanted to say I'm sorry again. Sometimes things jump out of my mouth before I think. I didn't mean to criticize or delve into your private life."

"Yeah, you did," he said. "And you're probably justified in your criticism. Just know that every deci-sion I've made to this point has been for my daugh-ter's benefit."

A decision that caused him a great deal of pain, if the remorse in his voice was any indication. "I'm sure that's the case," she said, knowing there had to be more to it. But she didn't intend to push him for more information.

Brett tossed the magazine aside, bent his knees and scooted up until he was propped against the black leather headboard anchored to the wall. "Have a seat."

Cammie perched at the end of the bed, moving as far away from him as she could without falling off the edge. She folded her hands in her lap to curb the impulse to send her fingers up his bare leg. "I get a little testy when it comes to this atmosphere. It reminds me of Mark."

He raked both hands through his hair. "Like I've said, I'm not Mark Jensen. I don't slap women around or take advantage of them. But after what happened between us last night, I could see why you'd think I might. I just want you to know I didn't plan for that to happen."

"That's good to know."

"But I have to admit I sure as hell enjoyed it." He topped off the comment with a fully formed grin.

Cammie glossed over the comment by turning her attention to the discarded magazine. "What were you reading?"

"An interview I did several months ago. Tim signs off on all articles, but I have this need to see how many times they've taken what I've said out of context."

"Well?"

"Only once so far," he said. "They asked if I was involved with anyone, and I told them no but I didn't elaborate. They took that to mean I'm looking for the perfect woman."

Cammie rolled her eyes. "You and every other man in the universe. First and foremost, perfect in bed."

"Maybe so, but no one wants a relationship without good sex. At least I don't." He nailed her with an intense, seductive gaze. "You never know where you might find that perfection."

Suddenly uncomfortable, Cammie came to her feet and pointed behind her. "I better get ready to go before Dennis takes off without us."

"Truce?"

"Sure." Cammie leaned to take his hand, but he didn't let go. Instead, he gave her arm a tug, just enough to throw her off balance. She landed squarely in the middle of his chest.

He looked at her a long moment before he said, "Maybe you better leave now."

Oddly, she had no real desire to move. "You're probably right."

"Do you want to leave?"

"I'm not sure."

"Tell me what you want, Cammie."

"I want..." *Not to want you.*

Before she could voice her true feelings, he wrapped his hand around her neck and drew her mouth to his.

He brushed his lips against hers in a series of teasing kisses most likely meant to dissolve her defenses until she could no longer reason. Either that or he was giving her ample time to get away before she was too far gone. But she was already too far gone.

Brett finally kissed her in earnest, reminding her of last night when this mistake had first been made. Countless objections ran through her mind, yet she couldn't form them into words or drown out the excitement his kiss generated, even when he rolled her onto her back and fitted himself against her. She couldn't breathe for many reasons—his body conforming to hers, the heady smell of soap on his skin, the scratch of roughened stubble against the smooth flesh of her face.

Don't do this invaded her brain. She pushed aside the cautionary words, even when she felt her shirt being tugged out of the waistband of her jeans and the cool wisps of air on her chest as he released each button.

When Cammie clasped his wrist during a passing moment of sanity, Brett stopped, laid his hands on either side of her face and looked into her eyes. "Since last night—hell, before last night—I've been thinking about us doing this. Do you think about it, Cammie?"

The way he said her name made her shiver. "No." A giant lie.

Brett smiled again, his blue eyes relaying a mystical power she couldn't seem to resist. He clearly didn't believe her. "Yes, I've thought about it," she finally admitted. "But I—"

He halted her protests with another hot kiss designed to destroy her defenses. She didn't try to stop him when he reached under her and pulled her blouse completely away. Didn't even attempt to escape when he moved against her so intimately that only one thing would bring them closer.

In one quick move, he unfastened the clasp of her bra and worked it off. They sighed in unison against each other's mouth at the first sensation of bare flesh. The last bit of Cammie's rational side seemed to melt away with the soft impressions of his hand on her breast, the erratic drum of her heart, his mouth pressed against hers. For some reason, Brett Taylor had his sights set on her. It both flattered and frightened her.

When he left her mouth and began to descend down her body with soft, warm kisses, Cammie vaguely realized they were quickly reaching that point-of-no-return moment. But she was so lost in the feel of his mouth closing over her breast, she barely noticed Brett had released the button on her jeans, then slid her zipper slowly, slowly down....

"Anybody home?"

CHAPTER SIX

PAT'S VOICE EFFECTIVELY hurled Cammie back into reality. She shoved Brett away and catapulted off the bed with the speed of an Olympian sprinter, grabbing clothes as she went. She put on her bra and redid her jeans as quickly as her trembling fingers would allow while chanting, "Oh, no, oh, no, oh, no…" The normally simple task of buttoning her shirt seemed astronomical at the moment.

Brett was still lying on the bed, facedown, hands above his head as if in surrender, his body shaking. Cammie suddenly realized he was laughing.

"Damn! Pat's got bad timing." He rolled off the bed, took a pair of jeans from a nearby chair and, with a groan and some difficulty, slipped them on. He grabbed a T-shirt, stopped beside her on the way to the door and softly touched her cheek. "I'll tell him you're in the bathroom. I'll go outside with him, then you can sneak out." He ran his thumb over her upper lip. "When it comes to explaining the whisker burn, you're on your own."

Then he left her with a soft kiss and a sexy smile. After Cammie heard the exterior door close, she went into the bathroom to splash cool water over her now-flushed face.

I've been thinking about us doing this. Do you think about it, Cammie?

She lowered her head and closed her eyes. Yes, she'd thought about him. For long moments, and often. She'd thought about kissing him more than she cared to admit, even before it had ever happened. Only this time it was much more than a simple kiss. She wanted him with a desperation that made no sense whatsoever. She wanted his hands all over her, his mouth all over her. And he wanted it, too. She'd felt it in his body, saw it in his blue, blue eyes.

But he was her employer and even worse—a singer. He would only hurt her, just like Mark had.

She didn't need a man like Brett Taylor, but she did need the job. She promised herself to end the game. Soon.

FOUR MORE STOPS ON THE TOUR, four days of pretending nothing had changed, four virtually sleepless nights. Brett was damn near on the verge of insanity. He sat on the sofa, aimlessly strumming the guitar—when he wasn't focused on Cammie conversing with her current copilot, Pat. She laughed and tossed her hair over one shoulder, then rubbed her hands back and forth over the steering wheel. A fairly innocent gesture, but it seemed downright erotic.

What had gotten into him? He'd had no business doing what he'd done to her in Fort Worth. What he still wanted to do to her again, and then some. He needed to focus on work and the upcoming schedule. Concentrate on his songs, not sex. After they left Albuquerque that night, they were heading to Vegas for two days of recreation and two sold-out concerts. Then on to California and more stretches of desert road. A good time for some serious songwriting, not seriously seducing the woman occupying the driver's seat.

He got up and paced, full of unbridled energy. Sexual energy. He could almost guarantee tonight's show would be damn good.

As soon as they pulled into the New Mexico State Fairgrounds, Brett immediately retired to the shower. He still had a couple of hours before the performance, but he needed to put some distance between him and Cammie, even if he couldn't quite forget the details of their last encounter.

The shower helped, but the process of shaving—not so much. He kept going back to that day in his bed. He kept remembering how good Cammie had felt, how she'd responded to him. Five more minutes—and one less band member—and they would've been engaged in some fairly fine lovemaking.

The serious lack of concentration caused him to nick his chin right at the cleft. After dabbing the cut, he took the razor and swished it around in the water, washing away the residual shaving cream, but not the recollections.

He braced both palms on the sink's edge, angled his body away from the granite vanity and lowered his head. He had no idea how he was going to deal with his Cammie predicament. Easy. He'd go out of his way to avoid her as much as possible.

"Brett, are you decent?"

So much for avoiding her. And decent? That was damn debatable considering his down-south reaction to the raspy sound of her voice. "Yeah."

When he heard the stateroom door open, Brett tried to brace for her arrival. Then he looked up to catch Cammie's reflection in the mirror. And damn if she wasn't checking out his ass. Not that he minded, since he'd been guilty of checking hers out, too. Quite a few times.

"Sorry to interrupt," she said. "The guys are ready to rehearse."

The small mirror was beginning to fog from the vapors of rasping breath. Brett wasn't sure which one of them sounded more winded. He had yet to turn around, probably best considering the fit of his jeans. And if she didn't leave soon, he couldn't guarantee he wouldn't take her down on the slate floor and have his way with her, as long as she was willing.

After he faced her, he realized the bathroom wasn't big enough for the both of them. Not in his current state. "Tell them I'll be out in a minute."

"Look, Brett, about the other day—"

"Not now, Cammie."

She released a frustrated sigh. "Fine, but we can't keep pretending we don't know each other. We have to work through this if we're going to survive the next few weeks. That means we need to talk about what happened like adults."

Talking was the last thing on his mind at the moment. "If you mean we need to discuss our make-out session, no way are we getting into that. I'm not going to risk losing my dignity in front of several thousand people."

Her eyes went wide. "Oh. I didn't realize it was bothering you that much."

He had to make her understand how close he was coming to losing control. "Bothering me? I'm so jacked up I can barely think. I figure that leaves me with three options, and none involves talking."

She folded her arms. "Please continue."

That's exactly what he planned to do. "I can take a cold shower, which probably won't work. I can take you into the shower with me and give you the wettest ride of your life. Or you can leave now before I forget why we shouldn't take up where we left off."

When she failed to move, he reached around her and grabbed the shirt hanging on the hook near the door, putting them in closer proximity. So close their thighs brushed. Man, this was sheer torture.

After mustering every ounce of willpower, Brett left the bathroom to finish dressing while Cammie rushed out, looking more than a little rattled. She could join the club.

A few minutes later, Brett strode into the living area, high on adrenaline and serious lust. "Hey, guys, how's everyone feeling?"

"Damn, boy, are you drunk?" Pat asked. "I haven't heard that much enthusiasm in years."

Brett frowned. "I haven't had a drop to drink. I've just got a lot of energy, so let's go expend some of it."

As they began to file out of the bus, Brett caught Cammie staring at him, a smile curling the corners of her mouth. Damn, she had a great mouth. Great everything, for that matter.

He sure as hell hoped performing would rid himself of the frustration. Otherwise, it was going to be a long, hard rest of the night.

CAMMIE MANEUVERED THE BUS through the desert terrain along the interstate, fighting fatigue and heavy-duty guilt. She'd tried to grab a quick nap while the band performed, but her mind had been too cluttered with images of Brett and what he'd said to her before the concert. Fortunately, he'd immediately retired to his stateroom after the performance. Now she was alone with her thoughts—and Brett only a few steps away, hopefully asleep.

Cammie turned on the satellite radio and tuned into a country station that ironically was playing Brett's latest hit. Nowhere to run, nowhere to hide to escape him. Over the drone of the engine, she thought she heard a noise from somewhere behind her and assumed it was only her imagination. Then she heard footsteps and sensed him moving toward her, another detriment to her composure.

She didn't want to face him right now. Didn't want to acknowledge he'd uncovered basic needs that she'd camouflaged with indifference and reserve for a very long time. He was everything she despised and feared in a man—his reputation as a player, his breath-stealing looks, his ability to make her lose all control. But that past revulsion, that ever-present fear, seemed to be fading in Brett's presence.

She yawned reflexively, her body reacting in protest over the lack of sleep. That didn't explain the immediate surge of heat when he stood behind her.

"Tired?" he asked quietly.

"A little."

"Want some company?"

Company would be nice, but she wasn't sure she needed that from him, even if she did want it. At least he was fully dressed, she realized when she glanced in the overhead mirror, the only saving grace. "Could you get me a cup of coffee? There's some left over in the pot. I'd get it myself but it might be a while before I find a place to stop." She questioned the wisdom in partaking of caffeine when her nerves already seemed sufficiently stimulated.

"No problem," he said. "Do you want anything in it?"

"No, thanks. Black's fine."

He left for a few moments, then came back with a cup that he set in the console's drink holder. Then he kicked back in the seat as far as his frame and the narrow space would allow. "Where are we?"

"Almost to Gallup." Cammie afforded him a quick glance and noticed he looked about as tired as she felt. "Couldn't sleep?"

"I've been thinking."

"About what?"

"About us."

The words sounded strange coming from Brett, giving Cammie an unexpected twinge of excitement. She personally hadn't considered them as anything but two people battling hormones. "What about us?"

"Tell me more about Mark," he said as if he'd reconsidered the topic.

"Not really much to tell. He's a jerk."

"How long have you known him?"

Cammie reached for the switch that controlled the windshield mist and wipers, giving it an angry punch, releasing the cleaner and setting the blades into action against the grime. Thoughts of Mark always conjured up hostility from deep within.

"I met him six years ago when I was a senior at Belmont, majoring in music history," she said. "I was at a nightclub where he was performing. He'd just released his first song and was still fairly unknown. I didn't know the first thing about him, but I thought he was kind of cute."

She caught Brett's smile from the corner of her eye as she continued. "They were having a karaoke contest during the break, something I indulged in every now and then for the prize money. Mark was signing autographs when it came my turn to sing. He had the bouncer find out my name, then he sent a note and invited me to join him onstage. After a lot of persuasion from Mark and my friends, I agreed. That was the beginning."

"What about the middle and the end?" he asked.

"I saw him when he wasn't on the road, mostly between stops. Six months after we met, he asked me to marry him."

"You were engaged?" Shock resonated from his tone.

"Not officially. Before I could give him an answer, his manager worked a deal he couldn't pass up and he left on his first major tour as an opener for Gil Markum two days after he proposed."

"Money takes precedence over personal issues, especially with managers," Brett added.

And Cammie had thanked her lucky stars for that fact many times over. "Actually, his manager was very supportive of our relationship. Mark was always a little bit wild and that tainted his image at times. I've often wondered if I wasn't being used as some sort of PR tactic. Like I could actually tame him."

Cammie glanced Brett's way and noticed his eyes looked heavy. She thought for a moment she might escape the rest of the interrogation, but she couldn't be so lucky.

"So that about covers the middle," he said. "What

did Mark Jensen do to you that caused you to break it off with him?"

Her hands tightened around the steering wheel. "Since we'd spent so little time together, I decided to surprise him a couple of weeks later in Little Rock. I drove eight hours, got in late, went to the hotel where he was staying and found him in bed with some groupie who didn't look a day over eighteen, if that."

"That's why you were so upset that morning in Fort Worth," he said.

"Exactly. Anyway, I told him I wouldn't marry him if he was the last man on the planet, and I left. I haven't seen him since. Not until the other day."

"And he never fought to get you back?"

Mark had fought, all right. He'd sent flowers and telegrams and harassing letters, telling her what a mistake she was making. He even had his band members call her. Mark Jensen didn't like to lose, and that included every aspect of his life.

Cammie blocked the disturbing images and continued. "He made an effort, but by that time I'd left school knowing he'd keep hounding me if I stayed. As it turned out, I had to help my grandfather with the company after he had surgery. I moved permanently back to Memphis and wouldn't take Mark's calls."

"Don't get mad when I ask you this, but did you ever consider forgiving him?"

Cammie took her eyes from the road long enough

to shoot him an acid look. "Forgive him? How could I ever forget, much less forgive him for falling into bed with someone else two weeks after he asked me to marry him? Maybe even sooner than that."

"Living on the road is hell," he said. "Some guys miss their wives and girlfriends so much they use that as an excuse to cheat—"

"He never missed me that much. We never even..." She was getting carried away with the baring of the soul. Some things were best left unsaid.

"You never even what?"

"Never mind."

She knew the moment Brett figured it out by the frown on his face. "Are you saying you never slept with Jensen?"

"No, I didn't, and frankly, I'm glad I made that decision."

"No wonder he's so determined to get you back," he said. "He's finally come to his senses and discovered what he's passed up."

She wasn't sure whether to be flattered or offended. "Is that in the way of sex with me, or a relationship with me?"

He rubbed his shaded jaw. "I personally suspect that's probably a pretty severe loss in both departments."

"Thanks, I guess."

They exchanged a brief, knowing look, followed by a lengthy span of silence as Cammie turned her complete attention back to the road, where it should have remained in the first place. After a few minutes ticked off, she started to comment on the weather, the full moon hovering above them, anything to veer from any talk of relationships and sex and, of course, Mark. But before she could speak, she glanced to her right to discover Brett had leaned his head back against the seat, his features slack with sleep.

Soon the only sound in the cab came from the lull of passing trucks, the occasional bump in the road and the cautioning voices in Cammie's head telling her she needed to be very, very careful from this point forward. If not, she could once again become another captivating singer's latest heartbreak casualty.

"IF HE WAKES UP and wants something to eat, tell him it's too late."

The comment jolted Brett out of sleep. When he opened his eyes, he saw Cammie still planted in the driver's seat, sipping her coffee, totally unaware of the dream he'd been having about her. A really dirty dream involving pulling the bus over, getting naked and getting down to business.

"Are you okay?" she asked when he groaned.

Brett turned his face away, guarding his eyes against the all-night diner's too-bright lights and Cammie's inspection. He sure didn't feel okay. He wasn't exactly sure what he felt. Disappointed it was only a dream? Mad because Bull's booming voice had forced him out of it? Sexually strung out? All the above.

His mouth felt dry, like he'd eaten a whole box of crackers, and his body still hadn't calmed down. "How long have I been asleep?"

"A half hour or so, right after our conversation about Mark."

He cleared his throat. "Yeah. That's the last thing I remember." That and her long legs exposed by the white sports shorts that had ridden up her thighs, and thinking how easy they'd be to remove. "Where are we?"

"In search of a three-egg omelet."

"Bull's hungry again?"

"Of course."

He scooted up in the seat, every inch of his body stiff from the damn uncomfortable position he'd maintained for too long. The song that began to play didn't help with his uneasiness, even if it did bring back some bittersweet memories.

In spite of that, he reached over and turned up the classic country tune.

Cammie sighed. "I love this song. It's one of my granddad's favorites. Yours, too?"

"Yeah. I used to sing it to someone." That admission would probably encourage more questions. Questions he wasn't sure he wanted to answer.

"Your wife?" she asked.

He could change the subject, or tell Cammie the truth. He chose the truth. "My daughter. I know that sounds crazy since it's a cheatin' song, but something about it used to calm her down."

"Maybe it was just the melody."

He smiled when he recalled those long-ago days. "Must've been. When she was a baby, she used to wake up every night at 2:00 a.m. I was on the road most of the time, so my ex-wife would call me and I'd sing Lacey back to sleep over the phone. She always wanted to hear it, even when she got older."

"I'm sure she cherishes those memories."

"I doubt she even remembers."

"I'm sure she remembers. I still do when it comes to my dad."

She'd had a good dad. "Again, it was a long time ago."

"I don't mean to pry, but how long has it been since you've seen her?"

Way too long. "About seven years, right after her fifth birthday. Not long after that, Jana remarried and then convinced the court I was an unfit father. She got full custody, and I got four hours of supervised visitation one weekend a month."

"And you haven't even spoken to her since then?" she asked.

He realized how bad that sounded. Probably because it was. "She used to send me letters and pictures from school and we spoke by phone. But eventually the letters and pictures stopped coming and so did the phone calls. I finally decided it was all for the best. Jana and Randy can give her a stable home, something I can never give her as long as I keep doing what I'm doing."

"I'm sorry, Brett," she said in a sympathetic tone. "I'm sorry for both of you. It's clear you still love her very much."

And sometimes love just wasn't enough.

The conversation had taken its toll on Brett's energy, and he'd probably live to regret confessing his sins to Cammie. For some reason, he wanted her respect as much as he wanted her, and he'd probably lost what was left of it. Without saying another word, he stood and headed toward his stateroom. "Are you going back to bed?" Cammie called after him.

"Yeah."

"Sleep well."

Not likely that was going to happen. He had too much weighing on his mind, and enough remorse to fuel a furnace. The realization that Camille Carson was chipping away at his emotional armor also made him nervous. He could handle the physical attraction, and had no problem seeing where it might lead. But getting too involved with her would only spell trouble for the both of them. If he hadn't already crossed that rickety bridge.

Regardless of what happened between them, she'd eventually leave, just like every other important person in his life.

LAS VEGAS SPREAD OUT before Cammie, brightly illuminated and gloriously seductive, even in the morning sun. She watched with amazement at the bustle of activity on the streets, casinos aglow, billboards sporting the names of some of the world's finest entertainers, including Brett's. She suddenly felt very limited in experience, never having seen anything quite like what she now witnessed.

She followed Dennis down the strip, turning off the main drag and into the rear parking lot of the massive five-star resort. As soon as she shut down the bus, she debated whether or not to wake her boss. Her dilemma was solved when she heard Rusty hollering, "Let's party!"

Brett emerged as she opened the door to admit the raucous group. The guys crowded in, all but Pat. When Cammie asked about him, Bull said, "He ain't feeling too well. I think it was a combination of beer, truck-stop chili and celibacy."

Everyone laughed—everyone but Brett. He seemed completely uninterested in taking part in the camaraderie.

Bull turned his toothy grin on Cammie. "Are you going to join us in some blackjack and watch us lose our asses...I mean, assets?"

She didn't dare admit she'd never played before. "As much as I'd like to watch you lose your asses and assets, I've had no sleep."

"Come on, Cammie," Jeremy said. "You're in the city that never sleeps."

Rusty rolled his eyes. "That's New York. But

no one sleeps here, either. Day or night. Too much to do."

She hid a yawn behind her hand. "Thanks, but no thanks right now. I'll see you guys this afternoon when I've had a long nap."

After the group made a hasty exit and rushed toward the hotel, Cammie stayed to pack. And surprisingly, Brett remained behind to watch her, just as he had that night in Fort Worth. The night that had changed the course of their relationship.

"No one can leave Vegas without at least pulling a one-armed bandit, Cammie," he said.

She stuffed a couple of T-shirts into her bag. "In all honesty, I've never gambled before."

"Really?"

"Really."

"I personally prefer poker," he said. "But the slots might be the best place for you to start. If you need to save your money, I'll float you a few bucks to play on. Consider it a bonus."

For what? Allowing him to cop a feel? "I personally plan to hang on to what I've got."

His smile arrived, slow as sunrise and just as bright. "Vegas is a great place to let loose. I think you'll like it."

She zipped her bag and threw the strap over one shoulder. "I'll probably like it better after some sleep."

Brett leaned against the divider, blocking her exit.

"I always come here in December, during the National Finals Rodeo."

"Is that to sing or to pick up another one of those?" She pointed to his belt buckle.

"Nah. But maybe I should take a break from singing and start roping again, in case the luck's run out of this buckle."

"I doubt that."

"You ought to come with me."

That nearly shocked her out of her sneakers. "Bud will be back long before then."

"Not as a driver. As a—"

"Cook, laundry aficionado and maid?"

"As a woman who likes to have a good time. You do know how to have a good time, don't you, Camille?"

She hated it when he called her by her full name. It made every part of her come to attention. "Yes, I know how to have a good time."

As she started past Brett, he caught her arm. "We still haven't talked about what happened the other day," he said.

Her pulse began to race in response to his touch. "Probably just as well. There's really nothing to talk about, is there? So let's just forget it."

"Can you forget about it?" he asked. "I sure as hell can't, and believe me, I've tried."

No, she hadn't forgotten one minute of their little interlude. She simply didn't feel it would be best to admit it at the moment. Not when the bed that facilitated said interlude was only a few feet away.

She ducked under his arm and moved toward the door. "I'll see you later."

"Cammie."

Her instinct told her not to turn around, but his voice had the pull of a high-power magnet. "Yes?" she asked as she faced him.

"Let me know if you change your mind."

"Again, we don't need to discuss it any further."

He took a few slow steps toward her. "I meant about letting me show you a good time. I promise you won't be disappointed."

She had no doubt about that. But she might be too foolish to live if she took him up on his offer. At least they wouldn't be sharing close quarters for the next three days. Maybe she'd be better off spending that time catching up on sleep.

WHEN THE BLARING ALARM startled Cammie out of deep, dreamless sleep, she fumbled for the bedside radio and muttered a mild oath. The last thing she remembered was emerging from the shower with her hair and body wrapped in a towel, thinking she'd just rest her eyes for a moment before retrieving the hair dryer. The towels had fallen to the floor and she was totally sprawled out on top of the blue silk comforter on her back, naked as the day she was born.

Even after four hours' sleep, she still didn't have the energy or desire to move, so she rolled onto her stomach and bunched a pillow beneath her. When she heard laughter filtering through the door connecting the suites, followed by Brett's deep voice, her body came to life. Gooseflesh covered her arms and legs, contrasting with the undeniable heat flowing through her from breast to toes and all points in between. She clutched the pillow tighter, confused by the desire, the sudden need to be touched...but not by just anyone. She wanted Brett to touch her again. Anywhere he pleased.

She let out a disgusted breath, tossed the pillow aside and flattened her face against the mattress. Absolutely absurd to feel this way. Hadn't she learned anything at all? Brett only wanted one thing—a quick roll in the sack. If she bent to his will, he'd eventually toss her aside like a holey T-shirt and move on to the next conquest. Then again, she could do the same. She wasn't searching for a permanent relationship, either, and they were both consenting adults. Maybe she'd been the good girl far too long. Maybe she should just go for it.

And maybe she'd have that opportunity sooner than she realized, she decided when she heard a rap at the door before it creaked open.

"Are you awake?"

She slowly propped up on elbows and ventured a look behind her, thinking he would have stepped quickly back into the other room when he noticed her state of undress. She'd been sorely mistaken.

Brett leaned against the now-closed door, his gaze

slowly skimming her body. Her bare backside was the only thing exposed, but she couldn't very well lean over and scoop the towel off the floor or crawl under the covers without exposing something else, so she opted not to move at all. Funny, she didn't really care if he looked his fill. And Brett didn't appear to be going anywhere anytime soon, either.

She scraped her brain for something innocent to say, but only one thing came to mind. One question that could produce an interesting answer.

"Do you need something?"

CHAPTER SEVEN

HELL, YEAH. HE NEEDED A DRINK. He needed her to help him out of his clothes. He needed to leave. If he were any kind of gentleman at all, he would've retreated the minute he caught sight of the fact she didn't have on a stitch. But no one ever accused him of being a gentleman. Now all he could do was gawk at her.

He couldn't take his eyes off her slim, golden back and one hell of a perfect butt where he located the mystery tattoo—a small red rose centered right in the middle of one cheek. He fought the urge to walk over to the bed and examine it more closely. And while he was at it, he'd run his hand along the valley and up those hills and whatever else she'd let him touch.

He cleared his throat and studied his boot to keep from acting on those urges. "You didn't lock the door." Talk about stating the obvious.

"No kidding."

"I just wondered if you'd changed your mind about joining me," he said as noncommittal as a man could with a growing ache in his groin.

"Join you in what?"

Was it an innocent question or was she playing a game? Maybe it was some sort of weird seduction. Maybe he was just engaging in some heavy-duty wishful thinking. "Gambling."

"I think clothes would be in order for that, don't you?"

He risked another look, only making matters worse. "Yeah. Might be less distracting."

When she smiled, Brett figured she had to be the sexiest woman he'd ever seen. She looked posed for a centerfold, her long dark hair damp and tangled, face glowing with a sexy blush, an incredible body laid out before him like a holiday feast. He better run now before it was impossible to move in any direction except toward her.

"How much time do you need?" he asked.

"How much time do *you* need?" Her grin deepened and she sounded like she was having a damn good time playing with him. Too bad that wasn't literal playing.

When he didn't answer, she scooted forward on her belly to the end of the bed and grabbed a towel from the floor. She sat up and covered herself as best she could, giving him only a peek of the rest of the bounty, but enough to shoot his blood pressure straight into orbit.

"I can be ready in about thirty minutes," she said. "You can go on with the boys. I'll find you."

He didn't really want to leave. He only wanted

one thing at that moment, but he knew better than to stay any longer. Four men waited in the other room. Four men with big-time imaginations and bigger mouths. "We'll be in the casino. Just ask the host to point you to our private table."

Before he could prepare, she left the bed, secured the towel and walked toward him. He clenched his fists at his sides and waited for her next move.

"I'm going to lock the door," she said, bursting his fantasy bubble. "As soon as you leave."

He reached behind him and fumbled for the knob. "Yeah. Good idea."

Brett stepped back into the suite with a dazed shake of his head. He turned to find Pat stretched out on the couch, Jeremy sitting cross-legged in front of the TV, Rusty slouched in a wing-backed chair and Bull drinking a beer on a stool by the in-room bar.

"Is she up yet?" Jeremy asked.

Rusty chuckled. "Don't know about Cammie, but Brett sure is."

Pat lifted his head and scowled. "I'm telling you, son, you need to have that looked into. You keep raising your flag every time you see her, we'll have to start saluting."

"You're imagining things, old man," Brett muttered.

"Nope, I'm not," Pat said. "You have a bad case of Cammie-itis, and there's only one cure."

Damn if Pat hadn't diagnosed him right. He wondered if anyone ever died from a perpetual erection. "I kind of walked in on her, that's all."

"Define 'walked in on her,'" Rusty said.

He damn sure didn't like the way they were enjoying his predicament. "She was kind of…" Brett began, growing warm at the thought. "She was… well…"

"Just say it, Taylor," Pat said. "She was nekkid."

Rusty and Bull rubbed their faces simultaneously while Jeremy's cheeks turned as red as a hothouse tomato. Pat dropped his head back onto the sofa and groaned.

Bull downed his beer and set the mug down hard on the counter. "I can't believe you came out of there so soon. You're a better man than any of us."

"Guess not or he'd still be in there," Pat added, encouraging more laughter from the group.

Bull slid off the stood and patted his belly. "If you're done ogling Cammie, let's go do what we came here to do."

Brett picked up a baseball cap and settled it on his head, thinking that was the best advice he'd heard all day. Yeah, just forget about it. If that was even possible. Probably not. "You with us, Pat?" he asked when he noticed his friend hadn't moved.

Pat stretched his arms above his head. "You boys go on ahead. I'm still feeling a little puny. I'll rest up now and join you after the show tomorrow night."

He looked at his long-time partner with concern. "Do you need to see a doctor?"

Pat frowned. "Nope. The day I see a doctor is the day I'll be ready to wear a suit and lie down in a satin-lined box with my toes turned up. Don't worry about me. I'm gettin' too old for this crap, anyway."

Before he could follow the guys out the door, Pat called him back. "I need a few minutes before you head out, son."

Brett pulled up the chair where Rusty had been seated, more than a little worried over Pat's serious demeanor. "What's on your mind?"

"Tim called," he said. "They want to know about the two slots on the album still needing to be filled. Are you workin' on anything?"

Not since he'd met Cammie. "I've got a couple of ideas rolling around in my brain. There's plenty of road time ahead to write."

"That's what I told Tim. He's worried something's distracting you and I figure he's right."

Brett shot Pat a dirty look. "What's that supposed to mean?"

"Don't get your dander up, Brett. He didn't say it was a woman."

"Nothing's distracting me." Hell, he sounded too defensive.

Pat forked a hand through his silver hair. "Brett, a word of advice. You've been alone a long time now—"

"I've got plenty of friends."

"Shut up, son, and let me finish. You've got very few friends outside the industry, and we're basically your family, which ain't saying much. I don't mean to lecture, but I've lived my life regretting I've never settled down long enough to have a family. Now it's too late for me, but for God's sake, don't wait until it's too late for you. Find a good woman and be a father to your kid."

Brett rubbed his jaw when it began to twitch. He hated it when Pat got sentimental on him. He was used to the macho bullshit, but he didn't like discussing emotions except within the context of his songs.

"Can't settle down unless you find someone to settle down with," Brett said.

"You think maybe you've found a prospect?"

"Who?"

"Don't play dumb, Taylor. Cammie's a great gal."

Nothing he didn't already know. "It's just a physical thing going on between us."

Pat slapped at the bill of Brett's cap. "I kind of like her, Brett. So do the guys, especially Bud. She's a truly nice girl. So before you take your johnson out of your jeans, be prepared to answer to us if you break her heart. We won't stand for it."

Brett came to his feet and shoved the chair away. "It's none of your damn business what I do, but I'll tell you right now I don't plan on anything of the sort. And if I wanted to nail the entire female population of Las Vegas, none of you could stop me unless you chained me to this chair."

Pat smiled. "Now, that's an idea."

Brett headed to the door, choosing to ignore the last comment. "Go to hell."

Pat, as always grabbing for the last word, said, "You know what they say about the best-laid plans... or is that the best plans to get laid?" He turned up the volume on the television and laughed heartily.

Brett rushed out of the room in order to regain some composure. Hell, yes, Cammie was a nice girl. It didn't take a genius to figure that out. And hell, yeah, everyone believed he was a user. A few weeks ago they would've been right. Until Camille Carson had come into his life, his needs took priority over a woman's feelings. But he did care about how Cammie felt. And because of that, he probably should stay out of her life.

He should just make it his goal to leave her alone. Accomplishing that was still a major dilemma.

THE LITTLE BLACK DRESS had called to Cammie like an old-fashioned ice cream soda. She should have turned away. She definitely should not have gone inside the store. If she'd been thinking straight, she would have exited on the casino floor instead of taking the elevator to the lower level where shops and boutiques lined the corridors. Instead, she'd bought the dress, and right now she seriously questioned her decisions. Both of them. The dress and the well-orchestrated seduction.

By the time she was close to being ready, guilt began to nag her over her intent. But Brett Taylor coursed through her blood like a shot of top-grade whiskey. She was high on him, and like her impulsive purchase, she had to have him. The only way to get him out of her system was to let him into her bed. Or so she thought.

This move was irrational, inadvisable and probably the craziest thing she'd ever done. But maybe it was time to go a little crazy. She was normally a sane, strong person. She could usually handle anything.

What she and Brett felt for each other had mostly to do with sexual chemistry, a strictly physical attraction. And what was wrong with that? She was a grown woman who, for most of her life, had always walked a straight line, avoided anything too daring or controversial. What could possibly be the harm in indulging her fantasies?

Because it was only a partial truth. Not only was she drawn to his sensuality, she longed to get under his skin and find the man beneath. She wanted to know what made him so sad. What made him so determined to be alone. What drove him every night when he gave his all for thousands of people, yet he didn't seem inclined to give himself to one woman. And if she could do that, she deserved an award.

With a large shade of doubt, despite the mental pep talk, Cammie applied the rest of her makeup, inserted her faux diamond studs and dabbed on her favorite perfume. She took a last look in the mirror and hoped she hadn't overdone it.

The halter-style dress had a triangular shape cut at the bodice, revealing a glimpse of cleavage. The hem ended a good four inches above her knee and the fabric adhered to every curve of her body. Of course, she was forced to buy black heels, bringing her total charges to an amount exceeding any balance she'd ever had on her credit card. At least she got paid next week. She smiled to herself. Indirectly, Brett had paid for this dress.

Clasping her small black bag to her chest, she inhaled a cleansing draft of air before leaving to search for the object of her desire…before she changed her mind.

"HELL, NOT AGAIN!" Brett had been cursing his luck for the past hour. He'd only won two hands and was about to give up when Rusty talked him into just one more. Now he watched the last of his chips sliding into the clutches of the dealer.

"You ain't concentrating, man," Rusty said.

Brett swung off the stool. "I give up for now."

Rusty shot him an evil look. "Hell, Taylor, you've got more money than the government. Why don't you just spend a little?"

Brett threw him a fifty. "You play for me. At least you're still on top."

Rusty smiled and shook his head. "And you wish you were on top right now, but not of your game. Just remember, if you walk out on the floor you're liable to get mobbed if someone recognizes you."

The reason why he'd intentionally skipped shaving and wore clothes fit for a farmhand. "I'll take my chances," he said, then walked away headed for who-knew-where.

Brett ambled to the bar for a beer, less than enthusiastic to be drinking it alone. He wasn't sure why he felt the need for one now. Of course, he was lying to himself. He knew exactly why he needed a drink, why he hadn't been concentrating at the table. He was having a lot of trouble focusing on anything but Cammie's image now burned like a brand into his brain.

Since she wasn't apparently going to show, he should find someone to get his mind off her. But he didn't want anyone but his all-fire sexy, hardheaded, great-kissing bus driver.

As he visually scanned the casino, Brett spotted a woman leaning over a table, seemingly interested in the screaming patrons engaged in the crap shoot. *Woman* was the operative word. She wasn't skinny and shapeless like a lot of women these days. Her long legs flowed out of a tight black backless dress that hugged every bend of her body, especially the rounded curves of her hips. The satin skin on her back looked real touchable. She could be any man's fantasy, but she wasn't Cammie.

He started to look away, but then she kicked up one high-heeled foot and laughed over the antics of a man who couldn't be a day younger than eighty, flirting with her like a teenager. She was probably a gold digger, someone looking for a rich catch. But damn, she did have great legs. She could also be married or a hooker or, in Vegas, she could even be a he. More important, she wasn't the woman he wanted. Then she turned toward him, and he realized she was exactly who he wanted.

Cammie.

Seeing her dressed like that left him initially stunned, then completely captivated. When she noticed him, she smiled and gave a teasing little shake of her head that made his heart race. Then she moved toward him in a slow, sultry gait. Now his heart seemed to stop.

"Hi," she said as soon as she reached him.

"Hi" was all he could manage, his eyes riveted on her softly painted face.

"I was just about to join you but I got distracted by all the excitement at the craps table."

"I'm done with gambling." He wasn't done with her, though. Not even close. "I was close to losing my ass."

"Really?" She leaned around him to inspect his backside. "Looks like all your anatomy is still in place."

Man, she smelled good, looked great, made him want to climb all over her. "I wasn't in the mood to hang around any longer."

"What *are* you in the mood for?"

Give him five minutes and he could tell her in

explicit terms. For that matter, he could show her. "I don't know. How about you?"

"I'm here to gamble," she said. "As a matter of fact, I thought you might show me how to play the slots."

He wanted to show her a lot of things, none involving a one-armed bandit. "What's it going to be? Pennies, quarters or dollar machine?"

"Dollars would be fine. But I need to find an ATM first."

"I'll take care of it." Brett headed to the nearest cashier cage, thankful for the opportunity to escape so he could pull it together. After he signed for cash on his account, he sought out Cammie again. He found her seated nearby on a stool in front of a dollar slot machine, legs crossed, her dress riding up her legs, giving him a bird's-eye view of her thighs.

He fed a hundred-dollar bill into the slot and tried to clear the uncomfortable hitch from his throat. "There you go."

She sent him a wide-eyed stare. "That's too much money, and it's your money."

He shrugged. "Don't worry about it. I'm ready to go for broke."

She picked up an amber-colored drink and sipped at the straw. "Tonight, Brett, I'm going for it all."

She slowly ran a fingertip over the rim of the glass, then proceeded to remove the straw and drew it through her pursed lips like she was enjoying a piece of licorice—or something else. Brett felt like a live wire had been attached to his spine and a charge sent the length of it. He moved behind her, close enough for the back of her head to touch the center of his belly.

"There are two ways to do this," he said, trying to ignore the pressure building below his belt. "You can push the button that says Spin—" he pointed to the lighted square "—or you can do it the old-fashioned way."

She looked up at him and smiled. "How do you prefer to do it?"

For a moment he was afraid he wouldn't be able to speak. He leaned closer to the chair, his body tensing with every word, every action, Cammie threw at him. If she did or said anything else the least bit suggestive, he might have to resort to self-mutilation to get his mind off what he wanted to do to her. "I prefer the way it's been done since the beginning."

Brett reached around her and pushed the credit button three times, then clasped her hand and placed it on the silver lever. Instead of releasing his grasp, he let his fingers glide up her arm to her slender shoulder. "Go ahead. Pull away."

She smiled up at him and dragged the arm down. Bells chimed. Three single bar symbols appeared in the window. "Did I win?" she asked.

"Fifteen bucks. Looks like you got lucky the first time."

She smoothed her hand over the dress, then switched her crossed legs, drawing the hem up another inch. "This is going to be easier than I thought."

With a pounding heart, he repeated the same motion of positioning her hand on the lever, only this time he curled his fingertips around the inside of her arm, grazing the side of her breast as he made his way up.

Cammie let out a little gasp of air as the cherries rolled into view. "You got your money back," he said.

"I enjoy getting a return on my investment. By the way, do you like my dress?"

Hell, yes, he liked it. And what was in it. And he'd really like to see it lying in a heap on the bedroom floor. "It's real pretty, ma'am."

She reloaded the machine and grabbed the arm on her own. But instead of pulling it, she fondled the ball on the end with red-painted nails, then encircled the silver lever and slowly stroked it all the way down the shaft.

Cammie made the same move once more while Brett looked on, perspiration forming on his upper lip. He could actually feel her doing it to him even though her hands were in full view.

He clenched his teeth in an effort to regain some control. He'd always had control. A lot of control. Now he was in danger of totally losing it to this woman. Again.

His hands inadvertently squeezed her shoulders with every seductive stroke. When she finally pulled the arm into position, he bent down and buried his face into the nape of her neck. "Are you through playing now?" he whispered.

"With this?" Cammie asked, running her hand slowly along the side of the machine. "We still have some money left."

Brett nibbled her earlobe. "That's the point. You're ahead. You should always quit while you're ahead." That particular advice seemed sound where they were concerned. Too late.

"If you say so," she said. "But I'm ready to take my chances."

He let out an exasperated breath and straightened. "Then, by all means, continue."

Cammie slid off the stool, quickly finished her drink down to the jingle of ice cubes and turned to face him. She closed in on Brett until their legs touched, then inched her fingers up the front of his shirt.

He grabbed her hand as soon as she made it to the top. "If you're not serious about this, Cammie, then you better leave now. Once we get started, I'm not going to want to stop."

She stood on the tips of her toes until her lips were barely an inch from his. "I was just about to say the same thing to you."

Then she pulled his head down and kissed him without regard to the crowded casino.

The clanging and ringing, whoops of cheer and shouts of frustration, vanished. All Brett could hear was the blood rushing into his ears, felt it rushing elsewhere. He had his hands on Cammie's bare back and she was doing things to his mouth that would cause a saint to sin. He didn't care if he made a total fool of himself in front of hundreds of people, all he could think about was this damn hot woman in his arms. He was in suspended animation...until he heard someone scream his name from somewhere down the aisle.

Jolted back into awareness, Brett clutched Cammie's wrist and tugged her toward the direction of the elevators and safety from the masses.

"Your money!" she shouted.

"Let someone else have it," he said as he practically pulled her along with him. "Maybe they'll get lucky, too."

ONCE WE GET STARTED, *I'm not going to want to stop.*
The words echoed in Cammie's brain as Brett led her past rows of slots and tables at almost a sprint. When they finally arrived at the bank of elevators leading to the exclusive club level, Brett pounded the up button and gritted, "Come on," while he glared at the doors as if he could force them open by sheer will. The car arrived a few seconds later and Brett lowered his head while several people filed out. Hand in hand, they rushed inside, only to be joined by an older, well-dressed couple who fortunately didn't appear to recognize him.

They rode in silence as the elevator crept to their

destination, pausing two floors below theirs to deposit the husband and wife. As soon as they were alone again, Brett pulled her back into his arms and kissed her thoroughly. Cammie wound up with her back against one marbled wall with Brett pressed against her. And when he cupped her bottom and brought her even closer, she wondered if they would even make it to the room before clothes started coming off.

Then the bell chimed, heralding their arrival on the top floor. This time Cammie took the lead, and his hand, and led him to her room's private entrance. She rummaged through her purse for the card key, pulling it out only to drop it on the floor, exactly as she had that first night he'd kissed her. Her hands trembled as she tried to retrieve it. Before she knew it, Brett grabbed it up and slid it into the slot.

The light flashed, the latch tripped and her heart seemed to momentarily stop. After they entered the room, she didn't have time to think before Brett backed her to the bed and took her down in his arms onto the mattress. She prepared to begin the journey of a lifetime, then all the kisses and mutual groping suddenly halted, followed by Brett's rough sigh.

He tipped his forehead against hers and muttered, "Damn."

If he was having second thoughts, she'd have to kill him. "What's wrong?"

"Condoms." He raised his gaze to hers. "Do you have any?"

Oh, sure. She snapped her fingers and faked a grin. "Darn, I forgot to pack them with my zebra-print panties."

He sent her a seductive half smile. "You have zebra panties?"

She rolled her eyes. "No, and I don't have any condoms, either. I thought guys always carried one in their wallet."

He rolled off her and streaked a hand over his jaw. "I haven't done that since high school. They don't hold up well. I learned that the hard way."

Definitely a story there, one she'd ask about later. "You could go to the gift shop and hope you don't get mobbed."

"Or I could go next door and get one from my shaving kit. It's either face Pat or rabid fans. Normally I might choose the fans, but my room is a hell of a lot closer."

"True."

Brett kissed her cheek, came to his feet and pointed at her. "Don't go anywhere."

He had to be kidding. "Where would I go?"

"Back downstairs to flirt with that guy at the craps table."

"He told me I reminded him of his granddaughter."

He grinned. "That's good to know. I'd hate to think you'd throw me over for someone twice my age."

"I will if you don't hurry up."

After Brett rushed out of the room, and the spontaneity had been ruined, Cammie tried to will away the misgivings. Of course he would be prepared enough to keep condoms readily on hand. Spontaneous sex was probably as much a part of his life as his songs. But why should she care? This was just purely physical attraction, or so she kept telling herself.

Still, she didn't have any intention of stopping what they'd started. As soon as he came back, she was going to lose herself in the experience and deal with the fallout later….

"Cammie!"

The sound of Brett's distressed voice sent her upright and to the adjoining door. She opened it to find Brett seated on the edge of the sofa next to an ashen and barely conscious Pat.

Brett looked up at her, alarm in his eyes. "Call 9-1-1."

CHAPTER EIGHT

WHEN SHE AWOKE the next morning in the ICU waiting room, Cammie's back ached from spending hours on the less-than-comfortable sofa. Her heart ached knowing that Pat was in a hospital bed, suffering from a yet-to-be determined ailment. She'd taken a thirty-minute break to return to the hotel and changed into T-shirt and jeans. After that, she'd fallen asleep against Brett's shoulder between periodic reports from the staff at hour intervals, while the guys had camped out on the remaining chairs. They'd all been very quiet, clearly scared to death, though they would never admit it.

But at the moment, she was the only one in the small room since the boys had left to find some breakfast. Brett returned a few minutes later with much-needed coffee. "Thought you could use this," he said as he handed her one paper cup. "No cream or sugar and probably strong enough to set your hair on fire."

She could use all the strength she could get. "That works. Thanks."

He took his place beside her and patted her leg. "How are you holding up?"

"I'm okay. How are you doing?"

He leaned forward and draped his arms on his thighs, clutching the coffee cup between his parted knees. "I'll be fine as soon as I know Pat's going to be okay."

She rubbed his back in a soothing gesture. "Pat's a strong guy. He'll be fine."

He straightened and sighed. "I hope you're right. He's been like a father to me. A better dad than mine ever was."

She sensed his turmoil as keenly as if it were her own. "He's a remarkable man."

"Yeah, he is." Brett sat silent for a moment before he set the untouched coffee on the table before them. "After Jana left me and took Lacey with her, I went pretty wild. Too much booze and too many women, anything to keep me from wallowing in self-pity. He told me, and I quote, 'Get your act together, son, or you're gonna burn out before your star even starts to rise.'"

Cammie immediately thought of Mark, only his wildness resulted more from self-indulgence than self-pity. "So he whipped you into shape, did he?"

He smiled, but only slightly. "He probably saved my life. Now I just wish someone would tell us what's wrong with him so I know what we're up against."

"I'm sure they will as soon as they know," she

said with as much confidence as she could muster. "And let's hope they know something soon. One more night on this sofa and I'll request to be Pat's roommate."

Catching her off guard, Brett smiled and pulled her close to his side before giving her a soft, innocent kiss. The growing connection between them was uncanny, the intimacy undeniable, as if they'd known each other for years, not weeks. As if they'd become more than only employee and employer. Maybe she was just imagining things. Or maybe it was simply the circumstance. Then he gave her a meaningful look before he kissed her again, a little less innocently this time, but not quite long enough to be deemed completely inappropriate. Or so she thought until Brett pointed to the windowed door and released a resounding groan.

Cammie discovered a trio of gaping band members with faces pressed against the glass, noses looking piglike, eyes wide and lips molded into distorted grins.

"Do you think they saw us?" Cammie said through a false smile and in her best ventriloquist imitation.

"I'd bet on it," Brett answered as he walked to the door. When he opened it, the gawking group entered in their usual melodramatic fashion.

Bull fell back against one wall and clutched his chest. "Call a doctor! I think I've come down with the love bug."

"Me, too," Rusty said, choking and gasping for air. "I need some mouth-to-mouth, so someone call me a nurse."

Brett scowled as he returned to the sofa. "Cut it out, guys. We're too tired for this, and Pat's situation isn't a damn joke."

"Lighten up, Brett," Bull said. "Besides, the two of you looked like Pat was the last thing on your minds a minute ago."

"Didn't look too tired, either," Rusty added.

Cammie felt a blush flowing over her cheeks while Brett studied the toe of his boot.

Bull chuckled and slapped Brett on the back. "Okay, we'll lay off for now. But you know us, we won't forget it."

Oh, joy. Cammie could just imagine what the future would bring in terms of teasing. Her future with Brett was much more up in the air. Future? They didn't have a future aside from a tour that could be indefinitely suspended, depending on Pat's condition. That might mean an early return to Memphis and saying goodbye to Brett and his band of merry men for good, and that somehow made her sad.

After everyone settled down, Rusty tuned the TV into a game show while the others dozed and chatted. At 9:00 a.m. a young doctor appeared and reported they were still running tests and he wasn't authorized to release more information. "Three at a time can go in to see him," he said. "But you can only stay for five minutes."

Brett told the others to go ahead as he remained behind with Cammie. They sat close on the couch, holding hands like teenagers. No words passed between them while they waited for their opportunity, only oddly comfortable silence until the group returned, looking lost and distressed.

Brett immediately shot to his feet. "How is he?"

Bull shook his head. "Damn, Brett, he looks like hell. It makes me sick to see him this way."

"Yeah, he can barely talk," Rusty said. "He doesn't deserve this."

Jeremy kept his head lowered as if the sight of Pat had been too much to bear.

"Let's go," Brett said, signaling Cammie to follow.

When they entered the room, Cammie swallowed hard around her shock. Pat looked so pale and helpless, a definite change from the strapping senior band member with the terrific sense of humor.

Brett approached the narrow bed and laid a hand on Pat's arm. "Hey, man, this is no way to get out of a gig. If you wanted tomorrow off, you should have told me."

Pat slowly opened his eyes and attempted a weak smile. "You know me, never could say no." When Pat offered his hand, Cammie stepped up and took it. "How are you holdin' up, gal?"

She smiled. "I'm okay. Just get better real quick. I'm having a heck of a time keeping these guys in line."

"That's probably what put me here." His smile

faded as he looked back to Brett. "What are you going to do...about the concert?"

"Don't worry about it," Brett said. "We'll manage. Tim's arranged for Bob Walker to sit in for you. He's in Arizona so he can get here quick."

"Good picker," he said. "Can't sing a lick, though."

Brett shrugged. "I'll just go it alone."

"Can't do it, Brett. New song needs some harmony." Pat lifted Cammie's hand. "This gal can handle it."

Cammie's mouth momentarily dropped open before she snapped it shut. "No way. I can't handle that."

"Sure you can, honey," Pat said. "You'll do a fine job."

Before she could respond, a nurse came in and reprimanded the pair for overstaying their welcome. When Cammie leaned down to give Pat a kiss on the cheek, he whispered, "If you won't do it for me, then do it for Brett."

How could she refuse either request? Yet how could she thrust herself back into a situation that she'd long since left, with good reason? "Okay. I'll think about it." The only promise she was willing to make.

As she left the room, Pat's suggestion left her stomach in knots and her mind in turmoil. Surely Brett wouldn't consider the proposition. After all, she hadn't performed in public in years. She did know Brett's music, but not well enough to pull off harmony. Singing lyrics with a radio was quite different from singing in front of a live audience, thousands of people hanging on every note, expecting nothing short of perfection.

Cammie hadn't noticed Brett trailing behind her until he grabbed her arm and guided her into a small alcove, away from the hospital chaos and prying eyes. "Pat's right. You should give it a shot."

She propped her hands on her hips. "You must be insane."

She started to walk away but he stopped her again. "I've heard you sing, Cammie. You could do it."

"I can't."

"You can." He sent her a teasing, sexy smile. "You're dying to try it and you know it."

He couldn't be more wrong. "Am not."

He pulled her to him and sent soft kisses over her face. "Say you will, Camille."

He was taking extreme advantage at the moment. "You're not playing fair."

"I'm not playing. I'm dead serious."

She pushed him back to arm's length. "Tell you what. I'll rehearse with you this afternoon. If it doesn't work, then you're on your own."

He picked her up off her feet and spun her around. "You'll be great. Hell, we might even have you signed before we leave here. You, me and Pat will make a great team."

"Whoa," she said when he placed her back onto

the ground. "I'm doing this for Pat's benefit, not mine."

Brett took her palm and planted a kiss on her wrist. "What about me?"

If he only knew the role he played in every decision in recent history. "Okay, so maybe a teeny part of me is doing it for you."

He looked more than satisfied with her answer. "Let's go tell the boys."

Brett took Cammie's hand and led her through the hallway with a spring to his step, as if they were kids on their way to a circus—which might not be so far from the truth.

"ONE MORE TIME," Brett said, tapping his foot in time with the beat.

They'd been going at it for two hours. Cammie felt exhausted from the work and her throat had begun to feel fatigued from the effort. No doubt about it—Brett Taylor was a talented, pain-in-the-patoot perfectionist. His earlier hits she'd had no trouble with, but even he seemed unsure about his latest endeavor. Unfortunately for her, his next release debuted tomorrow night and all the details had to be worked out.

Cammie took a quick drink and began to sing when the time came but Brett stopped again before finishing the first refrain. "Dammit, that's not it."

He walked away muttering a few mild oaths.

Cammie was about to tell him this whole idea wasn't working when he came back to her.

"Sorry, Cammie. It's not you, it's me. Let's take ten and try it again."

Brett left the immediate area, and while he was gone, Cammie dropped onto the stool, feeling drained of all energy.

"It really isn't you, Cammie," Rusty said. "He's having a hard time right now with a whole lot of things."

"I know, Rusty. He's missing Pat."

Rusty pulled up a nearby chair. "It's not just Pat. The last time he had a woman around during rehearsal, it was Jana."

"His ex-wife."

"Yeah. I think your singing with him has brought back a lot of memories."

Memories of the woman he loved and perhaps still missed. How could she have been so foolish as to agree to such a stupid masquerade? She didn't have the talent to take on something of this magnitude, or the ability to make Brett forget every woman he knew before her, especially his ex-wife. "Maybe this isn't such a good idea."

"I'm not saying that," Rusty said. "Just be patient. You're doing a great job. Something's been missing in the live performances for a while and I think you may have filled that spot."

Cammie smiled with gratitude. "Thanks, Rusty.

I'll stay, but only because of Pat, and because you're such a sweet-talker."

Before Brett returned, Cammie formulated a plan of action. If he was having trouble forgetting, then he needed to be reminded she was the one who needed his attention now. As soon as he returned, Cammie lifted her microphone and placed it immediately beside Brett's.

"What are you doing?" he asked.

"If we're going to do this right, I'm going to stand over here and inspire you."

"Inspire me?"

"That's what I said."

He frowned. "How?"

"Just wait and see."

The guys shuffled their feet and stifled their laughter, prompting Brett to give them a stern look. "We ain't got a clue," Bull said from his position behind the drums, arms raised as if Brett had a gun pointed at his chest.

Cammie started to bring the lyrics to her self-appointed spot on stage, but decided against it. Shuffling paper would definitely spoil the mood she was trying to create.

Brett grabbed up his guitar and began to strum.

"Do you have to play that?" she asked.

"No, but why the hell not?"

"Don't get testy. I thought we could go over the song first with only the band's accompaniment. Once we get it down, you can go back to playing."

Looking somewhat perturbed, he set the guitar aside against a speaker. "Anything else?"

She tried on an angelic smile, hoping to calm this devil in blue jeans and boots. "I think that about does it."

Brett turned to Rusty. "Okay, hit it."

As the introduction played, Cammie took Brett's hand that rested at his side. He seemed surprised by the gesture, but didn't pull away. Instead, he looked into her eyes.

The love song might have been initially inspired by Brett's former wife, but Cammie was with him now. She stood by his side, declaring lyrical devotion with a voice perfectly in sync with his. At one point after the second verse, and before the chorus, when the words spoke of making love, his arm slipped around her waist, pulling her so close they had no need for two microphones. Their united voices belted out a heartrending message, leaving Cammie feeling completely exhilarated.

When they neared the final refrain of the ballad, he moved his face closer to hers. And when the notes died down to a soft echo in the empty auditorium, they sealed the number with a spontaneous kiss.

Applause rang out, jolting Cammie back to reality and sending her away from Brett. Clearly they'd gotten totally carried away, and she suspected they might live to regret it.

"Hot damn, Brett," Bull shouted. "That was some singing."

Rusty patted Cammie's cheek. "Gal, you were definitely inspiring to the man here."

Brett seemed unusually distant, not even bothering with any comebacks to the band's ribbing. "Can you guys leave Cammie and me alone for a while?" he asked quietly.

"They want to be alone to take up where they left off," Jeremy said with an elbow in Bull's side. "Can't imagine why."

After everyone left the stage, laughing and tossing out innuendo, Cammie took a seat on the stool and waited. Brett stood without moving, hand to chin, as if contemplating what he wanted to say. She didn't understand his motive for asking the boys to leave, and she didn't care to speculate. "What is it?"

"This is all wrong," he said.

"What's all wrong?"

"What we're doing. It's not good."

His words pierced her confidence like verbal shards of glass. It was going to be over before it had truly begun. She should be relieved because she didn't need this responsibility or relationship. They didn't need it. But her heart fell when she thought of what could have been, followed by an internal indictment of her foolishness.

Cammie reached out and took both of his hands, prepared to bow out gracefully. "You're right, Brett. This isn't good."

He moved between her knees and bent to kiss the

top of her head. "I don't think you understand what I'm saying, sweetheart."

Sweetheart? She pulled away and searched his eyes. "Yes, I understand. You're talking about what's happening between us and how it's really gotten out of hand. I understand why—"

"I'm talking about your singing, this way of life. You're too good for it, Cammie."

Now she was really confused. "You mean my singing with you tomorrow? It's only temporary."

"Maybe not. You're damn good. This might be your big break. And it might mean you'll be so popular with the crowd that Tim's going to want you to continue with us. I don't want you to feel pressured. Or maybe I don't want you to be seduced by it. There's a lot of power in performing. And a lot of sacrifice."

Cammie was relieved that her future warranted his concern. She could handle that. He seemed very serious about what he'd said, but she was also determined to do right by Pat. "Look, I'm only a temporary addition. Nothing will come of it beyond my filling in for two performances. I'm not easily seduced." She felt the color rise to her face. "Not in the musical sense, anyway."

Brett laughed and pulled her from the chair, straight into his strong arms. "So you can handle it, can you?"

"I can handle it."

"What about me?"

"That remains to be seen."

"Do you trust me, Cammie?"

She paused while she considered saying words she never believed she'd say to any man ever again. "I do trust you, Brett. I put my voice in your hands, at least for the time being."

He softly kissed her. "I put my life in yours every night you're driving my bus. Now I can return the favor."

He kissed her again, his lips playing passionately against hers, his breath coming hard and heavy. Weary with relief, with desire, she wanted nothing more than to go upstairs and fall into bed with him. But at the moment, Pat's welfare was number one on the list.

She ended the kiss and rested her face against his shoulder. "Before we dissolve into the stage, I think we should go pay Pat a visit."

"Pat and his damn timing again. But you're right, we have to go tell him how well it went."

"He'll be very pleased."

"I'm very pleased."

And Cammie believed nothing could ruin her good mood.

"I'M SORRY, MR. TAYLOR, but we've suspended visitors for the time being. He's had a few setbacks this afternoon. We're having trouble keeping his blood pressure stable and he's been fairly agitated."

The doctor's words were body blows to Brett.

Pat had done so well that morning, no one believed they'd still be facing a crisis. "Is there something you're not telling us about his condition?"

The man removed his glasses and slipped them in his lab coat pocket. "We only know that he's had some arrhythmia, but it could be from dehydration due to food poisoning. Or it could be his heart. We're going to run a few more tests and then we'll know more. I'll keep you posted." Then he turned on his heels like a drill sergeant and strode down the corridor.

After the doctor disappeared out of sight, Brett crumpled onto the couch feeling like a deflated balloon. Cammie had gone for sandwiches, taking Jeremy along with her. Rusty and Bull claimed the chairs across from the sofa where they stared at various focal points throughout the room, avoiding eye contact.

"Think we should cancel the concert, Brett?" Rusty finally asked.

"I don't know. I can't think right now."

Bull tossed a candy wrapper into a nearby wastebasket. "I'm sure they'd understand."

"The promoters will be royally pissed," Rusty said. "We could've told them this morning. It would've given them some time to find someone else."

But this morning Brett hadn't known Pat could be worse off than anyone had thought. If something happened to Pat, nothing would be the same. He would be losing another person partially responsible for his success and sanity.

Cammie entered a few moments later carrying a large sack of hamburgers and fries. Brett took a whiff of the food and knew instantly he wouldn't be able to force one bite into his churning stomach.

"Here," she said, handing him a paper-wrapped bundle. "One bacon-cheeseburger, cut the onions, with mayo."

Brett took the package and tossed it aside. "I can't eat until I know he's okay."

She sat beside him. "Have they said what's wrong yet?"

"No. They're running more tests to see if something's going on with his heart. Hopefully we'll find out more later. In the meantime, we can't see him."

She smiled and laid a hand on his arm. "He's going to be okay. He's getting the care he needs and he's tough as nails. Are sure you don't want anything to eat?"

"Not now."

She dropped the sandwich back into the bag. "All right. You know what you can manage."

Cammie wasn't the kind to push him to do things he didn't feel like doing, something Brett was beginning to appreciate. Many people, including his manager, had taken on the role of nursemaid. If they weren't reminding him he needed more rest, they nagged him about getting too thin or needing a haircut. The nights he'd joined Cammie at the helm of the bus, she'd never scolded him about sleeping.

The thought brought a smile to his face and one to hers in return.

"What is it now, Taylor?" she asked. "Do I have mascara under my eyes and look like a raccoon, or maybe something's dribbling down my chin?"

He gently touched her cheek. Just having her there was the one positive in this entire nightmare. "You look as pretty as you always do."

"Thank you, Mr. Taylor. You're certainly a good liar." She smiled and went back to her sandwich.

He decided to use her as a sounding board. "Bull and Rusty think we might want to cancel the show."

Cammie's eyes grew wide. "No way. Pat's counting on us. How do you think that would make him feel if he knew we were canceling on his account?"

"She's right, guys," Bull admitted.

Rusty sighed. "Yeah, she is. Pat would skin us alive if he knew we canceled."

Brett nodded in agreement. "Then it's settled. Walker's coming in tonight." He checked his watch. "He'll be here by nine so we'll have to rehearse late. We'll stay until then. I'll give the hospital my cell number in case anything changes."

"Do you want me to stay here, Brett?" Cammie asked. "I think I've done enough damage for one day."

His first instinct was to keep her nearby for his

own sake, but that would be selfish. "Do you mind? At least until rehearsal's over."

"Of course not. You'll all feel better knowing someone's here with him. I can rehearse again in the morning."

Bull leaned over and laid his bulky hand on top of hers. "You're a real asset to this group, Cammie."

Rusty and Jeremy did likewise, hands stacked one on top of the other where Brett placed his on top. "Tomorrow's for Pat," Bull said.

"Yeah, for Pat," Brett repeated, silently hoping Pat would make another tomorrow.

At 2:00 a.m., Brett came for her. Cammie felt as though she'd been put through the wringer, her body longing for sleep in a real bed. Brett spoke with the doctor before leading her out of the hospital and into the warm night. At least the news had been favorable—Pat was doing better, although the test results had yet to be revealed.

He stopped and placed his arms around her when they reached the Hummer he'd rented for the duration. "It's nice out here," he said with a sigh. "You know what I'd like to do?"

"Pass out?"

"Take you to some remote place in the desert with no distractions or interruptions where we could just be together all night."

She wasn't exactly sure how she should respond, even if she did like the plan. A lot. "That sounds wonderful, but honestly, with Pat's issues, and the fact we're sleep-deprived, I don't think it's a good idea."

Brett tucked her hair behind her ear. "You're right. We have to stay close by in case Pat needs us, and you definitely need some sleep."

"I could probably sleep right here, right now, in the parking lot. But you need to rest, too. You still have back-to-back shows tomorrow night."

"True," he said. "But if you need me for anything during the night, I'm just a room away."

Sometimes she believed she was beginning to need him too much.

AFTER THEY ARRIVED at the hotel room, Cammie and Brett parted at their appointed rooms without even a brief kiss, only a polite goodbye. She chalked up Brett's sudden distance to fatigue. She wanted to try out the jetted tub but took a hot shower instead. Then she quickly dried her hair, dressed in a plain cotton gown and settled into bed. But try as she might, she could only toss and turn and contemplate her complicated relationship with the sometimes-mysterious man on the other side of the door.

She rolled to her side, fluffed the pillow and attempted to coax herself asleep by reciting the lyrics she had to remember tomorrow night. By the time she made it to the second song, she began to drift off, only to be awakened by the sound of an opening door.

She remained still as stone when she felt the mattress bend beside her. "Cammie?"

She rolled over to find Brett seated on the edge of the bed, his features unclear in the limited light, but she could see he was shirtless. "Yes?"

"Did I wake you up?"

"No." One more minute and he would have. "Is something wrong?"

"I can't sleep. I'm having a hard time shutting off my brain."

"I know what you mean."

"I was just wondering if you mind if I sleep in here with you. Just to sleep. I don't expect anything else."

He sounded so unsure, she couldn't help but smile. "Can you really do that, Brett? Sleep with a woman without wanting to *sleep* with her in the figurative sense?"

"It's been a long time, but I'm willing to try if you are," he said. "I'll stay on my side of the bed."

When cows sprouted wings. "I guess since it's a king, it's big enough for both of us."

"Are you sure?"

She flipped back the covers and patted the mattress. "Climb in before I change my mind."

"I can't sleep in my jeans."

She might not sleep at all if he wasn't wearing them. "Then take them off."

After he complied, Cammie rolled away from him again and tried to ignore the fact he was basically down to the bare minimum when it came to clothes. Although she'd only had a few hours' sleep in the past forty-eight, she would gladly make love with him all night. Instead, she decided to put him—and herself—to the ultimate test.

"Brett."

"Yeah?"

"You don't have to stay on your side of the bed. I wouldn't mind having you a little closer."

"Not a problem." He fitted himself to her back and draped his arm over her hip, his bare legs molded to the backs of her thighs. Having him so near gave her an odd sense of comfort, and a deep-seated longing.

If they could make it through one night without giving in to temptation, then maybe chemistry wasn't their only common ground. However, she'd wager her last dollar that one of them wouldn't last more than a few hours, and it could very well be her.

CHAPTER NINE

By THE TIME THIS WAS OVER, he'd deserve some kind of a medal of honor for uncommon valor in the face of temptation.

As Brett continued to hold her through the night, Cammie's breathing came steady and slow, while his sounded like he'd just run a marathon. He'd been so exhausted he'd mistakenly thought that once he'd found the right position with her in his arms, he'd pass out. Not a chance.

Every time Cammie moved against him, his body sprang to life. Her hair smelled great, and so did her skin, like his mother's favorite gardenias. He tried counting concert dates and his number-one songs, and when that didn't work he tried counting all the reasons why he was no good for a woman like Cammie. Why he shouldn't even consider making love to her.

Hell, who was he trying to fool? He wanted to sleep with her in every sense of the word. He wanted to touch and taste every inch of her, all the soft satiny feminine parts. He'd already sampled some of the finer points. Now he wanted more. He wanted it all.

But he'd be damned if he made the first move after all their talk about trust. So he found a semi-comfortable position, gave her a gentle squeeze and closed his eyes....

He came awake to kisses on his neck and fingertips trailing over his side. He slowly opened his eyes to find Cammie curled against his chest, soft and warm and obviously willing. He figured it was some sleep-induced response, but when she lifted her face and grazed his lips with hers, he wasn't so sure. "Cammie, are you awake?"

"Very." She rubbed her sweet little body against his and nearly sent him over the edge. "Apparently so are you."

Oh, yeah, he was. Cocked and loaded and ready to fire. He'd be playing with fire if he kept going since the one missing item that had previously halted their lovemaking could end it now. He'd just make this all about her for the moment and worry about the damn condoms later.

He began by kissing her slowly, deliberately, just a light exploration before he turned up the heat. She responded by leisurely rubbing her hands down his back and working her way to his butt.

This was the way it should be. Not some hurried act performed with the sole intent of sexual gratification. He cared a hell of a lot for the woman in his arms, something he hadn't experienced in a long time. The realization was unexpected, but he'd have to take it out and examine it later. He had more important things to consider at the moment, namely making her feel real good.

Brett took the hem of Cammie's gown, pulled it up over her head and tossed it away, leaving not a whole lot left between them except a pair of her skimpy panties and his boxer shorts. Just a lot of bare flesh that he intended to take his time exploring, beginning with her breasts. Cammie had other ideas. That became clear when she guided his palm to her belly, right above the thin lace band. Suddenly nothing seemed more important than pleasing her, even if it meant skipping a few steps.

He slid his hand beneath her panties and discovered she was soft and warm and wet. He began to gently tease and stroke her, inside and out, intending to bring her to the brink until she couldn't take it anymore. But he'd barely implemented the plan before she went off like a rocket.

She buried her face into his neck and muttered, "I'm sorry." She sounded innocent and apprehensive and maybe even guilty.

He brushed her hair back from her face and tipped her chin up, encouraging her to look at him. "Why are you sorry?"

"I just didn't expect that kind of reaction."

He kind of liked her reaction. "I'm hoping it meant I was doing something right."

She sent him a shaky smile. "Oh, yes. You could say that. Maybe even too right."

No such thing, in his opinion. Something else was going on with her, and he wanted to get to the bottom of it. "Are you having second thoughts?"

"No. I'm just overwhelmed."

Overwhelmed? He'd barely touched her. "Are you worried about where we go from here?"

"I'm worried about what you're going to say when I tell you something I should've told you before now."

He was almost afraid to ask. "What is it?"

"I've never made love with anyone."

He couldn't have been more stunned if the entire hotel staff had walked in on them. "No one?"

"No one."

The concept was unbelievable. Cammie was beautiful, sensuous, desirable—all the things that men instantly found attractive. And for some reason he was the first man she'd allowed to get this close to her. The thought of being her first disturbed him.

"How is that possible?" The only thing he could manage at the moment.

"If you mean *why* did I save my virtue, it wasn't exactly planned. I spent so much time around men at the business, I thought guys were all the same—crude and interested in only one thing. Not to mention my grandfather and Bud were like a couple of mother hens. And then there was that little prom-night incident."

This he had to hear. "Prom night?"

After covering up to her chin, she leaned over and snapped on the bedside lamp. "I know what you're thinking—Cammie is a living cliché—and you're right. It's that age-old story of studious girl goes to the senior prom with popular boy, minus the unplanned pregnancy. I thought, Everyone else is doing it, so why not? Let's just say Rocky had been drinking and he passed out before we got to the 'doing it' part."

He tried to stifle a laugh, without success. "His name was Rocky?"

She frowned. "Yes, and he was about as bright as a briefcase, and a liar to boot. He was so mortified over what he'd done that he told everyone in school that we did do the deed. I spent the two weeks until graduation trying to live it down."

"Rocky was an idiot."

"Yes, and a few years later, I met Mark, who had many of those same qualifications, and we know how wonderful that turned out to be. I didn't feel I was ready to take the next step until now."

Until now. Brett rolled onto his back. "Damn, Cammie, why didn't you tell me sooner?"

"So sorry I forgot to pack my I'm a Virgin button along with the condoms and the zebra panties."

He took her hand into his. "I'm sorry I acted so shocked. I mean, hell, it's not that common. Not anymore."

"Is this going to make a difference where we're concerned? If it is, I want you to leave."

Should he leave? He sure as hell didn't want to leave. He wanted her more than anything he'd wanted in a long time. "No way."

"Then where do we go from here?"

"Right where we left off."

He brought her back into his arms and kissed her again. He didn't know what would happen and right then he didn't care. He knew he might regret the decision. Like Pat had said, Cammie was special and he didn't want to hurt her. But they were good together. Destined to be even better.

When Cammie went for the waistband on his boxer-briefs, he caught her wrist. "If you go anywhere near Joe right now, it might be all over before we get started."

She narrowed her eyes. "You named it Joe?"

"Yeah. Joe knows how to please a woman."

"That's rather cocky," she said, then added, "No pun intended."

He couldn't help but laugh. Loud enough to cause Cammie to slap her hand over his mouth. "You're going to wake everyone up."

She had a point, and so did he. "You're right. I don't want to run into anyone when I go get the condoms."

Cammie let out an exasperated breath. "Next time, please tie the things around your neck."

He liked that "next time" thing. "You got it."

"Maybe I should go get it."

He kissed her chin and climbed out of bed. "You think I'd send you into a room full of barracudas to retrieve condoms?"

She pretended to pout. "You're not going to disappear and not come back?"

"Not a chance." Not this time, come hell or high water.

SHE'D ALWAYS KNOWN that if she took that final step, it would have to be with someone special. At one time she was willing to give herself to Mark. She'd made a mistake in thinking he was the right one. Maybe she'd made the same mistake by choosing Brett.

To heck with her doubts, she was sick of them. More than anything, she wanted Brett to make love to her. She was beyond the childish dreams of forever. She needed to discover what it felt like to be a woman, not the faithful granddaughter or someone's surrogate sister or just one of the guys.

He should be back by now. Maybe he'd reconsidered. Maybe she should have let him find out after the fact instead of confessing her inexperience. No. Honesty was the best policy no matter what happened from this point forward.

She sat up when she heard the phone, then the voices. The crew was up and about. Cammie plopped back onto the bed and with a frustrated yank pulled the sheet over her face. Someone was trying to tell her something, and she suspected it was that bitch named Karma.

Brett opened the door and asked, "Are you dressed?"

Cammie laughed and removed the covers from her face. "What do you think?"

He sat on the edge of the bed and rubbed her sheet-covered leg. "The boys are up and the hospital called."

Fear grabbed her and wouldn't let go. "Pat?"

"Good news. He's asking for us. As a matter of fact, he's giving the nurses hell."

"Thank goodness," Cammie said. "Guess this means we have to get ready to go."

"Guess it does." He leaned over and gave her a gentle kiss. "After the show tonight, we'll have the whole night to spend together. Alone."

"Promise?"

"Lady, I guarantee it." He took her hand. "But I can't guarantee I'll do my best tonight when you're all I'll be thinking about."

Cammie smiled. "Just think of something else." When she sat up and placed a kiss on the charming cleft in his chin, the sheet slipped down, revealing her bare breasts.

Brett hopped off the bed like he'd been shot. "Cover yourself, woman. Otherwise, I'm calling Pat and telling him he's going to have to wait."

"I'VE HEARD I'VE BEEN REPLACED," Pat said through a weak smile.

Cammie realized he might look gaunt and tired, but he was still as feisty as ever. "No one could ever replace you," she said. "But I am singing on key most the time."

Brett placed his hands on her shoulders. "She's doing better than that. She's got me singing on key."

"Praise be!" Pat said with more energy than she'd expected.

"So what's the verdict on your condition?" Brett asked.

Pat rubbed his stubbly chin. "Well, I ate some bad food, but my liver's good, which means I gave up the whiskey none too soon. And my cholesterol's a bit high. Other than that, I'll live."

Cammie worried he wasn't being completely truthful. "And your heart?"

"I've got a little bit of blockage," he said. "The doc told me I need to see a cardiologist when I get back home."

Brett frowned. "That's still a couple months away. Are you sure you're cleared to travel?"

"Yep." He turned his attention to Brett. "Do you mind stepping out, son, so I can give this gal here a few words of encouragement?"

Brett pointed at him. "That better be all you're intending to do. We don't want you to have another setback."

When Brett backed out of the room, Cammie

claimed a seat on the edge of the bed. "What do you really want to tell me?"

Pat took her hand and looked at her seriously. "Something's going on between you and Brett. Something more than singing."

The truth came alive in Pat's words, catching Cammie off guard. Pat was an honest man, and very perceptive, so she didn't dare lie. "I suppose you could say that."

"Some advice then. Brett's a hard one to figure. I love him like a son, but that don't mean I always understand him. All I want to say—at the risk of sounding like your dad—is be careful. Brett has a lot more to give than he realizes. It's going to take someone real special to convince him of that. But don't let him hurt you in the process."

Pat echoed the conflicting thoughts she'd been having for the past few days. Brett could hurt her and she knew it. She also knew how happy he'd made her in the brief time they'd been together. "I'm a tough girl, Pat. I'm not sure what it is that Brett and I feel for each other—or will feel. I only know that he needs me right now. I'm prepared for whatever happens."

"Good," he said, patting her hand. "Now you go knock 'em dead tonight and remember I'll be with you in spirit."

Cammie gave him a hug. "See you later. And stop giving the nurses grief."

Pat laid a hand on his heart. "You really know how to spoil an old codger's good time."

She left his room, taking with her his sage wisdom and kind smile, exactly what she would remember tonight before she took the stage. And she had little time to prepare for the first 6:00 p.m. performance. Very little time to make certain she looked her best.

CAMMIE HAD LEFT REHEARSAL, caught a cab to the mall on the strip and went on a frantic search for just the right look. She was now dressed in a new pair of dark-wash jeans and a black silky sleeveless top with a little silver embellishment right above her cleavage, which was a bit more exposed than she would've liked. She'd also chosen a pair of platform shoes so she wouldn't seem quite as short.

"Do I look okay?" she asked Rusty after she made her way behind the stage.

Rusty whistled when she did a quick turn. "Brett won't be able to hit a note when he sees you in those jeans."

"Thanks." She kneaded her hands. "So I guess this is it."

"Try to relax, Cammie," he said. "Don't think about the people out in the audience. The lights will be so bright you won't see much. Pretend it's another rehearsal."

Hard to do when she realized it was the real thing. "Okay."

A family of battering rams soon took up residence in her belly, and her palms had already begun to perspire. If she could just find Brett, she'd feel better. She hadn't seen him since she left the hotel that morning and she had to wonder if he'd purposefully been avoiding her.

"Five minutes," someone called from behind her. She could swear her heart lurched and lodged in her throat, which could make it darn difficult to sing.

Bull rushed passed her but stopped before taking his spot behind the drums. He gave her a quick kiss on the cheek. "Good luck, hon. You can do this."

You can do this, she chanted. She'd done it before. Just not in front of so many people in a first-class venue. And where was Brett?

A man with a clipboard approached her, flipped up a page and scanned the one underneath. "Are you Ms. Carson?"

She could deny it and make a quick getaway. "Yes."

"Stage left, just a little way past Mr. Taylor."

"Now?"

"Yes, ma'am. You're on in two."

Two minutes? In two minutes she was making her debut, if she could get her legs to move. Her hands trembled like a leaf in a breeze. She shook them repeatedly at her sides—until someone gripped them and she felt the kiss on her neck. "Lookin' good, sweetheart. You're going to make the men in the audience real happy."

Her runaway heart had been calm compared to the dance it did the moment she caught the first glimpse of Brett. He wore a navy tailored shirt that contrasted with his gorgeous blue in his eyes. His black felt hat had been replaced by a white straw, clearly indicating tonight he was playing the good cowboy.

When her hand automatically went to his smooth, shaven face, he kissed her palm and set her back away from him. "I think I'm in trouble. I won't be able to keep my eyes off you long enough to sing."

"Let's go, folks. Forty-five seconds!" the man with the clipboard called.

Brett leaned to give her a slow, sultry kiss. "It's your night to shine, sweetheart."

She wiped the residual lipstick from his mouth and smiled. "As long as my brain doesn't burn out before the second song."

"You'll do fine. Just follow my lead."

He turned her toward the stage and swatted her bottom, sending her reluctantly forward toward her position. She made her way to the microphone where a glass of water rested on a small round table nearby. She took a quick drink and glanced at the posted order of the songs to be performed. She said a quick prayer for Pat in hopes of making him proud, then cleared her throat.

When the ribbon of light peeking from under the curtain went down, Cammie took a hasty glance back at the boys. Rusty and Bull smiled at her and

Jeremy gave her a thumbs-up. Even Bob Walker waved, and she'd barely met him.

"Three, two, one…"

The introduction began.

The stage lights came blaring down in a brilliant red.

The curtain opened.

Showtime.

Rusty was right. She could barely see anything beyond the first few tables running perpendicular to the front of the stage. Having a few moments to tune into the atmosphere proved to be a blessing for Cammie. The crowd seemed more sophisticated and subdued than usual. She relaxed somewhat while waiting for the end of the instrumental, inhaling and exhaling several times in an attempt to calm her nerves.

Then the announcer introduced the headliner.

Brett didn't bound out as usual. Instead, he ascended on a recessed platform at the back of the stage like some wild angel, minus the halo and wings. As the spotlight centered on him, he strode forward to rousing applause, cries and whistles of the crowd.

Welcome to Las Vegas.

Cammie's heart clamored again when she met his gaze and he gave her a sexy wink. She managed to tear her gaze away to glance at the first number listed on the sheet. The gesture was pure reflex since she'd memorized every song in order of appearance.

Brett said a few words, mostly about enjoying Vegas. If asked five minutes later, Cammie couldn't tell anyone what he'd said beyond that. When the bars of the first song began to play, she worried her voice might fail her. But whether it be instinct or adrenaline kicking in, she belted out her portion of the vocals as if she'd done this every night of her entire life.

Brett turned to her and smiled as soon as the song ended. If she suddenly keeled over or her vocal cords disintegrated, nothing could ever be as memorable as that smile. It gave her the confidence to continue and the strength to do more than an adequate job.

After the fifth song, Brett paused to introduce the band and began with Pat's replacement. "I'd like to thank Bob Walker on bass guitar for filling in tonight. Our band's leader, Pat Jordan, is in the hospital. He's pretty sick, so we ask you to keep him in your thoughts and prayers."

Then he approached Cammie and took her hand. "This is, by far, the prettiest backup singer this band's ever had and she can stand proud with the best. Ladies and gentlemen, Camille Carson."

The crowd roared when he called her name. At first she thought the show of approval was a product of her imagination, but when the noise failed to calm, Brett led her to the front of the stage where she took a small bow. When she turned back toward the band, she found the guys applauding, as well.

Then Brett moved her microphone next to his for

their rendition of the song they'd sung earlier. The song that had ended in a kiss. Assuming she would remain back during the number, she sent him a look of confusion.

He leaned over and whispered, "Can't do it without some inspiration. If I don't kiss you this time, it's because Tim's in the audience and he'd kill me for ruining my single-guy-on-the-prowl reputation with the ladies."

Brett introduced the debut song and when the intro started, Cammie leaned toward him. "I expect to be repaid after the last show."

"You bet. And one more thing. Sing melody on the second verse."

"What?"

"Just do it."

Even though she couldn't understand the reason for the sudden change, it was far too late to argue. When Brett sang the first few lines, the emotional lyrics lilted over the vast hall like a soothing breeze. Brett's and Cammie's voices melded together during the chorus in perfect harmony, as if they'd always sung together.

When the second verse came, she did as she was told, singing the melody instead of the harmony. And then she realized he wasn't singing, just standing in place with guitar in hand and a sexy grin on his face. Heaven help her, she was performing solo. Now she'd have to throttle him later.

During a pause in the final refrain, Brett took her

hand and gave it a gentle squeeze. "You're unbelievable, Camille."

How could she possibly stay mad at this man?

When the song ended, regardless of his earlier concern about his reputation, he held her for a long moment. Most people would assume it was the embrace given to a good friend, but Cammie felt so much more. More than she should.

The rest of the concert seemed to fly by, each of Brett's songs supercharged with energy. Cammie became caught up in the chaos—the ultimate power trip—when the audience called for two encores.

Brett dedicated the finale to Pat, and Cammie watched offstage as he delivered a solo performance unparalleled to any she'd seen before. And as he lowered his head and the lights went down, she recognized she was dangerously close to falling in love with the man, not just the performer.

After the curtains went down, Brett hurried offstage, straight to Cammie's side. Despite all the harried activity, he made his way to *her*.

He took her in his arms. "You kicked ass, sweetheart."

"And I ought to kill you dead for that little surprise," she said.

He kissed her forehead. "Think about it. If I'd asked you beforehand to do it, you would've told me to go to hell. Right?"

"Probably. But why would you want me to sing when it's your show?"

"Because you've got a lot of talent, Camille Carson."

"And you've got a lot of nerve throwing me out there like that, Brett Taylor."

He laughed out loud. "You loved it and you know it."

"Okay, okay. It was a rush."

He kissed her lips this time. "Get ready, Cammie. Tonight's just the beginning of the journey."

CHAPTER TEN

THE HOUR BETWEEN performances passed quickly on a wave of adrenaline-induced energy. Brett barely left Cammie's side for the duration and occasionally sneaked a kiss when no one was watching. When the final concert went off without a hitch, including the duet Brett had originally forced on her, she felt as if she could break down the equipment singlehandedly.

"Time to party, Brett," someone called as soon as the curtain came down and the houselights went up.

Brett took her hand, led her down a narrow corridor and into a dressing room. "I have an after-party here in the hotel that I'm obligated to attend. I have to rub elbows with a few promoters and high rollers who've paid big bucks to be there."

Cammie saw their evening together coming to an abrupt halt. "Okay. I'll just hang around in the room and watch a movie or—"

"I want you with me."

Her optimism rose to an all-time high. "Are you sure?"

He slid his arms around her waist. "You bet. You're a part of the band now."

Not exactly the answer she'd wanted. "The show's over, so it's back to the bus duties for me."

"Maybe not. We don't know when Pat will be back on his feet. You might have to fill in for a while longer. If you're game."

As tempting as that might be, she had to be logical. "I guess we'll just have to wait and see." First and foremost, she had to find out what he expected of her tonight. "What should I wear to this little gathering?"

"Do you still have that dress from the other night?"

"Just got it back from the cleaners."

"That will definitely do." He gave her a brief kiss. "Now let's get out of here and get this party started."

SOME PARTY. CAMMIE basically stood in the background in the opulent ballroom and watched while Brett schmoozed with the attendees, including a few attentive female fan club members who'd won their admittance through a website contest. Every now and then, Rusty and Bull—dressed in their Sunday best—would stop by and converse before someone would steal them away. And once more she was left alone playing the role of wallflower. She could attempt to mingle but she wasn't in the mood. She could walk right up to Brett, who was talking to a fawning redhead, and insert herself in the conversation. Or she could call it a night and return to the room.

On that thought, she finished the second glass of champagne and decided to call it a night. Clearly the star had more important things to do, and spending time with her wasn't among them.

She set her glass on a roving waiter's tray and looked around for Brett, who seemed to have disappeared. She couldn't help but wonder if the redhead had absconded with him. Then again, he might have gone along willingly.

Feeling dejected, ridiculously jealous and totally out of her element, she pushed out the double doors and headed for the elevators. She'd barely taken a few steps before a hand caught her wrist and pulled her into a hallway feeding off the main reception area where she came face-to-face with the king of country music.

"Where have you been all my life, lady?" He sounded like an expert player.

"Where have you been the past few minutes?" She sounded like an insecure harpy.

"I just called to check in with Pat, and I was about to come looking for you."

All signs pointed to the opposite. "Really? I assumed you forgot I was there."

He inclined his head and studied her straight on. "Are you mad about something?"

Yes, and for no good reason. He didn't owe her anything, least of all his undivided attention. "I'm bored and tired. I'm going up to the room. Have fun."

When she turned to leave, he reeled her back in. "You can't go now," he said. "The fun's just about to get started."

"No offense, but I'm not going back in there just to stand around and blend in with the furniture. That's not my idea of a good time."

"It's not mine, either, but it's part of the life."

"Your life, not mine."

"Look, I know you think I was ignoring you, but—"

"You were."

"I was protecting you. If anyone gets wind of our relationship, then the press will be all over us and we'll never have any privacy."

That led to an all-important question. "Exactly what is our relationship?"

He tugged her closer. "We're two ordinary people just trying to get to know each other better."

She didn't feel ordinary in his presence, and he was anything but ordinary. "How do you propose we do that when we can't act like we know each other?"

"By going someplace where we can't be bothered. I have just the place in mind."

Temptation came calling again, overriding Cammie's common sense. "Where would that be?"

"I'm not going to tell you. I'm going to show you."

He took her hand and guided her to a service elevator where they traveled through a mazelike hallway and out into a back alley where he'd parked the SUV. After he helped her climb inside, and he'd settled behind the driver's seat, she shifted to face him. "What's going on, Taylor?"

"You'll see," he said as he drove out of the hotel lot.

"Not even a hint?"

He flashed a grin. "That would ruin the surprise."

And Cammie was surprised when they left Las Vegas proper and ended up on a road with little evidence of population. Fifteen minutes of silence passed before they came to a stucco structure situated far back from the rural street. Cammie couldn't make out much until they almost reached the end of the lengthy driveway.

The house, surrounded by native landscaping, seemed to blend into the desert surroundings. An expansive house that could pass as a remote compound for the rich and infamous.

Before Cammie could question Brett further, he'd already stopped beneath the portico, slid out and rounded the SUV to open her door. He helped her out, guided her to the entry and pounded out a code that opened the door to a two-story foyer. She tried to take in all the surroundings as he led her down the corridor, flipping on lights as they went.

Once they entered a massive great room with tower ceilings, Brett pointed to the beige leather sofa. "Get comfortable," he said as he released her hand. "I'll be right back."

After Brett disappeared, Cammie stepped out of her heels to give her aching feet some relief and walked around on the Mexican-tile floor. The room seemed an extension of the desert, the space washed in hues of sienna and clay. Earthenware pots held dried flowers in the same shades, and a Navajo rug in tones of black and red was suspended over the stone hearth. The furniture set out about the room had clean lines and some chrome, a mix of contemporary and Southwest motif. Beyond the seating area, a wall of windows drew her attention and she moved closer to discover a pool and hot tub set into the deck. The place was well-appointed, serene and very inviting.

Brett returned carrying an ice bucket containing a bottle of champagne in one hand, and a single red rose in the other. After he set the bucket on a nearby table next to two glasses, he offered her the flower. "This is for you," he said, looking a bit self-conscious over the romantic gesture.

Cammie took the rose and drew in the scent. "A flower before you deflower me." She'd clearly been bitten by the idiot bug. "I'm sorry. I'm nervous. It's beautiful."

He took the rose from her grasp and softly slid it down her throat to the open keyhole above her breasts. "Don't be nervous. We're going to take this as slow as you want. We've got all night."

If he kept that up, she'd rip his clothes off, to heck with slow. "How did you find this place?"

He set the rose aside and wrapped his arms around her. "It belongs to a friend."

"Male or female?"

"A guy. He's a record producer based in L.A. and this is his home away from home. I called him this morning and he was more than happy to let us use it for the night. He also had his housekeeper buy the champagne and the rose at my request."

Maybe he hadn't personally purchased the flower, but she still appreciated the effort. "He must be a good friend."

"Rick has a lot of money and a lot of friends, mainly women. He works and plays hard."

She looked around the area. "How many bedrooms does this place have?"

"Six. Two downstairs, four upstairs."

She brought her attention back to him. "Then you've been here before."

He let her go and slipped off the black sports coat he'd worn with his jeans to the party. "A couple of times when he had a party, but it's been a few years."

She could imagine what went on during those parties. She didn't want to imagine it. She didn't want to think of Brett with another woman, so she wouldn't. She'd just concentrate on their time together.

He lifted the bottle from the bucket. "Want some champagne?"

"I had two glasses at the hotel, but you go ahead."

He set the bottle back into the ice. "I'll pass for now. Maybe after we go for a swim."

She saw two immediate problems with that plan. "It's pretty cool outside."

"The pool's heated."

One problem solved. Now for the other. "I don't have a suit with me. In fact, I don't have anything with me, not even my purse."

"I took the liberty of packing you a bag earlier today," he said. "It's in the truck. Hope you don't mind."

She had no idea how he'd done that without her knowledge. "What did you bring me?"

He began to release the buttons on his white tailored shirt. "The usual. T-shirt, jeans and a toothbrush. Packing the red lace panties was the highlight."

Cammie couldn't be angry over him rifling through her underwear drawer when he took off his shirt, giving her a prime view of a prime chest. "Sounds like you've thought of everything but the swimsuit."

"I don't have one, either." He took her by the shoulders and turned her around. "We don't need one."

As he pushed her hair aside and slowly slid the dress's zipper down, Cammie shivered. "You're a bad, bad boy."

He brought his lips to her ear. "But I'm not a half-bad man, which you're going to find out if you'll let me show you."

When he parted the fabric and kissed her bare shoulder, she considered his request. When he pushed her dress down to drop at her feet, leaving her wearing only a strapless bra and matching panties, she didn't have the strength to argue.

He turned her back around to face him and gave her a long once-over. "There you go, instant little black bikini."

To complement her full-body flush. "True, but I'm feeling kind of awkward since you're still partially dressed."

"Not for long."

Brett made good on his promise by undoing his fly and working his way out of his jeans, one leg at a time. And when Cammie caught sight of his thigh-length black boxers, the word *Joe* scripted down one leg, and *Knows* down the other, she couldn't help but laugh.

"Where did you get those?" she said after she'd recovered enough to speak.

"Someone gave them to me."

That put a damper on her mood. "A woman who knows Joe?"

"Bull gave them to me last Christmas. It's always been an inside joke until I told you."

She supposed she should be flattered she'd been made privy to the questionable male humor. "Maybe someday I'll get to know Joe."

He grinned. "Maybe so."

Brett took her hand and led her through the glass doors that opened onto the deck. "Wait here," he said as he walked into the adjacent cabana.

He returned a few moments later with two beach

towels that he spread out on a double chaise longue. Then without saying a word, he strode to the deep end of the pool, stripped out of the Joe shorts and executed a perfect dive. Cammie could see little of anything due to the dark, dark night and virtually no light whatsoever. But, oh, could she imagine.

He surfaced a few feet away and slicked back his hair with both hands. "Turn on that lower switch behind you."

Still somewhat in shock, Cammie followed his instructions and turned to see the pool illuminated in light blue. Brett was still cast in shadows, but just knowing he had nothing on generated quite a bit of heat in her already heated body.

He swam to the edge next to the steps and propped his chin on his folded hands. "Now it's your turn."

She could jump in wearing her best underwear and risk ruining it. Or she could follow Brett's lead and bare it all. She opted to bare it all. Besides, he'd seen the better part of her, anyway, and in daylight. Plus, if they continued on this course, he was bound to see her naked at some point tonight.

With that in mind, she reached behind her, unfastened the bra and tossed it over her shoulder onto the table. Then came the panties that she shimmied down her legs while Brett looked on. She couldn't see his features in detail, but she could tell he hadn't moved an inch.

She followed his lead and walked to the opposite end of the pool to demonstrate her own diving expertise. When she emerged, he was right there in front of her. He caught her arm and tugged her close where she could feel how much he wanted her, and it felt so good to be wanted. Yet he did little more than kiss her softly as he moved back until he could stand. And for a few wonderful moments, they stood there kissing, hands in motion on each other's back, until Brett finally broke the kiss and tipped his forehead against hers. "Seems like I've waited forever for this."

"I know. We've had so many interruptions—"

"That's not exactly what I meant," he said as he pulled back and studied her face from forehead to chin before centering on her eyes. "It's been a long time since I've had the opportunity to give my undivided attention to someone special. I want to take my time with you."

Cammie was still stuck on "special." "We have all the time in the world, at least for now." Beyond that, she had no idea where they would go from here or what the future might hold. She only knew she didn't want this night to end.

He took her hand again and led her up the stairs where he guided her to the chaise built for two. "Have a seat. I'll be back in a minute."

After he walked back into the house, Cammie claimed the side of the chaise farthest from the door. She lay back, studied the host of stars in the sky and thought about what would happen next. Oddly, she wasn't at all nervous, only anxious for Brett's return. More than ready for his undivided attention.

He came back a few moments later and tossed several foil packets on the side table before perching on the edge of the chaise. "Just so you know, I want to be prepared this time. It's up to you how far we go."

She reached over and ran her palm along his arm. "I want to go all the way."

"Are you sure about this, Cammie?" he asked. "All you have to do is say the word and we'll stop, if you're not sure."

She thought he sounded tentative. "Are *you* sure?"

"Hell, yes."

"Then I think we've waited long enough."

But he still wasn't finished with the commentary. "I'll make it right for you, Cammie, I swear it. Just trust me to do that much."

Then he leaned over and kissed her again, this time without any restraint.

Cammie could no longer distinguish the warm breeze from Brett's steady breath coursing over her as he left her lips to kiss the curve of her throat, then her bare shoulders, before his mouth closed over her breast. As he lingered there, she sifted her fingers through his ebony hair as he shifted from one side to the other. With every pull of his lips, stroke of his tongue, her body responded in ways unknown to her. He lifted his head and took a downward descent with openmouthed kisses until he reached her belly.

Then he straightened and, to her surprise, stood and knelt at the end of the chaise. He clasped her hips, pulled her closer to him and bent her knees. For a moment she felt self-conscious and totally exposed. But then he placed delicate kisses on the inside of her thighs and she no longer cared. He moved higher until the tip of his tongue grazed the crease of her leg, and she involuntarily jerked.

Brett raised his head, his vibrant blue eyes reflecting the light coming through the nearby doors. "It's okay, Cammie," he said. "Trust me."

He continued with soft caresses, just a breath away from his destination, forcing the pleasant torture of anticipation on her while she waited for what would come. She might be inexperienced, but she wasn't ignorant. She'd talked openly about sex with friends and heard numerous descriptions about this level of intimacy. A level of intimacy she'd never granted to any man until now. But nothing could have prepared her for the sheer sensation when Brett's mouth hit home.

She gripped the cushioned surface, anchoring herself when he slid his hands beneath her hips and raised her higher. As he worked his magic, she was aroused beyond belief. Her body tightened with building tension, and the bliss almost bordered on agony. She fought to remain in control, thinking that if she gave in, she'd never recover. But she could no more fight the climax any more than she could fight her feelings for him.

"Please…Brett," she pleaded in a broken whisper, wanting more. Needing more.

She was only mildly aware Brett had left. She was very aware when he returned and moved over her. "I'm right here," he said as he draped her arms around his neck. "Just hang on to me, baby."

When he eased inside her, she closed her eyes and released a soft groan.

"Cammie, look at me." After she answered his command, he smiled. "Try to relax."

That seemed almost impossible, but she concentrated on his beautiful face to counteract the momentary pain. And then the pain gave way to pleasure and awe as he moved inside her. She wondered how she could feel both powerless and empowered at the same time. She questioned why witnessing his waning control was such a turn-on.

When his jaw tensed and his breathing became harsh and unsteady, she knew he was close to the edge. She also knew the moment he couldn't hold on any longer when his entire body tensed before he collapsed against her.

In those quiet aftermath moments, when Brett kissed her gently and held her tightly, she finally understood why lovemaking was so revered. She couldn't understand how anyone could take it so lightly. Being this close to someone, this vulnerable, went well beyond the act itself, at least for her. She was glad she'd waited. Waited for a man like Brett, who'd treated her with respect and care.

The onslaught of emotions overwhelmed her when he lifted his head and gave her a heartfelt look. "You're incredible."

So was he. More important, he'd done something totally unexpected—made her believe she could actually love again. She could love him, if he let her.

For the first time in his life, Brett had spent the past hour watching a woman sleep. Normally he wanted to get the hell out of Dodge before dawn, but right now he couldn't think of anywhere else he'd rather be.

Cammie had rolled away from him at some point during the night, and he'd woken up seriously missing her. Now she was on her belly with her face turned toward him, her eyes closed against the faint light streaming through the window across the room, her dark hair fanned across the pillow. The sheet was bunched low on her hips, exposing the rose tattoo that showed she could be a contradiction. Part innocent, part daredevil. All woman. And just looking at her made him feel things he had no business feeling.

Truth was, he still couldn't give her what she deserved—a solid, stable relationship with a man who wasn't a complete failure in the relationship department.

That didn't make him want her any less. That didn't stop him from wanting to make love to her again before they returned to chaotic life on the road. But he needed to keep everything in perspective and put some emotional distance between them. Easier said than done, and maybe too late to turn back.

"Baby, what are you doing to me?" he whispered.

He realized she'd heard him, or heard something, when her eyes fluttered open. And all the previous arguments for avoiding getting too attached went the way of the wind when she smiled. "How long have you been awake?" she asked in a raspy, sexy morning voice.

Long enough to know he was in big trouble. "A while."

She rolled to her back and didn't bother to cover herself, which didn't help his need for her one bit. "I slept like a rock," she said. "The last thing I remember was taking a shower and climbing into bed. And by the way, I'm still mad because you wouldn't shower with me."

If he had, he couldn't guarantee he would've been able to control himself. "You needed some time to recover."

She scooted over and laid her head on his chest. "You make it sound like I have some disease, like postvirginitis."

"I didn't want to hurt you any more than I already did."

She lifted her head and frowned. "I told you the first night we met that I'm not some fragile little thing you have to coddle. I just happen to be a late bloomer."

A sexy-as-hell late bloomer. "Yeah, I guess you're right."

She settled back against his chest and draped her arm around his abdomen. "Did you get any sleep at all?"

"A few hours." He had something he needed to say to her, even if he didn't have the guts to say everything he should. "I was just lying here wondering what I did to deserve to be your first."

"I was hormonal and you were available."

Damn. "You really know how to crush a guy's ego."

"I was only kidding. In all honesty, I wanted the first time to be memorable in a good way, not in the backseat of a car."

"Nothing like those memorable firsts."

"Your first number-one song?"

"The first time I held my baby girl." The thought jumped out of his mouth before he could stop it. But his daughter had never been more than a thought away since the day she was born.

Cammie sighed. "I'm sure that was a remarkable moment."

He wasn't one to share personal details, but he knew she would understand. "I was two weeks shy of my twenty-first birthday when she was born, and I was terrified. But when they put her in my arms, I realized I'd move mountains to do right by her." Even if it meant letting another man—a better man—raise her.

"You should try to reconnect with her, Brett."

He didn't see the point, and he didn't want to discuss it any further. "Can we move on to another topic?"

She lifted her head and showed him a serious expression. "I don't mean to meddle, but I care about what this is doing to you because I care about you."

He didn't know whether to be pleased or panicked. "Thanks, I guess."

She poked him in the ribs. "Relax, Brett. I don't expect diamonds or flowers, although I did appreciate the rose. I don't want to go steady and I don't expect you to declare your undying devotion. We're just two people who met during a time when we both needed someone to lean on."

He'd done most of the leaning. In fact, he wasn't sure what he would have done if she hadn't kept him grounded during Pat's crisis. "You're right. You came along and saved me and Joe."

She lifted her head and grinned. "Then I believe you and Joe need to show me some appreciation."

That much he could handle. He started by flipping her over and telling her exactly what he wanted to do to her, and she didn't seemed the least bit shocked over what some might consider crude. In fact, he could see that little spark of need in her eyes, felt it build when he kissed her, even more so when he touched her with his hands and mouth. He showed her that he could coax a climax out of her after he was deep inside her, something he'd learned through practice and experience. He thought about all the things he could teach her if given the opportunity, until thinking became out of the question and he couldn't do anything but give into one hell of a powerful release.

And when it was over—way too soon as far as he was concerned—he realized she had taught him a thing or two. But it didn't have a thing to do with sex, and her instructions had been subtle. She'd taught him to be a little more patient, and a little less quick to judge himself. She'd begun to make him feel almost whole again, and that he might actually be the man she needed. Only time would tell, and lucky for him, they still had time to see where this might lead.

When his cell phone began to buzz, he cursed the interruption and almost didn't look at the incoming text. But instinct told him it could be important, and he realized he'd been right in his assumption when he read the message from Rusty.

Get to the hospital now.

CHAPTER ELEVEN

BRETT DIDN'T SPEAK on the drive in to Vegas, and Cammie didn't press him to talk. As he navigated the remote road at a breakneck speed, she did maintain a death grip on the door handle, worried they might end up in the E.R. on a stretcher.

Once they arrived at the hospital, he swung into a parking space and barely shut off the SUV before he left the vehicle, leaving her behind. She sprinted across the lot and caught up to him in the lobby where he ignored the elevator—and her—and opted to take the stairs to the second floor where Pat had been moved to a regular room.

As soon as they pushed through the heavy fire door, Cammie's heart began to pound from the physical exertion and fear. She didn't feel the least bit better when they turned the corner down the main corridor to find Rusty and Bull standing outside the room opposite each other in the hall.

Brett converged on Rusty first. "Is he—"

"Leaving," Rusty said. "He's waiting for the discharge papers."

While Cammie nearly collapsed from relief, Brett

took Rusty by the collar, backed him against the wall and got right in his face. "You should've said that in the text, you son of a bitch."

She couldn't agree more, but she didn't agree with Brett turning his ire on Rusty. Obviously neither did Bull. He grabbed Brett by the shoulders and pulled him back. "Calm down, Taylor. That's not the whole story."

Brett shook off Bull's grasp. "Then someone sure as hell better explain real quick."

"He's going home," Rusty said. "He's quitting."

Cammie had kept her distance until Brett tore into the room. She immediately went in after him and found Pat seated on the bed, putting on his boots, and Brett standing there, glaring at him.

"What do you mean you're quitting?" Brett said, sheer anger in his tone.

Pat didn't bother to look up from his task. "I'll be sixty-one in two months. It's about time for me to retire. And this little episode made me face my mortality head-on."

"Look, you don't have to finish the tour," Brett said, a hint of desperation replacing the fury in his voice. "Cammie can fill in now and you can rejoin us next spring. That should give you plenty of time to recover."

Pat finally made eye contact with Brett. "You're not hearing me, son. I'm through with this life. Besides, there's a little gal back home in Little Rock who gave up on me years ago and married someone else. She's widowed now and she wants to give me a second chance. I'm gonna take it."

Cammie could tell from the hard set of Brett's jaw, his narrowed eyes, Pat wasn't getting through to him. Worse, he might never accept his father figure's departure.

Brett backed toward the door and reached behind him for the knob. "Then I guess there's nothing left to say but good luck."

With that, he was gone, leaving Cammie stunned by his careless disregard. Pat's chuckle drew her attention. "It's not funny, Pat. He should be horsewhipped for being so rude to you."

Pat scooted over on the bed and patted the mattress. "Come sit a spell and I'll tell you a few things about the main man."

She was torn between humoring him and going after Brett to give him a piece of her mind, what was left of it. She chose to show Pat the respect his boss hadn't and claimed the spot beside him. "First of all, let me just say I understand your decision, even if it does make me sad to think you won't be on board to keep me company. But I don't understand how Brett could walk out of here without thanking you for all you've done for him."

Pat sighed. "Brett and I are even on that count. He kept me around for ten years and I've got a nice pension to show for it. In return, I put up with his nonsense and bad moods, but then, I know him better than he knows himself."

"I don't doubt that," Cammie said. "We've spent a lot of time together lately and I still feel I don't know him."

"And that's why I'm going to tell you exactly what to expect. He's going to be mad as a badass bull and he's going to brood."

Lovely. "For how long?"

"As long as it takes for him to realize he's going to do fine without me. In the meantime, you'll need to have the patience of a saint. And you need to remember that whatever he says or does, it's not about you. It's about his dad leaving him, although he'd be hard-pressed to ever admit that."

Cammie realized Pat did know Brett and what made him tick. She also recognized she couldn't save him from himself, and being his verbal punching bag wasn't anything to celebrate. "Maybe it would be best if I leave now. Every time he looks at me, he's going to be reminded you're not there."

Pat took her hand into his. "You leaving now would only make it worse. I know it's a hell of a lot to ask of you, but hang in there. You could be the one person to bring him out of his pity party."

That was definitely a tall order, and improbable. "I'll try, but only because you asked."

"You'll try because you care about him." He inclined his head, narrowed his eyes and looked at her straight on. "Maybe you even love him a little bit?"

She marveled at Pat's wisdom, and cursed her own transparency.

"Believe me, he's easy to love, and hard to hold on to. But he's worth it, Cammie. Just don't give up on him."

As if Pat's departure wasn't bad enough, more sorry news waited for Brett in his stateroom. The tan over-size envelope sat centered in the middle of the mattress, a note from Rusty paper-clipped to the front.

Tim sent this by courier to the hotel. He said it looked important.

Important, yeah, and from the looks of the attorney's return address in Texas, he'd bet his last buck he knew what it was about.

He toed out of his boots, stretched out on the bed and turned the packet over twice. He'd like to ignore it, just like he'd like to ignore his mentor leaving him high and dry. But delaying the inevitable could cost him in the long run.

After tearing open the envelope, he withdrew a petition to have his parental rights terminated, clearing the way for Jana's husband to adopt Lacey. From what he could tell, he had until September to fight it, but he had another fight he had to take on first.

He tossed the papers aside, fished his cell from his jeans pocket and hit the speed dial to contact the party responsible for this surprise attack. When she answered, he dispensed with formality. "Thanks for blindsiding me, Jana."

"Don't act so shocked, Brett. This has been a long time coming, and you have no one to blame but yourself."

He tightened his grip on the phone hard enough to break the damn thing. "What about your blame in all of this?"

"I don't know what you mean."

"Hell, yes, you do. You're the one who kept Lacey from me for all these years. First, you stripped me of my rights to see her except for one freakin' weekend a month. When I did have a break, she was always busy with something. Camp or a sleepover or a cold."

"Excuse me, but you can't blame me for your schedule. And you're the one who stopped calling her."

His mind traveled back to that day six years ago, and he got mad all over again. "Did you forget what she said to me that last time I talked to her? Just in case, I'll repeat it. It had something to do with you telling her I drank too much and chased *whores*. *Whores,* Jana. That's a pretty adult word to be coming out of a six-year-old mouth."

She sighed. "We've been through this, Brett. She overheard a conversation I had with Randy."

"I don't give a damn where she heard it. The point is, she did hear it, you never took it back and she'll probably never forget it."

"Guess the truth hurts, doesn't it?"

He gritted his teeth so hard he thought they might

shatter. "I didn't start drinking until you took Lacey and left. And I sure as hell never cheated on you."

"Yes, you did," she said. "You had an affair with your career. Fame and fortune was the only thing that ever mattered to you."

She was dead wrong. Every drop of blood, sweat and tears had been for his family, especially his child. "You sure as hell didn't have a problem taking my money in the divorce settlement. And you never even gave me a chance to prove I could handle the singing and the family life. You just took off with our kid without even saying goodbye."

"I left a note."

He'd burned that note and downed half a bottle of whiskey that night. "Oh, yeah. After seven years together, you might've had the decency to say goodbye to my face."

"I knew you would talk me out of it, or at least try. In spite of all your faults, you've got charming people to get your way down to a science. Heaven help any woman who gets involved with you. You'll only bring her a whole lot of heartache."

He grabbed the papers and clenched them in his fist. "Admit it, Jana Beth. You're still pissed off at me and you've been using our kid as a pawn to make me pay. Well, I'm done paying."

"Sign the papers, Brett."

"Go to hell, Jana."

After he hung up, he hurled the wadded documents against a wall and followed suit with his cell phone, breaking it into several pieces that scattered across the area.

"Pat didn't mention you were inclined to throw things."

He spun around to see Cammie standing at the now-open door. "Don't listen to everything Pat tells you. He's full of crap."

She folded her arms across her middle and leaned a shoulder against the frame. "Seems to me he's pretty much got you pegged."

Ignoring the comment, he stretched out on the bed on his back and studied the ceiling to avoid her condemnation. "What do you want, Camille?"

"If you're done with the tantrum, I just wanted to let you know that I'm about to head out. The guys want to know if you have a dinner preference."

Yeah. The other half of that old bottle of whiskey. "I don't give a damn about eating right now."

"That's right. You only give a damn about feeling sorry for yourself. Pat left, your dad left and my parents died. It sucks and it hurts."

"Pat's leaving wasn't a surprise." But it had stung like a hornet. "Everyone eventually leaves. Life's a bitch."

"And we only have one of them. So you can waste precious hours wallowing, or you can appreciate what you have and get on with the business of living."

When he ventured a glance he found her standing at the end of the bed, glaring at him. He considered telling her about the termination papers, but he didn't have the energy to get into that. "If you're done with the lecture, I'd like some privacy."

She held her ground. "You can have all the privacy you want, as soon as I say what I need to say to you. You can throw whatever you like and you can even throw me out. You can pretend nothing ever happened between us, and that's fine. But you're not going to be able to get rid of me because I promised Pat I'd fill in for him until the tour's over. So get used to it."

When she turned and left, slamming the door behind her, Brett considered going after her. He owed her an apology. He owed her a lot more than that. He wanted to tell her how much she meant to him. How much he'd come to care about her. How close he was to landing right in the middle of loving her. Then Jana's words came back to him.

Heaven help any woman who gets involved with you. You'll only bring her a whole lot of heartache....

A quick, clean break would be best. Cammie deserved a better man. The man he might never be.

THE STADIUM WAS EXPECTED to be bursting at the seams with fans later that evening, yet the outdoor concert appeared as if it might not happen when the threat of a severe storm hung over the stage. But as if the country-music gods had willed it, the threatening clouds peeled back and exposed the radiant California sun before the end of the rehearsal.

Yet the storm between Brett and Cammie still prevailed. Now her nerves were frayed and close to being completely shot. She and Brett had barely spoken to each other since their last tense conversation right before they left Las Vegas, or the two days since they'd arrived in Los Angeles. He'd acted as if nothing had happened between them that night in the desert house. She couldn't help but feel cheated and used and discarded like yesterday's newspaper.

Fortunately, Bonnie and Karen had flown in for a minivacation, serving as her companions during their free time. They'd gone shopping, swimming and sightseeing, and not once had Brett's name come up in the context of their relationship. If the women had been made privy to any information, they hadn't let on. When it came to the music part, the guys hovered around her as if they'd become self-appointed bodyguards to protect her from her boss's foul mood. Regardless of their motives, they'd kept her mind off the fact Brett was bent on behaving like she didn't exist, as he had the entire rehearsal.

The heat was about to do Cammie in as they rehearsed the final song for at least the tenth time. Brett was his usual obsessive self, maybe even more so.

After he said, "Again," Rusty formed an obscene gesture behind Brett's back.

Feeling totally drained, Cammie plopped down

on a stool and swiped the beads of perspiration from her forehead. If King Brett was trying to drive home a point by working her to death until she lost five pounds due to dehydration, he was succeeding.

"Get up, Camille. We're not done yet." Brett seemed bent on calling her by her full name now, as if to put more distance between them.

At the moment she'd like to sock him in the nose, or other sensitive regions. Unfortunately, she wasn't a violent person. Then a sudden devious thought crept into her mind. If he was hell-bent on playing the mean man, she had no choice but to be a mean girl. No bodily harm involved, of course. Just a little refreshing wake-up call to calm him down.

She slowly slipped off her perch and walked to the small thermos where Brett happened to be standing. "May I?" she asked sweetly.

He stared at her for a moment, not so much in suspicion but with annoyance. "Help yourself." He turned away, then added, "Just hurry up."

"No problem. This won't take long at all." She took two large squeeze bottles and filled them full of the icy water. Leaving the tops off the bottles, she started toward Brett, who now had his back to her. She winked at Jeremy, then looked at Bonnie and Karen seated on the ground below and smiled.

Bonnie began to laugh when realization dawned and Karen yelled, "Go, girl!"

Cammie took both bottles and dumped them on the unsuspecting star's head. When he spun around, water dripping from his hair onto his T-shirt, she smiled and handed him the bottles. "Now that you're cooled off, I'm ready to continue."

From the furious look on Brett's face, she figured she'd probably gone too far and could be instantly fired. Well, that was just too bad.

Brett hurled the containers to one side and sent her a fierce look. Even so, the way he slicked back his hair made Cammie's heart execute a little hip-hop.

"Rehearsal's over," he said irritably. "Everyone be here by six." Then he disappeared down the steps and into the tunnels below the stadium.

The band remained fixed in their positions and Cammie worried they resented the antics responsible for Brett's spontaneous departure. Then the laughter spread, first with Rusty, then Jeremy and lastly Bull, who Cammie suspected had been laughing all along. Before she knew it the entire road crew had joined in.

Cammie hugged her arms to her middle and tried to look contrite, even if she wasn't. "Sorry, guys."

"Guess you showed him, Cammie," Rusty said.

Bull laughed again. "Damn, I wish I had a camera to record the look on his freakin' face. Looked like someone slapped him up the side of his head with a cow patty."

"A really cold cow patty," Cammie said, bringing about another round of laughter that continued as they filed off the staged and headed into the tunnel leading to the lot.

Halfway to their destination, a lanky guy with longish light brown hair stopped to speak with the guys as the girls hung back and waited. Cammie thought he looked familiar, but she couldn't put a name to the face. "Who is he?" she asked Karen.

"His name is Cruz something," she said. "He's with the opening group that's called…I can't remember."

Cammie did. "DHD. I saw it on the schedule."

"Stands for Down Home Devils," Bonnie added. "Devil or not, I could get down with him."

Karen grinned. "Give me half an hour and a hotel room and I could tear that up."

Bonnie laid a hand above her breasts. "You're married, Karen. But I'm not. And if Doug doesn't put a ring on my finger soon, I might try to get me some of that."

"He's not interested in us," Karen said. "He keeps eyeing Cammie. You should introduce yourself."

Cammie did notice his covert glances. Yes, he was cute—in a scruffy sort of way. But he wasn't nearly as tall as Brett, six feet at best. And although he had piercing brown eyes, they weren't as magnetic as Brett's. He wasn't Brett, period. "Sorry, but I'm not interested." She'd had her fill of singers. Enough to last a lifetime.

After the group of guys said their goodbyes and

disbanded, Cruz moved past her and directed a wink at her. "Check you ladies later."

Karen hooked an arm through Cammie's. "He means he'll check you out later. And you should check him out, too."

Cammie had no intention of going there. She only wanted to go back to the hotel, shower and take a long nap. She also planned to have a serious conversation with Brett after the evening performance. She understood he was still hurting over Pat's departure, but that didn't give him the right to be so irritable. She could no longer tolerate his avoidance or his bad temper. If he refused to man up, look her in the eye and tell her she'd only been a diversion, she seriously questioned whether she could stay on for the remainder of the tour.

IF BRETT WAS IN THE THROES of emotional turmoil, it wasn't obvious when he took the stage. At least not to his audience or to Cammie. He was as dynamic as she'd ever seen him. He was also full of surprises. During their special song, he moved over to sing in her microphone, as if he wanted to reenact their performances in Vegas.

Of course it was an act, and she didn't intend to play along. But by the second time around with the chorus, the undeniable chemistry became apparent…until she snapped out of it and shifted away from him. When he appeared altogether confused, she shrugged and went right on singing without giving him a second glance. Yet she was still very aware of his presence and her continuing desire to be near him. She had to be strong. Had to be.

After the show ended, Cammie came to a decision. Life was too short to hang on to the hope that they would ever reestablish a relationship. For that reason, she intended to enjoy herself tonight—exactly what was on her mind when she exited the stage. She planned to freshen up at the hotel, slip on the new knock-'em-dead blue dress Karen and Bonnie had convinced her to buy and then pay a visit to the hotel lounge. The place came highly recommended by Jeremy, who had spent the past two nights holding up the bar.

She'd made it through half the tunnel maze when she came upon the mysterious Cruz, one shoulder leaning against the cement wall, hands in the pockets of his well-worn jeans.

"Hey," he said as she came within a few feet from him.

She almost didn't stop but decided to be polite, then be on her way. "Hey. Good show tonight."

"You, too." He pushed off the wall and offered his hand. "By the way, I'm Jamie Cruz. People call me Cruz."

At least he had nice manners, and a snake tattoo crawling up his forearm, reminding her of Mark. Not a good thing. "Nice to officially meet you, Cruz. I'm Camille, but most people call me Cammie."

"I know," he said. "I asked Rusty about you before the show."

Karen and Bonnie had been right about his interest in her. "Don't believe everything you hear." Namely that she was single and on the prowl.

"Same goes for me," he said. "I was wondering if you might want to have a drink with me in the hotel bar since we're staying at the same place."

That's where she'd planned to go, but somehow that didn't seem too wise, especially with Cruz tagging along. "Any other time I might say yes, but in case you haven't heard, I drive Brett's bus as well as sing backup. We have to head out early so I should probably call it a night."

He smiled, yet it didn't pack the same punch as Brett's did. "Just one drink. I don't know about you, but after a show, it takes me a while to wind down. I also know sometimes it's nice to find a friend in all this craziness."

She did agree with him on that point. "True, but I'm fairly tired. Maybe some other time."

"Are you sure? I'm buying."

She noticed Brett rounding the corner, and when he caught sight of her, she swore he picked up the pace. She hoped he'd keep on walking, but no such luck. He strode right up to them and came to a stop at Cammie's side. "The car's on its way," he told her without taking his eyes off her companion.

Cruz stuck out his hand for a shake. "Thanks for the opportunity, man."

Brett stared at his hand a moment before accepting the gesture. "No problem." He sounded as if it was.

"I was just asking Cammie to have a drink with me," Cruz said. "You need to tell her all work and no play can burn you out."

Brett sent Cammie a harsh look before turning back to Cruz. "She doesn't drink. And even if she did, I wouldn't be too pleased if she spent her free time hanging out in a bar after a show."

How dare he try to dictate what she did in her spare time. "Don't listen to him," she said. "I have a drink on occasion, and I'd enjoy having one with you." Apparently she'd stooped to typical high-school antics—flirt with a new guy to make the other guy jealous.

Cruz looked victorious. Brett—not so much. He looked like he could blow a gasket. And she honestly didn't care. "Meet me in the lobby in an hour."

"Sounds good," Cruz said as he backed up a step. "See you later, Taylor. I'll take good care of her."

Brett didn't even wait until Cruz was out of sight before he launched into a tirade. "What was that all about, Cammie?"

"That was about me having a drink with a nice guy, and FYI, I'm well within my rights to do so."

Cammie tried to get past Brett, but he caught her hand before she was successful in her departure. "Nice guy? How the hell do you know that when you just met him?"

She could no longer contain her anger. "It's really none of your business what I do, Brett."

"I'm making it my business."

She wrenched her hand away. "You don't own me, Brett. Directing my social life isn't in the contract. I'm not your property."

"No, but you are still my employee, and I have to look after the band's reputation. If it gets out that you're ready and willing, every bastard in the industry will be hunting you down."

That was rich coming from him. "Having a drink with someone in the industry does not mean I'm ready and willing."

"He's a stranger, dammit."

"So were you when I met you. Now if we're done, I need to go."

He released his hold on her hand. "Not until we're through talking about this."

She rubbed her temples, her head beginning to pound from the stress of one too many confrontations in one night. "We have nothing to say to each other. Everything you've done since Vegas speaks volumes."

Cammie did an about-face, walked down the hallway and out into the misty night. She scanned the back lot and didn't locate the car hired to transport them to and from the venue. Great. Hopefully the guys would be along soon with a cell phone to find out what the hold-up might be. In the meantime, she could seek shelter back in the tunnel, or she could wait in the rain. Going back inside seemed favorable, although either scenario promised a chilly atmosphere.

When she turned around, she discovered Brett leaning back against the cinder-block wall adjacent to the opening, hat in hand. Droplets of water had formed on his skin, and the halogen light above made his blue eyes seem almost unearthly. He looked like a beautiful dark angel, and she wanted nothing more than to run to him. But that would be just plain stupid.

Brett pushed off the wall and walked to her, his expression softening with each step. "You don't have to go out with that guy to prove a point. I know I don't have any claim on your time, but I don't want to see you get hurt."

The man was concerned about her feelings, yet he had dealt her the harshest blow anyone could endure. "Hurt? *You* don't want me to get hurt? I can't believe you said that after what you did to me."

"I'm sorry, Cammie."

He sounded sincere, but an apology wasn't enough. "And I'm supposed to accept that as an answer."

"It's the only one I've got."

"It's not good enough. You act like it's my fault Pat left."

"I said I'm sorry, Cammie. What more do you want me to say?"

She wanted him to beg for forgiveness, to tell her

he cared about her, that she hadn't only imagined the strong emotional connection between them. "All I want to know is why, Brett. Why do you keeping shutting me out? Don't you realize you're punishing me?"

His gaze drifted away. "It's no good, Cammie. When it comes down to it, I'm no better than Mark Jensen in a lot of ways. A singing career and serious relationships don't mix."

He just didn't quite get it, and she wondered if he ever would. "First of all, you aren't anything like Mark. Second, for some reason you're just not willing to own up to the fact that you are capable of more than you realize. Anything can work if you want it badly enough and you set your mind to it, including a relationship. All you have to have is the same desire you have for your singing."

"I've learned from experience that commitment to anything but the job doesn't work in this business. At least it hasn't for me."

Cammie considered not saying anything else, but she always tended to hang on until all possibilities were exhausted, especially when she strongly believed in something. And she did believe in Brett, more than he believed in himself. "I don't understand why you're so determined to drive everyone who cares for you away."

He continued to stare at the ground. "You're right, you don't understand."

"I want to."

"I can't talk about it, Cammie. Maybe one day, but not now." He finally raised his gaze to hers. "Don't set yourself up again for another guy to cut you down."

She had no intention of doing that. "Then make me an offer."

He paused as if weighing her suggestion, but then he emotionally shut down right before her eyes. "I can't offer you anything, Cammie. Not a damn thing."

CHAPTER TWELVE

BRETT TOSSED ASIDE the notepad onto the coffee table and gave up on the lyrics that just wouldn't come. The noise in his head was second only to the sounds assaulting his ears. "Turn down the freakin' TV, Rusty!"

His friend emerged from the bedroom and scowled at him. "Why don't you turn down the attitude?"

"You'd have an attitude, too, if you were trying to write a song with some ball game blaring in the background."

Rusty sat on the sofa and stared at him. "It's not the songwriting that's got you so rattled. It's Cammie."

He didn't want or need advice. "Aren't you and your wife going to dinner?"

"She's still getting ready, and you can't brush me off like that. We've been in the trenches together for a long time and I can read you like sheet music. You're so obsessed with your bus driver you can barely function."

"I'm not obsessed with her," he said. "I'm pissed at her."

"These days you're pissed at everyone. You're in love with Cammie and for some reason you can't handle it. A lot of men would give their right arm to have a woman like her."

Hearing the word *love* was a shock to his entire system. "Yeah, like that guy named Cruz. She's going out with him as we speak."

Rusty swiped a hand over his face. "I figured he was going to make a move on her, but I didn't think for a minute she'd fall for it."

He'd been asking himself that same question for the past hour. "Well, she did. I ran into them talking after the show, and right when I was about to tell him to get lost, she told him to pick her up in the lobby."

Rusty chuckled. "Oh, man, you are so far out of the loop it's not even funny. She was trying to make you jealous."

He had a hard time buying that. "Cammie's not a game player. She's a straight shooter."

"Maybe so, but you're not giving her a whole lot of choice. If going out with Cruz gets your attention, even if it's negative attention, then she'll do whatever it takes to make you notice her."

Rusty could be onto something, but Brett still had a hard time believing it. "That's a pretty extreme way to get my attention."

"It worked, didn't it?"

Damn. "Yeah, it worked. And I have half a mind to stop her before she makes another big mistake."

Rusty came to his feet. "I think you should because I doubt he told her he's got a wife and kids back home in Kentucky."

"That's great," he muttered as he stood. "You should've told me sooner."

"Good luck," Rusty said. "Just remember that if you step in, she'll be royally pissed."

Just thinking about the cheating bastard even attempting to touch Cammie made him seethe. "If I don't, she could get royally hurt."

CAMMIE TOOK A SEAT on a gold brocade sofa that was about as comfortable as a cement slab and flipped through some fashion magazine while she waited for Cruz. And if he didn't show up soon, she'd return to her room and curse being stood up for the second time in her life. But in this case, that might not be a bad thing. She had to agree with Brett—she didn't know a thing about this guy. However, the hotel bar was a safe place to get to know him, as long as she kept her wits about her and her drink in her possession at all times.

"Hey, Cammie."

She looked up from the magazine to see Cruz crossing the lobby. He'd changed into another T-shirt with Bad to the Bone emblazoned across the front and a better pair of jeans. Now she felt completely overdressed.

She came to her feet and tossed the magazine aside. "I almost gave up on you."

"Sorry I'm late. I had to make a couple of phone

calls." He took a step back and whistled. "That's a great dress."

"I really should probably go up to the room and change," she said. "I don't get out much and I thought—"

"Don't change," he said. "I like you just the way you are."

At least someone did. "Are you ready to go?"

"Sure."

He took her hand, taking her totally by surprise, and started across the lobby toward the lounge.

"Take your hands off her, Cruz."

At the sound of the familiar voice, Cammie glanced over her shoulder to see Brett boring down on them, a fierce look on his face.

"Stay out of this, Brett," she said. "This doesn't concern you."

"It does now." He pointed at Cruz. "Did he tell you he's married?"

She turned her shock on Cruz. "Is that true?"

The man had the nerve to look innocent. "Well, yeah, but she's not here right now."

Brett stepped between her and Cruz. "Because she's home with the kids, you bastard."

Cruz slid his hands into his back pockets and took a stab at an innocent look. "Hey, you know how it is, Taylor. It gets damn lonely on the road. My wife understands how it is. Now why don't you just move aside and let Cammie decide what she wants to do."

"She's already decided," Brett said. "She's leaving with me."

Cammie inserted herself between them and planted her palms on their chests, holding them arm's length apart. "Actually, I don't plan to spend my evening, what's left of it, with either of you, so both of you need to go away."

Cruz leered at Brett before he brought his attention back to Cammie. "Seems to me I'm treading on sacred ground here. I should've known Taylor would've gotten to you first. I'm guessin' you didn't find him to your liking. If you go with me, I'll show you a real good time."

Cammie didn't have time to brace herself before Brett stepped between her and Cruz. "You low-life son of a bitch," he said in a menacing tone. "She's more woman than you can handle. Now get the hell out of here before you regret it."

Cruz narrowed his eyes. "I might be a son of a bitch, Taylor, but at least my daddy liked me enough to stick around."

While Cammie looked on helplessly, Brett grabbed Cruz by the shirt and shoved him backward, sending him against a marble column. But before he could go after him, a massive security guard appeared from nowhere and wrenched Brett's arms behind his back, subjecting him to the full force of Cruz's fist to his jaw. A throng of staff and two more security guards tore through the lobby and ushered Cruz outside as he yelled obscenities directed at everyone involved.

After Cammie came out of her stupor, she turned to see Brett sitting on the sofa, blood oozing from the corner of his mouth, and his jaw showing signs of swelling.

The security guard approached her and pointed at Brett. "Is he with you?"

She almost denied it, but right or wrong, Brett had defended her honor. "So to speak."

"He says he doesn't need a doctor, but he needs to put some ice on that lip."

"I'll take care of it." She walked to the sofa and frowned at Brett. "Come on, Marshal. Miss Kitty's going to take you to your room."

The cut in the corner of Brett's mouth prevented more than a partway grin. "Didn't know you cared."

She would not give him the satisfaction of returning his smile. "Right now, I don't. I just can't stand the thought of you bleeding all over the nice Oriental rug."

When they reached the elevator, Cammie and Brett rode in silence to the top floor. It brought to mind another hotel in another city, another elevator…another lifetime, it seemed to Cammie. In this instance they stood miles apart, Cammie on one side of the mirrored wall, Brett on the other.

As Brett studied the floor the entire trip, Cammie wondered if he'd been thinking about a few days ago when they couldn't seem to keep their hands off each other. She wanted to reach over and smooth the lock of hair falling across his forehead, touch his cheek above his swollen jaw spattered with evening stubble. But she was still too angry to provide that kind of comfort. At him for believing she needed rescuing. At herself for being gullible once again.

After they reached his room, Cammie grabbed a washcloth from the bathroom, filled it with ice from the bucket and handed it to him. "Here. This should keep the swelling down."

He touched the ice to his jaw and winced. "Thanks."

She crossed her arms over her middle. "For your information, if I'd known Cruz was married, I would not have agreed to the drink. You have my permission to say I told you so."

"It wasn't your fault. Guys like him come a dime a dozen and it's easy to get pulled in by their lines. Just be more careful next time."

Did he really believe there would be a next time? Worse, he didn't seem to care if there was. "I'll see you in the morning."

Before she could get out the door, he called her back. And like the fool she'd become around him, the fool she'd been tonight, she turned around to find him perched on the arm of the sitting-area sofa. "What?"

"Can you stay awhile?" He apparently read the reservation in her eyes when he added, "I just want to talk."

She should tell him no, but he looked so pitiful,

she decided to throw him a bone. "Okay, but only for a few minutes."

Brett crossed the room and opened the minibar's refrigerator. "Do you want something to drink?"

"No, thank you." She wanted to get out of there as quickly as possible, before she made a second colossal mistake tonight.

Brett returned with a beer, sat on the opposite end of the couch and engaged in ritualistic label-peeling. "I wanted to say I'm sorry about causing a scene."

"On one hand, I'm glad you told me before I left with him," she said. "However, the macho posturing wasn't pleasant. But I'm partially to blame, too. I should have never agreed to the drink."

"Then why did you?" he asked without looking at her.

Time for the admission she felt she had to make. "I was so angry with you I guess I thought it was a good way to get your attention." For some reason that made him smile, which made Cammie feel like an immature idiot. "I know. It was a really childish thing to do."

"Rusty told me that's what you were doing."

Wonderful. "You told Rusty?"

"He's the one who told me Cruz is married."

Might have been nice if Rusty would have told her. "Well, it's over and I'll be much more cautious in the future."

He set the beer on the coffee table and leveled his gaze on hers. "I swear, Cammie, I never wanted you to feel that what happened between us didn't mean anything. I was trying not to hurt you, and I did, anyway."

Yes, he had, but that was one confession she refused to make. "It's done. No harm, no foul." No truth in that, either.

He leaned back against the cushions and sighed. "I've failed a lot of people in my lifetime, and history keeps repeating itself."

"Are you referring to your ex-wife?"

"Yeah. She was the first."

Cammie tucked her leg beneath and prepared to have some answers to her questions, provided he cooperated. "What exactly happened between the two of you?"

He stacked his hands behind his head and stared at the ceiling. "We grew up together, we married too young, we had a kid, I got my big break and we grew apart. She hated this way of life, and eventually she learned to hate me."

"I can understand why she might feel that way about the business." Even if she would never understand how anyone could ever hate Brett. "I've seen firsthand what it means to be in the spotlight and all the temptations that go along with it."

"Unlike that idiot tonight, I was faithful to her," he said. "Not that I didn't have opportunities. A lot of opportunities. But my mother drilled it into my head that when you take a vow, you keep it. I sure as hell tried until the bitter end."

She found both his honesty and his convictions admirable. "And you've never been involved with anyone since that time?"

He leaned forward, took a drink of the beer and dangled it between his parted knees. "I've had a few female friends over the years who I could call when I needed to."

She suspected more than a few. "Friends with benefits?"

"More benefits than friendship," he said. "It's sometimes hard to know who your friends are in this business."

"And it doesn't bother you to live like that?"

"Sometimes." He took a long swig of the beer and set it back down. "But it's the only life that works for me right now."

Cammie felt sincerely sad for him, and a little for herself. "I'm sorry you feel that way. I, on the other hand, want more than just casual sex and false friendships."

He sat quietly for a few moments before he said, "Let's start over, Cammie."

"How do you mean?"

"It ain't going to be easy, but I want to be your friend. I think I need that more than anything right now."

Now she was really confused. "I'm not sure we've ever really been friends."

"Not true," he said. "I've told you more about my personal life in less than a month than I have with anyone in ten years. I really appreciate that about you."

She supposed that was something. "I guess we can try."

He looked genuinely pleased. "That's all I'm asking."

And she hoped it wasn't too much to ask. Even now, if he so much as touched her, she'd forget about friendship for one blissful night in his bed. Yet that would only lead to more hurt and heartbreak.

Fatigue began to set in, sending Cammie off the couch. "Okay, friends it is."

"Where are you going?" he asked.

"To bed, which is where you should be going. We have to be up early in order to get to San Jose and have enough time to rehearse. I'm still pulling double duty for the next two weeks, remember?"

He stood and hooked his thumbs in his pockets. "Not so. Bud's flying in tomorrow morning to take over for you."

"Since when?" she said around her shock.

"Since he decided you needed a break."

On one hand, she was glad to have Bud back. On the other, she worried what might happen if he got wind of her extracurricular activities with the star of the show. "Just promise me one thing, Brett."

"Name it."

"Don't let on to Bud about what happened with us. He'll go ballistic."

"WHAT'S THIS I HEAR about you and Brett?"

Cammie had barely boarded the bus before Bud launched in with a question she didn't care to answer. But if she didn't say something, he'd only continue to hound her.

After tossing her bag onto the sofa, she returned to the cab, gave him a quick hug and sat in the seat beside him. "It's nice to see you, too, Bud. How's the baby?"

He presented a proud-daddy grin. "She wasn't quite cooked to done, but she was done enough. She's getting fatter by the day."

"You make her sound like a Thanksgiving turkey. You should have stayed home the entire month as planned."

"My mother-in-law came in and I'd had about all the woman talk I could stand," he said. "Besides, I figured I might be needed more here."

It had become all too clear why he'd come back early—to police her. "I'm getting by fine, Bud. I could have managed until you got back."

He rubbed his scruffy chin. "Maybe so, but you still haven't answered my question about you and Brett."

She shrugged. "I agreed to sing backup to fill in for Pat, at Pat's request."

"I ain't talkin' about the singing. Rusty says the two of you really heat up the stage together. I'm wondering if it's just the stage you've been heating up together."

Cammie hoped her flushed face didn't give her away. "We're friends, Bud. That's it." That much was true, for now.

"If you say so." Cammie thought she might be able to escape until he added, "How come you haven't called home?"

She tried unsuccessfully to tamp down the guilt. "I called Granddad in Vegas. He told me the business is doing well and they have two contracts for college charters during football season."

"They're worried you might not come back home."

No surprise there. "They don't have to worry about that. This is only a temporary situation. Once the tour's finished, I'll be heading back to Memphis and the business." Funny, that notion didn't seem all that appealing. Necessary, but not that much fun.

Bud stared out the windshield for a time before he nailed her with a serious stare. "Are you sure nothing's going on with you and Brett aside from the singing?"

"I'm sure." She couldn't have said that a few days ago. "Now can we get on the road?"

"Might be nice if we waited for Brett to get here."

Cammie glanced back at the closed stateroom door where she thought he might be. "I assumed he was already here."

"Not yet."

As if they'd willed his appearance, Brett scaled the stairs and stepped inside, looking freshly showered, clean shaven and extremely sexy, even in black

T-shirt and jeans. "One of the tractor trailers blew a tire," he said. "So it's going to be at least another hour."

Bud shut down the bus and shifted toward Brett. "Have you been happy with Cammie's services?"

If Brett was at all rattled by the question, he didn't show it. But he did lay a palm on her shoulder. "Cammie's been great, and you weren't kidding when you said she could sing."

From the disapproving look on his face, Bud was clearly bothered by the gesture that seemed fairly intimate. "I'm just glad to know you appreciate her. She deserves that, and your respect."

"You can count on it." Brett finally dropped his hand and hooked a thumb over his shoulder. "I'm going back inside to meet with Tim in the restaurant."

"Just be sure you're back when we're ready to roll," Bud called after Brett as he left the bus, raising a hand in acknowledgment.

Cammie climbed out of the seat before she had to tolerate more questions. "I'm going to do some laundry while we wait."

"I'm not done talkin' yet, Camille."

Bud's use of her given name meant this wasn't going to be good. "What else do you want to know? I brushed my teeth twice a day and ate right, although I did miss my curfew a couple of times. But hey, at twenty-seven, I figure it's acceptable to stray now and then."

"How far have you strayed?"

Too far to take it back. "Don't worry, Bud. Your little Cammie's a big girl and she can take care of herself."

With that, she headed to the back of the bus before she gave herself away. Yet Bud could probably see through her lies like she was made of cellophane. Could probably see the way she felt about Brett in her eyes alone. If he knew how much she cared about him, he'd escort her off the bus and ask more questions later.

Lucky, lucky Brett. How convenient that he'd made a hasty exit before he'd had to undergo the third degree.

"WHAT'S GOING ON with you and Cammie?"

Ignoring Tim for the time being, Brett signaled the waitress to refill his coffee, although he'd like a shot of eighty-proof whiskey. "Nothing's going on, Tim. She's filling in for Pat."

"That's not what your band says."

Damn the band. "Exactly what does the band say?"

Tim adjusted the purple tie that looked like a noose around his flabby neck. "I hear you've gotten pretty cozy with her onstage. I'm not saying that's a bad thing at all. In fact, it's a good thing, having a lady with talent like that backing you up. But…"

There was always a *but* with Tim. "You're worried she's going to ruin my rep with the ladies."

"No. I'm worried what's going to happen after the tour's over. Chemistry onstage is one thing, a serious relationship offstage is another."

Brett smiled at the waitress as she poured the coffee. "Thanks."

She grinned like a kid when she backed away. "Yes, sir, Mr. Taylor."

Tim pointed at the woman's back. "That's what I mean. We need to keep that adoration going. No need to mess it up with you going off and getting married again."

Married? Where the hell did that come from? "I promise you I'm not getting married in the foreseeable future, if ever. And as far as Cammie's concerned, once we're done with the tour, that's the end of it. She's going home and so am I. We'll probably never see each other again." That reality hit him with a force he didn't expect, right in the heart.

Tim leaned forward and dumped half a canister of sugar in his coffee. "I've been meaning to talk you about that very thing. How do you feel about Cammie going into the studio and backing you up on a couple of tracks?"

"It doesn't matter what I think," he said. "She'll never agree to it."

"She might if you asked her nicely. I see a future for that little gal, and I'd be glad to manage her. She could even open for you and then we'd have men coming to see her and women coming to see you. Best of both worlds."

Brett didn't like the thought of men lusting after Cammie, nor did he like to think of her thrust into a life that she admittedly didn't want. "You're getting way ahead of yourself, Tim. First, she has no intention of breaking into the music scene. Second, she's too good for it." Just like she was too good for him.

Tim sat back and rimmed the cup with a bulky thumb. "You should ask her just to be sure."

He could ask, but he already knew the answer—no. "I need to go before Bud takes off without me."

"One more thing," Tim said. "Don't forget the studio's sending a crew to Seattle to shoot the rest of the video for the next single."

Just what he needed, something else to do. "Fine. Any idea what they have in mind?"

"They mentioned they don't want good ol' Texas boy and they don't want the band. They want sexy with you and a woman. They're holding casting calls for prospective actresses to play opposite you." Tim released a gruff, seedy laugh. "I'd pay to have that job."

Great. He'd be expected get personal with a perfect stranger. Not that he hadn't done it before, and not only in front of a camera. "Let me know the details so I have some time to prepare. And tell them to pick someone who's older than twenty and isn't texting her damn boyfriend all the time like the last one."

"I don't know what you're bitching about. A lot

of men would give their right eye to make out with a sweet young thing."

"It's not as easy as you think," he said. "It's kind of hard to generate chemistry with someone you met two minutes before you step on set."

"I'll do what I can, but it's not up to me. You'll just have to live with what they give you."

Something suddenly occurred to Brett. A great idea. "I want Cammie in the video." That would guarantee some hefty chemistry.

Tim shook his head. "They're pretty strict about who they use, Brett."

"Make it happen, and I'll try to talk her into cutting the track with me." And the devil could be living in a deep freeze before he convinced her to take on either project. He'd have to pull out all the stops to persuade her.

"I guess it could work," Tim said. "She's a good-lookin' woman and real sexy."

Didn't he know it. He'd have no trouble making a video with Cammie and pretending he wanted to make love to her. Only he wouldn't be pretending.

Brett pushed back from the table and stood. "I'm going to do my best to get her to agree, but just so you know, she could shoot me down."

"Or she might surprise you and say yes."

CHAPTER THIRTEEN

"No way."

"Come on, Cammie. It's not a big deal."

Being immortalized in a video was a huge deal. "Oh, look. You can see the Golden Gate Bridge from here."

"Sweetheart, pointing out the sights isn't going to keep me from trying to talk you into this."

She turned from the hotel window so Brett could see exactly how little she welcomed this ridiculous suggestion. "I don't know the first thing about making a video, much less acting in one."

He brought out his best sexy look, the one that would make her crawl over hot coals to get to him. "You just follow the director's instructions and take it from there."

He made it sound so simple. Too simple. "I'll let you know when we get to Seattle."

His smile faded out of sight. "I need your answer by tomorrow. If you won't do it, they'll be forced to find some tall, leggy blonde to rub up against me all day."

He'd stooped to an all-time low with that argument, and she did have to admit thinking about Brett wrapped up with some nubile actress could easily sway her to his side. If she let it. "Good. I hope you have a marvelous time with the blonde and the mutual rubbing."

"I don't want anyone but you," he said. "Besides, it's for 'When You Know It's Real,' and no one knows that song better than you do aside from me."

The song they'd sung together every night. Their special song. "Would I be expected to sing?"

"No. They'll play the studio track during the shoot, so the audio won't be an issue. We just have to act like we want each other."

That wouldn't take a whole lot of effort. And that in itself seemed dicey. The friend thing had been going so well, she didn't want to mess it up. For the past two days, they'd done nothing more than share meals and talk and rehearse on the bus. No touching. No hanky-panky. No sneaking off into the stateroom to hide from Bud and make good use of Brett's big bed. Not that she hadn't imagined doing that very thing.

"Will you just think about it?" he asked.

"Fine. I'll think about it." And then she'd give him another emphatic "no." Right now she was curious about the box Brett had been sorting through when he summoned her to his room.

She brushed past him, claimed a seat at the table and took inventory of the items strewn over the glass top—a folded piece of paper and several guitar picks. "What is all this?"

He pulled back a chair, turned it around and straddled it backward. "It's some stuff Pat sent me." He held up the yellowed paper. "This is the first song we wrote together on the bus. I didn't know he'd kept it. Never realized Pat was so damn sentimental about things."

"What about the guitar picks?"

Brett picked up a black plastic triangle and studied it. "Pat stole them from the bands we opened for, and eventually performers who've opened for us. He liked the challenge of taking them without getting caught."

Very weird. "Wouldn't they have just given him one if he asked?"

"It's all a part of the game. All done in fun with no harm intended. It's what makes everyone a part of the family."

A somewhat dysfunctional family. Cammie gestured toward the cardboard container. "Can I look?" she asked tentatively, not wanting to intrude.

"Sure." After he shoved the box in her direction, she removed a medallion dangling from a silver chain.

Brett slowly pulled the pendant from Cammie's grasp. "Pat liked the idea of a saint watching over us while we traveled. He swore it kept him safe for the twenty-odd years he owned it. He told me on the phone the other day that he wanted me to have all of it for luck."

"You spoke to him?"

He dropped the medallion back into the box. "Yeah. I called him after this came. I thanked him and I apologized for being an ass the day he left."

She was go glad he'd put away his pride. "Good. I'm sure he appreciated it, especially the apology."

Brett's gaze drifted back to the box. "I remember the first day I met him. Pat was between bands and decided to audition. After he finished, he looked me over and said, 'Damn, you're nothing but a pup. Here's another one I'll have to raise.' He was so freakin' confident I was going to hire him. And I did. Been a fool not to."

"I agree," she said. "Pat's one in a million."

"He's one of a kind." Brett's shoulders slumped slightly, as if the energy seeped out with the memories. "He'd been around a long time so he was the best thing that could've happened to my career. He guided me on many an issue. He never let me know that's what he was doing, but I finally figured it out. He never took credit for all the success, either. He had a lot of offers from other bands over the years, but for some reason he stuck it out with me. Guess he saw something no one else did."

Cammie saw it, too—the wounded man behind the superstar. The man who had so much going for him, yet still seemed unsure at times. "I'm going to miss him and I barely knew him, so I know it's going to be tough on you for a while."

"Yeah, it is." He got up and poured the last bit of coffee from the pot. After he sat down, he began to speak again. "Last night, during one number, something wasn't quite right with the bass playing. I thought Pat must've had something to drink before we went on. I was going to give him one of my 'what in the hell is wrong with you' looks, but he wasn't there. That's when it hit me that he's never coming back."

Cammie hated the pain in his voice and expression, yet she was truly happy he'd finally opened up to her. "You'll see him again, Brett, somewhere down the line. It's not like he's completely out of your life."

"Yeah, but it's not the same thing as having him around all the time." He stood, carried the cup to the counter, then turned to face her. "What are your plans for the rest of the day?"

She took a quick check of her watch. "We have four hours to kill before rehearsal, and I'm starving. Do you want me to call room service?"

"I want to go out somewhere and take a walk."

Cammie assumed he meant alone. "Okay, I'll see you later."

"No way. You're going with me."

"For a walk?"

"Yeah."

"Aren't you afraid someone might recognize you?"

He picked up his cap and set it low on his brow. "I'll take my chances."

Spending quality time with Brett, away from the hotel and chaos, was worth a few chances. "All right. But we have to get an umbrella. And I get to say where we eat because it's my turn. I personally want to go—"

He suspended her tirade by putting a fingertip to her lips. "If you don't shut up it'll be time for the show before we get where we're going."

She pulled his hand away. "I want to go to Fisherman's Wharf and eat seafood."

He frowned. "You know I don't like seafood."

She rolled her eyes. "You don't like fish and there's a lot more to choose from. Try eating some crab."

"Most guys spend most of their life avoiding crabs."

Men could be so crude, even the incredibly cute ones. "Very funny. You should really try to expand your horizons."

He seemed to consider that for a few minutes. "I'll make a deal with you. I'll try the crabs, if you'll agree to the video thing."

Leave it to him to bargain with her. She wasn't all that keen on putting herself out there for the world to see. She had absolutely no idea what to expect.

But if Brett was willing to take a chance, then so should she. "Okay, I'll do it."

He picked her up and swung her around before setting her back on her feet. "You won't regret it. In fact, you just might enjoy it."

SHE'D BEEN POKED, pulled, positioned and powdered. She'd changed clothes more times than she could count—an outfit for the scene on the boat crossing Puget Sound, one for the pier, another for the stroll downtown. She'd been praised for her bone structure, and insulted because she walked like a guy. And now she stood barefoot on a pebbled beach in a place known as Deception's Pass, wearing a gauzy white top covering—of all things—a little red bikini. Worse, the once-sunny skies had opened up, releasing a deluge not ten minutes after they'd climbed down some rickety steps to get to this remote part of the park.

She was freezing to death and wouldn't be surprised if her teeth left her mouth to go skittering across the water like skimming stones. "What is the hold-up?"

Brett—who wore a white tailored shirt and rolled-up jeans—didn't look at all uncomfortable. "They're just trying to get it right. It always happens at remote locations. But at least this is the last shot."

"Good, because I'll be dead from exposure after this one."

He had the gall to grin. "It's barely raining now and it's not all that cold."

"Easy for you to say. You're wearing cotton and denim, not a piece of tissue paper and two pieces of yarn."

He raked his gaze down her body and back up again, slowly. "If it's any consolation, you look real good. Especially wet."

The innuendo in his tone didn't help her current chills. "I look like a drowned rat in a block of ice. I am not enjoying this."

"Pretend we're in the Bahamas."

"That's kind of hard to do when you're surrounded by pine trees and it smells like Christmas. Not that I'm complaining. This is an absolutely gorgeous place, if you're wearing appropriate clothing."

"Well, since you're suffering, then I'm going to suffer, too." He worked the buttons on the shirt, stripped it away and tossed it on a nearby boulder.

The unbelievable backdrop had nothing on Brett Taylor's beautiful body. Once she got past the impact of his bare chest, Cammie's attention turned to a drop of water sliding down his sternum and onto his board-flat belly before disappearing into his waistband, like the raven's wing on his tattoo. She'd give anything to be that drop of water, and suddenly she wasn't quite as cold.

"Okay, folks," the director called from his perch above them. "This is for the final chorus. Make it sexy and make it look like you mean it."

Brett slid his arms around her waist. "You heard the man. Act like you mean it."

That would so not be a problem, and suddenly she was very warm.

"Cue music."

As the song began to play, so did Brett. He toyed with the opening on her blouse, then lowered his head to nuzzle her neck. Her hands automatically landed on his arms to experience the play of his muscles. Then he slid his palm to the small of her back and nudged her closer. He kissed her forehead, then her cheek, and placed another at the corner of her mouth.

She looked into his incredible blue eyes that were almost a match to the Pacific and everything else—everyone else—faded away, as if they were truly alone on a remote beach with no concerns other than being together. And as the final refrain began to play, the lyrics—richly sang in Brett's remarkably deep voice—began to sink in....

It's the way you see through me...the way you make me feel.... That's when I can't deny it...when I know that it's real....

What she felt for him had become very real. All too real. She couldn't deny she loved him. Every flaw. Every insecurity. Every beautiful part of him, inside and out. And she simply didn't care what that might mean as soon as he kissed her. A deep, moving kiss that continued long after the recording had stopped. Much longer than would be deemed appropriate for two people who were supposed to be playing a part.

The round of rousing applause and whistles interrupted the kiss, yet Brett didn't let her go. "This is why I chose you."

If only he'd meant that in every way possible.

ON THE DRIVE BACK TO SEATTLE, their conversation had died with the combination of fatigue and a return to reality. Brett wasn't one to make too many demands during the shoots, just a trailer where they'd showered and changed, and some food. But this time he'd ordered a private car to take them back to the hotel where they would immediately board the bus, bound for Denver.

Cammie slept soundly against his chest, his arm wrapped around her shoulder. He felt such a fierce need to protect her, only she didn't need his protection, except maybe from him. During that final shoot, when they'd been wrapped up together, for the first time the lyrics he'd written solely to produce another number-one hit had meant something. Because she meant something to him. More than he wanted to admit. He'd begun to believe he could take the next step in this relationship, until past failures stopped him cold. She'd eventually grow tired of his moods, the demands on his time, this crazy life he'd known far too long. He couldn't imagine doing anything else, but right now he couldn't imagine doing without her.

"Do you want me to let you out at the entrance, Mr. Taylor?" the driver asked.

"No. Let us out at the bus around back."

"Yes, sir."

As the driver navigated the car through the parking lot, Cammie straightened and stretched her arms over her head. "I haven't packed my stuff yet," she said.

He already missed having her so close. "While you were in the shower, I called the hotel and had one of the staff members do it for you."

She smiled. "That was nice of you."

"And you deserve it." She deserved a lot more than that.

When the car came to a stop, they both slid out and entered the bus to find Bud waiting in the driver's seat. He took one look at Cammie and scowled. "You look like you're on your last leg."

"Just about," she said as she walked into the main cabin.

Brett stood behind the driver's quarters and peered through the windshield to find the lot deserted. "Where's the other bus?"

"Already on their way, following the equipment trucks," Bud said. "We'll catch up to them sooner or later."

Knowing Bud's tendency to speed, Brett had no doubt they would. "Just drive carefully and don't worry about catching up to them."

Bud sent him a confused look. "Since when do you concern yourself with my driving?"

Since Cammie had come on board. "I'm just saying we have two days to get there, so take it easy."

Cammie returned, looking a little more awake than she had the past few hours. "If you two don't mind keeping it down, I'm going to bed now. Or maybe I should say I'm going to berth now."

That wasn't going to happen. "Since Bud's driving now, you can have my bed. Me and Bud can share the berth."

"You're okay as a boss, Brett," Bud said. "But I ain't climbin' into a berth with you."

He wasn't in the mood for Bud's smart-ass humor. "I meant we'll trade off. When you drive, I sleep and vice versa." Like he really needed to explain that.

"Lighten up, Taylor. I figured that's what you meant."

Cammie folded her arms across her middle and frowned. "Don't I have any say in the matter?"

Brett and Bud simultaneously said, "No."

"You need your rest more than I do," Brett added. "I tend to stay up later, anyway."

She dropped her arms and looked altogether frustrated. "Fine. I'll be glad to take over your bed, and that's exactly where I'm going as soon as I get my things together. Night-night."

As soon as Cammie turned around, Brett grabbed the curtain and slid it partway shut to conceal the cab. "Feel free to take off now. I'm going to close this so I can have some privacy."

Bud didn't make a move to leave. "Why do you need privacy?"

"Cammie's going to bed and I'm going to do some writing, if it's any of your damn business."

Bud raised his hands from the steering wheel. "Fine. I just want to make sure that's all you plan to do."

As far as Brett was concerned, that remained to be seen. Maybe not tonight, but anything was possible after the shoot today. "See you in the morning," he said, then pulled the curtains completely closed. Just for the hell of it, he strode to the control on the wall and sent the wood divider sliding across the closed curtain.

"Boy, you've done it now. He'll think something really nefarious is going on."

He turned to see Cammie sitting on the sofa, one arm draped over the back. "I thought you were going to bed."

"I'm not that sleepy anymore," she said. "But at least I'm thawed out."

He dropped down beside her and laid a hand on her thigh. "You handled everything pretty damn well."

"Except for the complaining," she said. "But I swear if I'd had a pair of hiking boots I would've been all over those hills in a heartbeat."

"You're a hiker?"

"Used to be. I hiked quite a bit in high school and in college."

He narrowed his eyes and inclined his head. "Were you a tomboy, Camille?"

"What gave it away?" she asked. "Maybe that 'she walks like a guy' comment?"

That plain pissed him off. "Someone said that to you?"

"Yes, but it's probably true." She raised her hand as if taking an oath. "I confess I was a dyed-in-the-wool, sports-playing, dress-avoiding tomboy."

"I thought you said you were studious?"

"I'm also an overachiever."

He learned more about her each passing day, and he liked everything he'd learned about her so far. "I wondered about that until you showed up in the casino wearing a dress." A man-killing dress that had almost done him in.

She dropped her hand and laid it on his. "I decided to take a walk on the wild side and see what all the hype was about. I didn't mind being dressed up that night, but I don't plan to make a habit of it."

He leaned back and laughed. "You beat all I've ever seen, Cammie. A woman trained in classical music who likes to climb hills."

She bent her elbow on the back of the sofa and leaned her cheek into her palm. "Okay, so I'm also a little schizophrenic."

"You're the most intriguing woman I've ever met."

"I'm sure you've met more interesting women."

None like her. Never like her. "Think what you will, but you're wrong." When she hid a yawn behind her hand, he added, "You're also sleepy."

"Yes, I guess I am." She pushed off the sofa and faced him. "Do you need anything from your room before I retire?"

He needed to be with her all night. He also needed to ask about Nashville, but he figured she'd been through enough today. "My toothbrush and shaving kit."

She headed away and came back with his stuff, then disappeared into her designated bathroom. She returned a few minutes later and smiled down on him. "Good night, and thanks for the experience today. Other than the cold, I did enjoy it."

He stood, leaving too little distance between them. He wanted to kiss her. He wanted to take her hand, lead her into his bedroom and show her how much she meant to him in the best way he knew how. But he didn't want her to think that's all he wanted from her, although right now he wasn't sure what he wanted. "Hope you get some sleep," he said, deciding to leave it at that. No kissing. No touching. Just a friendly good-night.

Cammie threw a wrench in his plan by slipping her arms around him and giving him a hug. They stayed that way for a few moments, holding on to each other, until she finally let him go.

"You're a good man, Brett Taylor," she said as

she backed down the corridor a few steps. "Better than you realize."

Brett continued to stand there long after Cammie had closed the stateroom door. She made him want to be a better man. A man she could count on. He still had a few demons to conquer, but he decided then and there to prove his worth to her. If he succeeded, anything was possible.

CHAPTER FOURTEEN

DENVER, CHEYENNE, Omaha, Kansas City. More unfamiliar cities and sold-out concerts and crazed fans. But now they were bound for Tennessee, headed home. As far as their roller-coaster relationship was concerned, Cammie had no idea where that was heading, but she suspected nowhere.

She did have to hand it to Brett—he couldn't have been more considerate over the past ten days. During rehearsals and concerts, he'd treated her like a queen, frequently asking if she needed anything and getting it if she said yes. He'd even had single red roses delivered to her hotel rooms. At night, he'd treated her like a pariah, making certain the band was on board until the wee hours of the morning. She'd gone to bed alone to deal with the loneliness and desire for him that wouldn't go away.

Yet she couldn't discount the occasional glances or the casual touches between them on the bus. She couldn't ignore the chemistry that still existed between them onstage. She also couldn't help but wonder why Brett seemed so silent and moody tonight.

Maybe it was simply a little bit of letdown now that the tour was finally over.

Before she headed for bed, she gathered a few dirty cups and glasses from the table and set them into the sink where she'd drawn some soapy water. Her attempts to wash them were thwarted when Brett said, "Leave those for now and sit down."

After wiping her damp hands on a towel, she joined him on the sofa and crossed her legs before her. "What's on your mind?"

He streaked one hand through his hair. "I have something I need to ask you but I'm not sure how you're going to take it."

He sounded so blasted serious she wasn't sure, either. "Just ask."

Leaning forward, he laced his hands together, forearms resting on his thighs, and focused on the floor beneath his boots. "Tim wants you to cut a track with me for the new CD."

Every dream she'd ever possessed told her to say yes. Every instinct told her to say no. She answered with a question. "Why?"

"Because he says you're too good a prospect to pass up. He has this idea that he's going to manage you and build your career."

"He's making a huge assumption that I actually want a singing career. I don't." She couldn't let herself want it. "I have to consider the family business. My grandfather's not getting any younger, which he mentioned on the phone yesterday. He's terrified

I'm going to get caught up in the jaws of the music-industry machine."

Brett looked totally perplexed. "Do you plan to drive buses the rest of your life?"

Not willingly. "I owe my grandparents that much."

"And you don't owe yourself a chance to have a shot at a music career." He posed the statement as a comment, not a question.

She realized how it all sounded—that she was willing to settle, at least when it came to a career. As far as her personal life went, just the opposite. "Call me old-fashioned, but I eventually want marriage and kids, hopefully before I turn thirty in three years." When she noticed the alarm in his eyes, she added, "Don't worry, Brett. I know we don't want the same things."

He seemed to consider that for a moment before he stared at her dead-on. "You'd really ignore once-in-a-lifetime opportunity for an ordinary life?"

She surely wasn't surprised he'd feel that way. "Maybe it's hard for you to fathom, but having a family means a lot to me. Fame and fortune doesn't."

"I get that," he said, although Cammie doubted he did. "Why don't you come to Nashville and at least tour the studio, see what it's all about?"

She sighed. "It wouldn't matter, Brett. Songwriting is the only part of the music scene I'd be interested in pursuing. But everyone knows how hard it is to break in."

"Not if you have connections."

She refused to use those connections—namely him. "I want to do it on my own, if I do it at all. At the moment I don't have anything that would interest anyone."

"You have that song you've been working on."

The song hadn't come up since the day he'd heard her sing it. "Why on earth would you believe someone would want to record it?"

"Because it's good," he said. "Real good."

"I think you're crazy."

He smiled and touched her face lightly, yet it weighed heavy on her heart. "You know I am, but that doesn't mean your song's dead in the water. If you'll let me see it again and maybe make a few suggestions, I'll give you an honest opinion."

She saw no real harm in letting him take a look. "Okay. But I'm warning you, it's a hopeless cause."

"I'll be the judge of that. Go get it."

"Now?"

"Yep."

After unfolding her legs, she slid off the sofa to retrieve the weathered spiral from the cabinet above the flat-panel TV. When she turned around, she discovered Brett sporting an amused expression. She'd been caught red-handed engaging in covert activity with a ring binder.

"Have you been hiding it from me?" he asked.

He was too intuitive for her own good. "Hiding it from me, actually. There are a lot of memories in these pages. I think I just wanted to forget everything for the time being. But if you have anything to contribute, have at it."

She leaned back against the counter and watched him open the notebook to the dog-eared page containing her most recent effort. When he scanned the text, closed the book and fell silent, Cammie collapsed onto the sofa. "Don't just sit there and leave me in suspense."

"I was right," he said. "It's good."

"Then what's wrong?"

"I've been lying to you," he said, again failing to make eye contact.

Figured. "The song sucks."

He refused to look at her directly. "This isn't about the song. It's about me. About us."

She feared she knew what that might entail. "Just spill it, Brett. I can take it, whatever it is."

"Tim isn't the only one who wants you to come to Nashville," he said. "I want you there, and I want you to stay with me."

She hadn't let herself hope that he'd propose seeing each other after the tour was over. Granted, she could be reading too much into it. "Define 'stay with you.'"

Brett finally made eye contact, yet his expression didn't provide one clue as to what he was thinking. "I have a big house and a big pool and a big bed. Or you could have your own room. I have three more."

Maybe he just wanted his temporary bus driver

to fill in as a temporary bed buddy. "I still don't understand your motives."

"I'm ready to try and see how we work outside of this atmosphere, Cammie," he said. "I really like being around you. Hell, I like being around me. I couldn't say that before we met."

She was flattered by his comments, thrilled that he wanted to pursue a relationship, but not too stupid to stay cautious. "Yes, things have changed with you and between us, in a good way. It's pretty remarkable. But I wonder how long that would last and how much time you're going to give us. Do I plan to stay a few days or weeks, or until you decide you're done with me because you're afraid to get too close?"

"I want you there for as long as it takes to explore what we have together. I want us to be a… you know."

She almost laughed at his obvious discomfort, but she didn't find his hesitancy all that funny. "A couple?"

"Yeah. We can do things normal couples do. Go out on dates, that kind of thing. Get to know each other better."

"I assume you mean inside and out of bed."

She could swear he was starting to sweat. "Well, yeah. I figure if we're going to do it, we should go all in."

Cammie would love to go all in—emotionally and intimately—but she feared the possible repercussions to her heart. "Can you really give up your freedom and your other female *friends?*"

That brought about his frown. "There hasn't been anyone else but you since you came on board."

"Not that I'm aware of." She sounded like a suspicious girlfriend.

He left the couch and leaned back against the counter as she had. "I was with you almost every day until at least midnight."

"That still leaves seven or eight hours during the day."

"So what do you want from me exactly, Cammie? A promise ring?"

"A promise that you can be faithful to one woman."

"As long as that woman's you."

"And you'll talk to me if we hit a rough patch instead of running away?"

He looked a little hesitant, the ever-present uncertainty in his eyes. "I'm pretty screwed up in that department. Truth is, I used Pat's departure as an excuse to stay away from you. I figured if I gave you a tough time, you'd eventually realize I'm not worth the effort."

She smiled at his insight. "You've been subconsciously putting me through a test to see if I'm going to give up on you. And guess what?"

"You're still here, taking what I throw at you. But from this point forward, I promise I'll do whatever it takes not to disappoint you."

Soul-baring was so unlike Brett, and so, so welcome. Still… "To be perfectly honest, I'm scared." Scared of shattering into a million little pieces if he rejected her again and then never being able to put her heart back together.

"I'm willing to take the chance. Question is, are you?"

Was she? "It's a huge step, Brett. I've never lived with anyone aside from family, but I know it's not always a picnic."

"I know," he said. "But we won't know until we try."

"True."

He pushed away from the counter and rejoined her on the sofa. "You don't have to decide right now. We still have a couple of days and a few hundred miles to go."

Even that didn't seem like nearly enough time to make such a monumental decision. "Okay. I'll definitely give it some serious thought. Right now I'm going to finish cleaning the kitchen."

She returned to the sink and began to wash and weigh the pros and cons. She had so many things to consider—namely her grandparents' reaction. She couldn't just leave them high and dry to pursue a relationship that might not last. But she couldn't keep letting their needs take precedence over her own unless she wanted to remain at a stalemate. And she thought about Bud's reaction if he learned she'd been lying to him about her real relationship with Brett—that was unthinkable.

When Brett's arm came around her, a mug gripped in one hand, his other resting on her hip, she momentarily stopped thinking. "You forgot this."

She hadn't forgotten how good it felt to have him so close. "Thanks."

"Can I do anything else for you?"

She thought of several things, none involving dishwashing. "Not that I can think of at the moment."

When she felt him push her hair aside, she froze. When Brett's warm lips drifted over the back of her neck, she darn near quit breathing. "What are you doing?"

"Just trying to show you what you'd be missing if you turn me down."

A little more of that, and she'd probably agree to anything—to a point. "Are you having some sort of domestic goddess fantasy? Because if that's the case, and you want me to come home with you to do your dishes, the answer is no."

"I have a housekeeper." He traced his tongue along the shell of her ear, sending a series of chills down her spine and a surge of heat elsewhere. "But I have to admit, watching you do the dishes turns me on. Watching you do anything turns me on."

Pretending to ignore him, she took another glass from the counter and began to wash it. "Do you plan to seduce me senseless until I agree?"

"Is that a problem?"

"If that's the only reason you want me to come home with you, then yes, it is."

He took her by the shoulders and turned her around, a hint of anger in his eyes. "I live in a world where sex is as readily available as cell phones. If I wanted to screw a different girl every night, I only have to tell a roadie to scour the crowd and find me a willing woman, and there are plenty out there. I don't have to give her roses or tell her the details of my sorry past to get her into bed, only the promise of a good time. I sure as hell don't have to invite her to my house. So if you think that's all I want from you, think again."

He'd definitely put it in perspective, and she felt somewhat ashamed over her assumption. "I'm sorry."

"You don't owe me an apology, but I do owe you an explanation. I'd be lying if I said it hasn't been killing me not to touch you. Sometimes I want you so bad it hurts like hell, and it's not just about sex. So I'm sorry if you still feel that way. I just wish I knew how to convince you that what I want from you is something I haven't wanted since my marriage ended."

She reached up and rested her hand on his jaw. "I'm convinced. Now kiss me."

The minute his lips touched hers, she ignored the warring emotions, the fleeting fear of being totally powerless in his arms. She didn't notice the lights of passing vehicles filtering through the shades, or the occasional jolt beneath their feet. She was too lost in wanting him, too keyed up with anticipation. She was only mildly aware that the counter's edge bit into her lower back, and very aware of the proof that Brett wanted her when he pressed against her.

He broke the kiss and framed her face in his palms. "Every night when I go to bed alone, all I can think about is you. I think about making love to you, and only you, every minute of every day. I swear, Cammie, I'd lay you down right here, but…"

"But what?" It sounded like a fantastic idea to her.

Brett released her and stepped back. "You're going to have to come to me this time. That's the only way I'll know you're sure."

He walked away, leaving her with a desire that transcended anything she'd felt before in her life.

Cammie turned on the faucet and dabbed some water on her face, then made her way to the berth where she found Brett stretched out on his back, a forearm covering his eyes. And bunched on the floor next to the small bed—his shirt, jeans and shorts.

The thought of him naked underneath the covers was almost her undoing. But she remained motionless, hovering over him, waiting until he acknowledged her presence.

When he didn't, she sighed. "I'm here."

"So am I. It's your move."

He seemed so sure she'd crawl all over him at that

moment, and although she truly wanted to, she decided to make him wait and wonder.

She walked into the stateroom, closed the door behind her and leaned against it for support. If she had any sense, she'd make him suffer another day. Okay, maybe another hour. At least a few more minutes...

WELL, HELL.

Brett rolled onto his side and tried to get comfortable, but he couldn't find a satisfactory position that didn't add to his misery. He should've left well alone following the conversation. He shouldn't have kissed her. He had no one to blame but himself. He could have carried her into his bed right then, before she had a chance to change her mind. But he'd been determined to allow her to take the next step. Apparently she wasn't going to give him the satisfaction. Literally.

Brett's entire body tensed when he heard the door reopen. He didn't dare look up...or hope too much. He remained still as stone until he heard the overhead light click off, sending the compartment into darkness. But when she tugged the sheet away and the narrow mattress bent, he could barely stay still.

As she squeezed in beside him, it didn't take him long to figure out she wasn't wearing a stitch. And even though the bed was barely adequate for a man his size, it took no time at all for them to find a comfortable position—her leg draped over his bare thigh, her head resting on his chest and her fingertips coming dangerously close to the end of his tattoo.

Somehow, someway, he had a moment of clarity. "We need to go into the room in case Bud decides to check on us during a fuel stop."

She planted a kiss on his neck. "The divider's closed."

"He can still open it from the other side."

When she planted another kiss low on his belly, he wasn't sure he'd be able to move except to maybe pole vault off the bed. "It's kind of a thrill knowing we could get caught," she said.

For her maybe. "He'll kill me and spare you. Plus the condoms—"

"Are on the floor beside us."

Damn, she'd thought of everything—up to this point. "Are you sure you don't want to go to my bed? Seriously, Bud's going to be really pissed if he finds us here. I can handle him, but I'm worried about you."

She raked her nails down his thigh, coming awfully close to Joe. "I'm not going anywhere for the time being. That is, if you still want me."

"Oh, yeah. Me and Joe need you real bad right now."

She laid her hand on his chest and pressed her fingertips against his pounding heart. "But will you ever need me with this?"

I already do…

The thought exploded inside his brain with the

force of a grenade. He didn't know exactly when it had happened, but he'd fallen lock, stock and barrel in love with her. He wanted to tell her, but the words wouldn't come. "I'm learning, Cammie. Just give me a little more time."

"That's all I need to know."

She took the lead then, rolling on the condom with unexpected ease, although he could tell her hands were shaking. But she wasn't so nervous that she showed the least bit of hesitation when she moved on top of him and guided him inside her. He didn't know how he'd gone so long without this, without her.

She rocked back and forth to an erotic beat in sync with the motion of the bus. He touched her without mercy, brought her closer and closer to a climax. He heard the catch of breath in her throat and the soft moan as she swayed above him, letting him know she was almost there. With one more stroke, she softly cried out, and that led to his downfall. He shook with the force of his own climax and after it finally subsided, he experienced the emotions that before could only be found in his songs.

Just the way she said his name meant more to him than a thousand triumphs on stage. The way she accepted him, flaws and all, meant more than a hundred top-ten hits. He held her tighter, but he couldn't seem to get close enough even though they were as close as two people could be.

Cammie shifted as if she were going to move away. "Don't," he said, almost too harshly.

"I'm not going anywhere," she said softly, as if she understood his frustration.

Brett turned to his side, taking her with him. "Stay with me."

"What about Bud?"

"I don't give a damn about Bud."

"Brett—"

"Stay with me," he repeated. "Don't leave me." *Don't ever leave me.*

"I promise I won't."

"You son of a bitch."

Brett came awake with a start and glanced over his shoulder to see Bud standing by the berth surveying the scene, a murderous look on his face.

Cammie faced the wall and he was molded to her backside like a spoon. Fortunately, she was covered. Unfortunately, he wasn't, since the covers were bunched at his feet, giving Bud a bird's-eye view of his bare ass.

"You *sorry* son of a bitch," Bud repeated when Brett took his time pulling the blanket to his waist before he shifted onto his back.

Cammie came awake and rolled over, surprise replacing her sleepy expression when she noticed Bud. She sat up, tugged the sheet to her chin and sent him an acid look. "Do you mind, Bud?"

"Hell, yeah, I mind. Your grandfather would kill me if he knew I let this happen, Camille Carson."

"It's not her fault," Brett said quickly. "It's mine."

Cammie turned her frown on him. "You don't have to explain anything to him, Brett."

Brett rubbed his eyes and stared at Bud. "I don't suppose you'd buy it if I told you nothing happened."

Bud's gaze roved to the floor where a silver packet had been carelessly discarded alongside Brett's clothes. "No, I wouldn't buy that."

"Harold Eugene Parker, stop treating me like I'm a child."

Bud's face turned a bright crimson in response to Cammie's comment. "Dammit, Cam, I told you never to call me that!"

"Harold Eugene?" Brett couldn't stifle his laugh if his life depended on it, and it might.

"Shut up, Taylor," Bud said. "You've already stepped in a knee-deep pile of manure, so don't push your luck."

Cammie rolled her eyes. "Don't you have something better to do, Bud, like fuel up? I assume that's why we've stopped."

"I'm not moving, because the stud here has some explaining to do."

Brett lunged off the bed, taking the blanket with him, bumped his head and swore loudly. "First of all," he said with a finger pointed in Bud's chest, "we're both over twenty-one and free to do as we please. Second, nobody forced anybody into bed. And third, this isn't the first time."

Bud glared at Cammie. "Do you know what you did when you let this player have his way with you?"

Cammie slid farther down onto the pillow and dared to smile. "In case you haven't noticed, I'm not that skinny little teenager with braces and a training bra you used to tell what to do."

"You wore braces?" Brett asked.

"For two years."

"Yeah? So did I."

"For crying out loud," Bud muttered. "Who gives a flying flip who wore braces? I'm sure her teeth are the farthest thing from your mind right now, Taylor."

"Not necessarily." Brett dropped down on the edge of the bed and gave Cammie a brief kiss. "She has great teeth."

"Thanks, sweetie," she replied. "So do you."

Bud let go a string of curses that would have any mother going for a bar of soap. "Stop with all the sweet talk, dammit."

"Okay, Bud, here's the deal." Brett took Cammie's hand. "This isn't an over-the-road romance."

"No, it's not," Cammie chimed in. "As a matter of fact, I'm going to Nashville with Brett."

Brett didn't bother to hide his shock. "You are?"

She looked up at him and grinned. "I can't stand the thought of you all alone in that big empty house and no one to talk to but your housekeeper and your horses. Not to mention, I can't wait to use your pool."

"I forgot to tell you the deck overlooks the lake. It's a great place to write and talk, or we don't have to talk at all. We'll do whatever you say."

"I say it sounds like a wonderful idea."

"Don't I have anything to say about this?" Bud growled.

"No," they answered in perfect unison.

Brett pointed toward the front of the bus. "So if you don't mind, Cammie and I would like to get some sleep."

After Bud shook his head and walked away, Brett lifted Cammie into his arms, sheet and all, and deposited her on the bed in his stateroom. Then he secured the door before he came back to the bed. "There's something to be said for locks."

When she unraveled herself from the covers and stretched her arms out to him, he didn't hesitate to jump right in with her. Yeah, he was definitely ready to go all in.

He rolled her onto her back and hovered above her. "So I guess this means your answer is yes."

"Yes, I'm saying yes." She frowned. "That is if Bud chooses to deliver us there."

"He'll take us there, all right. Bud ain't no angel and I don't think he wants me spilling stories I know about him to his little Cammie. And I sure as hell know he doesn't want the rest of the band to find out his real name."

"That's blackmail, Brett."

"Sometimes that's the way you have to roll to

get what you want around here." And damn, he wanted her.

"You're not going to blackmail me, are you?"

"No, but I am going to keep you in this bed all day."

"Works for me." She landed her sweet little hands on his butt. "Speaking of rolling, let's make some noise and give Harold Eugene something to stew over."

"Just what do you have in mind?" he asked, although he already knew the answer when she slid her hand between them and homed in on her target—good ol' Joe. And as usual, Joe immediately rose to the occasion.

Brett drew in a sharp breath and grinned. "Nashville, here we come."

CHAPTER FIFTEEN

THE APRIL SUN BEAT DOWN on Cammie's shoulders and back, sending her into a euphoric state second only to the bliss she'd experienced over the past three weeks. She didn't care to move from her comfortable position in the redwood chaise, although she would eventually have to go inside in order to avoid sunburn. She wouldn't risk being in pain when Brett touched her—and boy, had he touched her quite a bit.

She thought about all those evenings they'd spent at home, dining on meals Brett's housekeeper had prepared in advance, then making love in several rooms and in several incredible ways. In Brett's presence, she'd become completely uninhibited. So uninhibited that she'd decided to work on her tan on the upper level deck just outside the bedroom, topless, something she'd never done before. That seemed to be the direction her life had taken—a course of self-discovery with a man she'd never allowed herself to hope for, let alone love.

She also loved his house—a modern, multi-level wooden structure overlooking the lake. The size alone indicated its owner had a lot of money, but not an ounce of pretension when it came to the interior. The decor inside was simple and masculine—dark earth-tone sofas set out about two living areas, a media room, a sound studio and a high-tech kitchen normally only seen in designer magazines. Yet she'd been bothered that two of the bedrooms had barely been furnished, prompting a few ideas of how she would add her own touch. Maybe paint the room at the end of the hall a nice sage-green and talk him into buying something bigger than the twin bed he'd put in there…and she was getting way ahead of herself.

They still had far to go, but in some ways they'd already come a long way. They'd even ventured into Nashville proper last weekend, dined in a four-star restaurant and explored Music Row out in the open, like a normal couple. A normal couple who had to pause now and then for Brett to sign a few autographs for fans who clearly had recognized those haunting blue eyes beneath the brim of his cap. He'd also taken her on the studio tour where they'd tested out the equipment by singing together. However, she still hadn't agreed to participate on the CD, but she was coming mighty close.

Cammie couldn't recall when she'd been happier, but the elation frightened her. She didn't know how long it would last, especially after what she'd discovered that morning at the market. She had no idea if Brett knew about it, and if he did, exactly how he'd reacted to it. She would find out as soon as he returned from the meeting with his producer, the fourth this week. In the meantime, she intended to enjoy the calm before the probable storm.

After she stretched her arms over her head, Cammie dangled one hand over the side of the chaise—only to have a wet tongue streak across her knuckles. She opened her eyes to Brett's drooling black retriever staring at her expectantly. "I see you've been taking lessons from your master, Merle."

"Yeah, and his master says that's the best view he's seen all day. I just hope I'm the only one getting a show."

Cammie looked up to find Brett standing at the sliding door, sunshades covering his eyes and a surprisingly serious expression on his face.

She sat up on the edge of the chaise, her arms crossed over her bare breasts. "You don't have to worry. I haven't seen a soul all day except for Merle. I sure missed you, though."

He strode to the chaise, leaned over and gave her a brief, almost perfunctory kiss before he claimed the adjacent chair. "What have you been up to? Aside from sunbathing naked."

His tone was borderline irritable and she wondered if the meeting hadn't gone well. However, she knew something that might take his mind off his troubles. She took a chance and lowered her arms and braced her palms on the edge of the chaise. "I'm only half-naked. I still have on my bottoms."

He grabbed the discarded terry robe from the table and tossed it at her. "Put that on. Otherwise, I won't be able to concentrate on our conversation."

A conversation she didn't particularly want to have in light of what she needed to tell him. "Spoilsport," she muttered as she slipped on the robe and cinched the tie at her waist.

He took off his sunglasses, set them on the table and pinched the bridge of his nose as if he had a headache. "Tell me about your day."

She'd start with the mundane details before she lowered the boom. "Well, I got up and took a shower after you left. Then I had some breakfast in the sunroom with Merle, who eyed my bagel the entire time. Then I had lunch, a fantastic Greek salad Naomi made me. She's great, by the way, and very efficient. I hope you pay her well. Oh, and I hope you don't mind, I gave her the night off so I can test your grilling skills."

"You should've asked me first," he said. "Tim's coming to dinner. Now I'll have to call her and tell her to come back."

She'd clearly overstepped her bounds. "I can cook dinner," she said. "I went to the market after lunch and picked up four rib eyes." Time to reveal the dreadful part of her day. The part that could send him over the edge. "That's where I discovered this."

Cammie leaned back, felt around for the magazine, then brought it out from beneath the chaise. She held her breath as she held it up for his inspection.

He surprised her by shrugging, not shouting. "Just your run-of-the-mill gossip rag."

Cammie pointed at the line in the corner of the front cover. "Did you read it?" She turned it around and did the honors for him. "'Another Country-Music Heartthrob off the Market? Look Inside to See Brett Taylor's Latest Conquest.'"

"You just have to ignore it, Cammie," he said. "This is the same rag that claimed Naomi's my long-time mistress and her sons are my illegitimate sons, all because I picked her up from the cleaners when her car broke down."

He didn't realize that what they'd written this time was true. But he would.

She opened the pages to the brief blurb listed under the current social-happenings heading. "It says here, and I quote, 'Country-music crooner Brett Taylor, thirty-three, was spotted on the Nashville streets cozying up with former bus driver and current backup singer, Camille Carson, twenty-seven. Seems Ms. Carson has more than driving and singing skills if she can tame this confirmed bad boy.' And they even have a picture."

She turned it back around to show him the photo of the two of them walking out of the bar where they'd had an after-dinner drink. Again, Brett didn't seem all that shocked by any of it. He did seem distracted.

"Doesn't this bother you?" she asked when he didn't respond.

"It's bound to happen," he finally said. "I'll let Tim handle it."

"As in confirm it?"

He grabbed his sunglasses and stood. "I don't know, Cammie. I have more important things to worry about right now."

Things he clearly had no intent of sharing with her. Unwilling to let him off the hook, she followed him into the bedroom where she found him emptying his pockets onto the bureau. That's when she spotted the stationery next to his keys. Purple stationery with darker hearts swirling across the top and handwritten words filling the first of what appeared to be two pages.

Cammie couldn't contain her curiosity, even if she risked suffering his wrath. "A letter from a fan?"

He kept his back to her as he shrugged out of his shirt and put on a T-shirt. "Not even close. It's from my kid, and she's definitely not a fan."

At least he'd told her that much, and now she knew the source of his distress. "Do you mind if I ask what it says?"

He sat on the cowhide chair in the corner and slipped off his boots. "Be my guest, but I've gotta warn you. Your opinion of me is probably going to drop to an all-time low."

"I doubt that." She didn't doubt the content was going to be disturbing.

After picking up the letter, she perched on the edge of the mattress and began to read. The first line alone broke her heart. She could only imagine what it had done to his.

Dear Dad,
Or maybe I should just call you Brett because you haven't been my dad for a long time. But I still remember when you were my daddy. I remember when you used to sing me that crazy song before I went to bed. I remember when you came to get me after a concert and I'd hide behind your truck. You liked to scare me but I wasn't scared because I knew you wouldn't really hurt me and you didn't back then. But you hurt me a lot of times because you never showed up at my softball games or when I showed my horse. I guess you just had more important things to do.

Mom told me she sent you the papers for you to sign so Randy can adopt me. I don't understand how a dad can give up their kid without asking that kid if that's what they want. I know Mom's made it hard for you to see me and I know I said something bad to you the last time we talked on the phone. I just wanted to say I'm sorry and that I really want to talk to you one last time. I want to hear you say why you don't want me anymore. But if you don't want to call me, that's okay. I still love you, anyway.
Love, your daughter for now,
Lacey

Cammie set the pages aside and took a swipe at her eyes with her sleeve. She glanced at Brett to see he had his head lowered, his hands tightly clasped together. She didn't know what to say, or if she should say anything at all. But she had to try to get him to talk, if only to ease some of his burden. "What are you going to do about this, Brett?"

He streaked both hands down his face and leaned his head back against the chair. "I don't know."

"She mentioned something about papers. Did you get them?"

"Yeah," he said without looking at her. "The day we left Vegas. They were waiting for me when I got on the bus."

That certainly explained his erratic behavior. "Why didn't you tell me?"

"Because it's not your problem. It's mine."

He still had a lot to learn about relationships. "When two people are together, that's part of the deal. You share your problems and I share mine."

"Yours aren't nearly as bad as mine, so that makes it one-sided."

Not as far as she was concerned. He might not want her comfort, but she was going to give it to him, anyway. She pushed off the bed, crossed the room and climbed into his lap, where she rested her head against his heart that had to be breaking. She prepared for a rejection, but he rubbed her arm gently, as if she was the one who needed soothing.

"She still loves you, Brett," she said. "She wants you to be her father again."

His hand stilled against her arm. "She has a dad, and he's a decent guy. He can give her what I never could. A life where people don't invade your privacy because they think they have the right. He can give her his time."

She lifted her head to look at him, stunned by the abject pain in his face. "But he's not you, and he never will be. Maybe if you call her—"

"I don't see the point," he said. "It'll only make it harder to let her go."

"Then you've already decided."

"She's better off without me."

"I don't agree, and you're definitely not better off without her. You're hurting like hell and it's not going to ever go away."

"Well, I guess that's just a burden I'll have to bear. She'll probably thank me for it later."

Or she could hate him for it—a thought Cammie chose to keep to herself. He was already suffering enough.

He nudged her off his lap and stood. "I need to take a shower. Tim's supposed to be here around six-thirty and that's only two hours away."

Just like that, he'd raised that same old emotional wall. A wall she'd hoped to tear down. Now she wasn't certain she ever would. "Fine. I'll use the guest bath to get ready." She'd begun to feel like a guest, anyway.

Brett responded with a simple "Okay," then disappeared into the adjoining bathroom and closed the door, in turn shutting her out.

Cammie felt she had to do something to encourage him to respond to his daughter, and that gave her an idea. It could very well backfire on her, but she didn't believe he really wanted to let his daughter go without a fight. But if that happened to be the case, she worried she could be next.

CAMMIE HAD BARELY tossed the Caesar salad before the doorbell sounded. When she heard Tim and Brett engaged in casual greetings, she swept through the kitchen and out onto the stone patio carrying Brett's earthenware dishes.

"Hey, there, Cammie."

She set the plates down and turned to see Tim standing at the patio door wearing khaki slacks and a red golf shirt, an unlit cigar stump dangling from the corner of his mouth. She sincerely hoped it stayed unlit, at least during dinner.

She crossed the patio and shook his hand. "Can I get you something, maybe a beer or mixed drink?" *Maybe a pamphlet on the dangers of smoking cigars?*

"Scotch and water sounds good."

"I'll get it," Brett said quickly, leaving Cammie alone with Tim for the time being.

She gestured at one of the white cushioned chairs

she'd taken great pains to clean the past week. "Have a seat."

After he complied, she took the chair opposite him and waited for Brett to return to bring the drink. She plucked at a thread dangling from the hem of her shorts, then smiled at Tim tentatively as she tried to think of something to say to break the awkward silence. "How are things going with Brett's career?" *Brilliant, Cammie.* Like she hadn't witnessed Brett's booming success firsthand.

Tim leaned back, an exaggerated grin on his face that dwarfed the nub of the cigar. "All I'll say right now is everything's going to work out fine for both of you. I've got it all laid out. I'll wait for Brett to explain."

Baffled by the comment, she barely managed a smile. She'd assumed Tim was there to go into detail about Brett's next tour and recording schedule. She suspected he could very well try to convince her to cut the track.

Brett walked onto the patio balancing three drinks in his hands. He set the first in front of Tim. "One Scotch and water, light on the water just the way you like it." Then he handed her a red can of soda. "And the hard stuff for you." After he sat down with his bottled beer, he turned his full attention on his manager. "What are you doing here, Tim?" he asked, revealing he was as clueless about the reasons for the visit as she was.

Tim took a long drink and shook his head, comically jiggling his jowls, reminding Cammie of a bulldog she once owned. "Good stuff." He set his drink down on the glass-topped table and hitched his pants. "I'm not going to beat around the bush. I'm here because I wanted to confirm that we're all set for Cammie to record with you."

Exactly as she'd predicted. "Wait a minute. I still haven't agreed to this."

"Just hear me out, Cammie," Tim said. "We want to recut 'When You Know It's Real' just like you did it on the tour. We're going to hold off releasing the single until we have you on the track."

Cammie hesitated. "I don't know, Tim. I'm not sure I'm ready for this."

"You're not even going to consider doing it?" Brett asked.

What they were offering was a life-altering experience. She wanted to say *Sure, why not?* But she didn't like to be pressured. "I didn't say I wouldn't do it. I still have some reservations, though."

Tim rested his elbows on the table and steepled his fingers together. "This is a good opportunity to hone your skills, Cammie. Many a singer would jump at this chance."

"But I've never considered myself a singer in that sense."

"The moment you sang onstage with Brett Taylor, you acquired that label. It's not a derogatory designation. Hell, it's a damn honor."

Brett held up his hands to silence Tim. "Can I say something here?"

Tim sat back and sighed roughly. "Go ahead."

He turned to Cammie. "All I'm asking is that you sing with me on one track. Hell, it's a lot easier going into a studio where you don't have to worry about performing in front of thousands of people. You just have to contend with a few producers…and me."

"That's what worries me."

"Just give it a shot. If it doesn't work out, no sweat."

Not knowing where they were going in their personal lives only added to her concerns. "Can I have a few days to think about it? After all, you're not going to the studio until next week."

"All right," Tim said. "But I need an answer by the end of this week. Now there's something else I need to cover here." His expression turned somber. "I don't have to tell you that I was none too pleased about this living arrangement."

Cammie looked toward Brett, who didn't return her gaze. "This is the first time I've heard that."

"Well, I'm not pleased," he continued. "But I've faced the fact that you're adults, you choose your path even if it affects your career."

"Glad you see it that way," Brett said.

"What about affecting his career?" Cammie asked, not willing to go on until Tim clarified his position.

"Brett has a reputation with the ladies, but that's

only part of it. Country-music folk are like one big family. Marriage is the acceptable norm, not shacking up. Now, no one exactly knows you and Brett are living together, but I'm trying to keep it out of the news."

Clearly he hadn't seen the tabloid. "And if it leaks out?" she asked.

Brett put his hand on her arm. "It's okay, Cammie, I—"

"No, let him finish. I want to know what could happen."

"Hard to say." Tim flicked his ashes away with fingers as stubby as his cigar. "Might be nothing, could be some repercussions. Decreased ticket sales, CD sales."

"But not likely," Brett added. "People are more liberal in their views these days. After all, I sing about drinking and infidelity and divorce, not to mention sex. It all goes on behind the scenes."

"I know that, Brett," Tim said, a touch of scorn in his smile, his tone condescending. "Now, if you two were married, that would make a difference. But it would also create a whole new set of problems. Brett's biggest fan base is made up of women who fantasize that they could be the one for him. If he gets hitched, that fantasy is over."

Cammie inched forward and aimed her glare on Tim. "And I know that many women find a man who loves someone enough to marry her and have kids with her very sexy. Just look at the country legends who've been married for years. Men with names like George and Allan and Brad." She snapped her fingers and pointed at the current burr in her backside. "I believe one of them is named Tim. I still see them playing to packed houses."

Tim frowned. "You two aren't planning to elope, are you?"

"Absolutely not," Brett said, the first words he'd spoken in a while, and he'd said them a little too forcefully for Cammie's liking.

She'd deal with Brett later. Right now she required further clarification. "So you're saying we're supposed to pretend that we don't know each other. Is that right?"

"I'm saying it would be best if we keep your little romance under wraps, at least until we release the new album. No handholding onstage, no overt displays of affection."

She let go a cynical laugh. "Obviously you haven't seen the local tabloid yet. It seems they caught us pretending to be a couple, complete with a photo."

Tim shot an acid look at Brett. "Why didn't you tell me about this?"

"I've handled it," Brett said. "I called my publicist a while ago. She's going to demand they print a retraction next week."

On the verge of losing complete control, Cammie sprung out of her chair. "I suppose I can live with that. This arrangement is only temporary, anyway, kind of like a summer vacation." She picked up Tim's drink and resisted the urge to dump the contents in his virtually nonexistent lap. "Let me freshen this up for you."

She should have known the past few weeks were too euphoric for something like this not to eventually come about. She remembered Mark's complaints of how he had an image to uphold, that he was expected to dress a certain way, behave a certain way. She assumed that losing some of yourself was all a part of the trade-off to become a success in this business. Obviously Brett's image would be tainted if he had a woman in his life, especially one that performed with him.

She hadn't heard the door slide open again, but from the corner of her eye she caught Brett standing in the entry to the kitchen, an empty beer bottle in his hand.

"You don't have to do this, Cammie."

"Do what?" she said, dumping a shot of Scotch into Tim's glass, then filling it with water and ice.

"Run away. Tim's just trying to tell you how it is. I don't like it, either."

"But you agree with it. Otherwise, you would have never asked for the retraction."

Brett moved forward and angled his hip against the counter. "No, I don't. But things will be different after the new CD's out in a few months. We can reassess the situation then."

"So now I'm a situation?"

"I don't know what you want from me, Cammie. I'm doing the best I can under the circumstances."

She handed him Tim's drink. "You're doing it again."

"Doing what?"

"Closing yourself off to the possibilities of finding something real with someone, only now you're using your career as an excuse."

He looked as if he might throw something, like Tim's drink. "I've worked long and hard to get where I am, Cammie, and sometimes this career dictates your personal life."

"Only if you let it, Brett. But maybe it's time I go before you start to resent me."

He set Tim's drink on the counter and framed her face with his palms. "I'm sorry," he said. "It scares the hell out of me to think what I'd do without the singing. But it scares me more to think about what I'd do without you right now."

Right now. That was the key. "I'm terrified that I'm going to be collateral damage if this whole thing blows up in our faces."

He kissed her softly. "Just be patient with me, baby. I'll figure it all out."

She hoped he did, before it was too late.

CHAPTER SIXTEEN

LATER THAT EVENING, after the dishes had been put away and Tim had taken Brett outside for a private conversation, Cammie went to bed alone. Brett joined her but he didn't stay long. He'd left her with a quick kiss and the excuse he wanted to go downstairs and work for a while.

Although she couldn't be certain it was just an excuse, Cammie suspected there was much more to it than his work. She'd let him go without any argument, believing it best to leave him alone with his thoughts. But at half past two and he still hadn't made an appearance, she began to worry and decided go downstairs to check on him.

Normally she'd be able to hear the strains of music coming from the basement-level room by the time she reached the kitchen. Instead, she noticed the usual household sounds: the steady hum of the air conditioner, a drip from the faucet, the creak of the floor underneath her feet, but nothing else that would indicate Brett was still working.

Cammie descended the stairs, stopping short before she came into his view. Brett sat on the beige carpeted floor, his back propped against one paneled wall, eyes closed, long legs stretched out before him, a nicked, well-worn guitar resting in his lap. At first she thought he'd fallen asleep, then he slowly shifted and ran a hand over his face.

"You look tired," she said as she padded into the room.

His eyes met hers and she knew immediately something was troubling him.

"Just a little writer's block," he said. "What are you doing up?"

Cammie sat down on the high-backed stool next to him, resisting the impulse to hold him even though he looked like he could use a hug. "I couldn't sleep a wink. My feet were cold and I didn't have any hairy legs to slide them under. Not to mention that king-size bed gets a little lonely."

She followed up with a smile, but Brett didn't return the gesture. Instead, he stared off into space as if he hadn't heard her.

"I had lunch today at the Sunset Grill," he said from out of the blue. "Met an old friend, someone who was in my original band." She was surprised by the sudden disclosure but let him continue without any response. "His name's Jerry Neill. Do you know him?"

"No. Should I?"

"He plays for Mark Jensen's band."

It seemed fate was on a cruel mission to cram her past down her throat. "What did he want?"

"Actually, I called him. Since Bob Walker's decided not to stay with the band, I need to find another replacement for Pat. Jerry's one of the best bass players in the business. Got a pretty decent voice, too. He left me early on for a better offer but we've always been pretty good friends. Anyway, I heard he's not happy with Jensen so I asked him to join us."

That would go over like a lead balloon with Mark. "Did he accept?"

Brett stretched and rolled his shoulders. "He's thinking about it. The biggest problem is going to be Jensen. Jerry's still got a couple of months left on his contract."

"I can understand his concern. Mark will probably make it pretty tough on him because of me. Unless he doesn't really know about us."

Brett set the guitar aside. "He knows, all right. Jerry told me Mark's been asking a lot of questions about you to anyone who might know anything. Some people thrive on making trouble, especially people you've pissed off at one time or another."

"Surely you haven't made anyone mad," she said dramatically, finally extracting a smile from Brett.

"I've done my share."

Cammie slid off the stool and joined Brett on the floor, hugging her knees to her chest. He curled his arm around her shoulders, yet still seemed pensive. "You know, Camille, you're sitting next to a conglomerate. Sometimes I don't know where the company ends and I begin. I'm just property to most people."

"Not to me." She reached up to smooth away a strand of hair from his forehead. So many questions invaded her mind. How did he feel about her, where were they going, if anywhere? But she didn't have the courage to ask him point-blank.

Cammie settled on a question that might lead to the more serious topic of the state of their relationship. Or he could exile her back upstairs. "Out of curiosity, what attracted you to me?"

"The great way you filled out your jeans."

"Gee, thanks."

"Hey, I'm just being honest." He hesitated for a moment, then shrugged. "Before you, I hadn't met anyone who didn't look at me like I was a god. They want the larger-than-life star. Or at least my body. You were different."

Cammie rested her head on his shoulder. "I want your body, so why am I so different?"

"At first you didn't want any part of me. I think that was my attraction to you from the beginning. You didn't come on to me or act like I was something special. You weren't impressed with all the glory. You see something else in me. God only knows what that something is."

When Cammie sought Brett's eyes, her soul shook with the realization of how much she loved him, how much she needed him...and how much she needed to know how he really felt about her. "Now that the chase is over, what happens next?"

A look of apprehension passed over Brett's face, his dark brows furrowed into a frown. She sensed the conversation had gotten a bit too heavy when he failed to answer.

Lighten up, Camille. Don't back him into a corner.

She kissed him softly and playfully rubbed his thigh through the soft-washed denim of his jeans. "Why don't we go upstairs and I'll show you what comes next."

He took his arm away. "You go on up. I've got to finish this tonight." He stood and shuffled through the pages of a notebook. "I'm running out of time."

So am I. She rose to her feet and held out her hand. "Surely you can spare a few minutes for the sake of a desperate woman—"

When Brett refused the gesture, she felt as if someone had run a stake clean through her heart. "You don't understand, Cammie. It's not a game. Tim's on my ass big-time—he says I'm not concentrating. You and I both know he's right. I've got to cut two more tracks for the new album and they've got to be fresh. If this project falls short, then someone will come along to claim my place, someone younger with bigger dreams."

Tim was obviously the reason for his bad mood. "You're only thirty-three. That's a little young to worry about being replaced."

"You get old quick in this business. Hundreds of

singers—eighteen-to-twenty-year-olds—are champing at the bit to move me out of the way. Not to mention those that are my age or older. People like Mark Jensen. It's a constant battle to stay on top."

It was a side of him that she'd seen before, right after Pat left. The brooding Brett Taylor. His mood had little to do with being driven to succeed and more to do with fear of failing in every aspect of his life—professional and private—just like Mark. Only Brett dealt with his fears by withdrawing into himself instead of relying on the bottle.

She could only offer reassurance. Whether it would make a measurable difference remained to be seen. "Mark isn't half as talented as you are. He doesn't write any of his material and most of his ticket and record sales come from a lot of butt-shaking in the direction of screaming women. It wouldn't be fair even to compare yourself to him."

His expression stayed serious, almost cold. "Nothing's fair about the music industry, Cammie. It takes a lot of blood, sweat and ass-kissing to get anywhere in this town. And a hell of a lot of luck. I've got some nice things now, but it took me years to get them. Boats, houses, buses, a production company. But in one minute—" he snapped his fingers "—gone. Just like that."

"You worry too much, Brett."

"Lately I haven't been worrying enough." He tossed the tablet aside and came to his feet. "Did you know Jensen's a nominee for Male Vocalist?"

Cammie wasn't surprised by the information, just surprised he'd waited until that moment to mention it. "I've never paid much attention to that."

"Well, he is, so it looks like more than a little butt shaking's going on. In fact, he had three top-five songs last year, two went number one."

After all the success Brett had enjoyed, he was still plagued by serious insecurities. "Come on. Mark isn't even close to being your competition and he certainly doesn't measure up to you in the butt department."

Brett picked up his guitar and turned his back on Cammie, but not before shooting a cynical glance in her direction. "At one time you must've liked his ass, at least enough to almost marry the son of a bitch."

His sudden reversal in attitude astounded her. Just a few minutes ago he'd listed all the reasons she was special. Now he seemed poised to go off like a time bomb. Did he really believe Mark Jensen was still a threat to their relationship? Or was it the fact she'd been involved with Mark long before they'd met, coupled with the possibility of Mark garnering the accolades that Brett so obviously coveted?

He strummed a few chords, walked around the room and, when she didn't leave, reluctantly faced her again. "I don't know how to make it more clear to you, Cammie. I can't come with you upstairs because what I might need or you might need takes a backseat to the work."

She cringed at his harsh words, but she wouldn't

let it go. "So you're saying even if you wanted to make love to me right now, you couldn't because work is more important?"

"Yeah. Welcome to the world of country music. It ain't all it's cracked up to be." He went back to his random strumming.

Cammie couldn't leave now. Not now. He might turn away, but she had to take the chance. "What about emotional needs?"

The sound the guitar made was tuneless, hollow. "You get what you can when you perform."

"What are you afraid of?"

Brett stopped, dropped his hand from the guitar strings and raised his eyes to her. "I told you. I'm afraid of being washed-up before I'm ready."

Cammie took two hesitant steps toward him. "That's not what I mean. I'm talking about feeling something beyond what you get from your music and performing. Don't you ever get tired of being alone? Do you ever wonder if there's anything else?"

She took another step until they were almost touching. "Or do you think a commitment to something or someone other than your music won't mean as much as singing to strangers, that you can't have it both ways? How do you know you can't have it all?"

"I can't risk finding out, Cammie."

Seeing the despair in his eyes, the futility in the hard line of his mouth, made her want to reach out to him in some way, make him realize how good they were together. "So where does this leave us?"

He lowered his eyes. "Honestly? I don't know right now. I like things the way they are. Don't make this any harder than it is, and don't ask more of me than I can give you right now."

Cammie reached for his guitar and, surprisingly, he relinquished it to her even though he looked put out by the gesture. She rested it against a table, then slipped her arms around his waist. Brett remained very still, fists clenched at his sides, as she touched her lips to the pulse point at his throat. "Are you mad at me for asking, or are you mad at yourself because you care more than you're willing to admit? Maybe you're just afraid if you let yourself care you won't have any excuse not to let go of the past. After all, it's much easier not to take a chance than to risk getting hurt again."

He said nothing, which made her believe she was on the right track. At least she could hope. Hope might be all she had left once she was finished.

She whisked a kiss over the cleft in his chin, then laid her hand on his cheek. "I should be afraid. I'm risking as much as you are, maybe more. But I'm not afraid of what I feel for you."

His expression looked pained, like he was battling his emotions, his desire, every step of the way. "Don't, Cammie."

She ignored his demand and plied his face with soft kisses. "Don't you think I know how good it feels to be in front of that crowd? Performing is a rush, but as great as it is, it can't compare to what I feel when you're inside me. When I lose all control while you have your mouth and hands all over me."

She could see his resistance waning, could sense immediate surrender when his respiration picked up speed. "So don't be mad at me, or afraid."

Cammie slid her hands underneath Brett's shirt and ran her fingertips over his chest, waiting and hoping he'd respond. And he did by tilting her head back and kissing her breathless. Then suddenly he stopped.

"I'm sorry," Brett said, one hand still wound in her hair. "I can't do this right now."

She'd never felt so humiliated—and defiant—in her life. "All signs point to the contrary."

"Let me rephrase that," he said. "I could make love to you right now, up against the wall without a thought. But it wouldn't be fair to you."

"The bruises on my backside would be worth it."

"I'm serious, Cammie." His expression confirmed that. "I don't want to hurt you more than I already have tonight."

That certainly wasn't up for debate. "You'll hurt me more if you keep pushing me away, and I don't mean in a physical sense."

"I'm trying to include you, but sometimes I have to deal with things on my own."

She felt he wasn't trying hard enough, but she was too tired to revisit the same issues tonight. "Fine. I'll leave you alone. I'm going back to bed."

As Cammie started away, Brett caught her hand,

wrapped his arms around her and hung on for the longest moment before he let her go. "Cammie, I know this life of mine isn't easy on you, and it might not get any easier for a long time. If you want to go, I won't stop you. If you can live with one day at a time, I want you to stay. But it's your decision to make."

Not exactly what she wanted to hear, and a decision she'd have to make sooner than later. "I'm pretty stubborn, so I guess you're not going to get rid of me that easily. Besides, there's no swimming pool at the old home place."

Brett smiled in his beautiful way. "Now you want me for my pool."

Cammie turned away before he could see her tears. "And don't forget your body."

Once again, she went to bed alone, Brett's words tumbling around in her restless mind. He might never love her the way she needed to be loved—unconditionally. Even if they somehow made it past this current bump in the long road, she could always play second fiddle to his career. And someday soon, she would have to choose between settling for what he could give her, or standing her ground, even if it meant leaving him.

Just before dawn, Brett came to bed and made love to her again, slowly, sweetly, taking his time, talking to her in soft whispers as if she was the most important thing in the world to him—even though she acknowledged she wasn't and never would be.

She clung to him long after it was over, fighting the tears as he held her.

"I want to believe people can have it all," he said, breaking the silence. "But sometimes I think that might be too much to ask."

"It's not if you really love someone." Now that pivotal moment of truth. "And I do love you, Brett."

Her worst fears came to pass when Brett failed to respond. The possibility they could have a future together faded with his obvious inability to love her back, his lack of faith in what they had, and himself.

But Cammie would still cherish these moments in his arms, knowing in her heart they would probably be some of the last.

BRETT DROPPED THE PHONE back onto its cradle after hanging up from the disturbing phone call.

"Who was it?" Cammie called from the down the hall.

"Just my publicist." A very nervous publicist. She'd spent the past twenty minutes explaining to Brett that word was out in Nashville he and Cammie were living together. Of course, the story appeared in two well-known tabloids, not any of the more reputable country-music magazines.

But that wasn't the only revelation. The topic had come up during an interview with Mark Jensen. The jerk had said Cammie had dumped him to pursue another singer with more status—namely Brett. He didn't dare mention it to Cammie. He could tell she was upset enough about not attending the award ceremony with him tonight. In fact, she'd been upset for the past week, and he thought he knew why, even if she wasn't saying why.

Little by little, his life was wearing her down, as well as his inability to commit completely to her.

She walked into the bedroom but stayed right inside the door, arms crossed beneath her breasts, a shoulder pressed against the frame. "What time do you have to leave?"

He took his belt from the bureau and slipped it through the loops. "The walk-through starts in about an hour and I should be home by four. That's just enough time for me to come back here, get dressed and get back to the auditorium by five-thirty for the damn red-carpet walk."

"Then why bother to come back here? You could just take your clothes with you."

After he tucked in his shirt, zipped his jeans and hooked his lucky buckle that didn't seem so lucky anymore, he faced her. "I thought maybe we could spend some time together."

"Save your spare fifteen minutes, Brett. I don't need them."

"Look, I know you're mad about not going with me tonight, but—"

She straightened and sighed. "I'm not mad. I'm resigned. This is just the way it is. The way it will always be."

"Not always," he said. "I'll have a break at the end of the summer."

"Two whole weeks before the CD's released," she reminded him, although she didn't have to. "Let's not forget all the personal appearances and press conferences and preparation for the upcoming tour. And I believe a few more award shows where you'll amass another dozen or so trophies."

He didn't feel up to explaining again the pitfalls of his career or arguing with her over the schedule. Not when he had one of the most important milestones hanging in the balance—his first nomination for Performer of the Year. "Yeah, it's going to get crazy. Nothing I haven't dealt with before."

"Of course. All on your own."

He didn't know what to say to her to make it better, so he chose to switch the subject, which wasn't much better. "Tim's still riding me about you singing with me. What do you want me tell him?"

"No."

"That's it? Just no?"

She straightened and strolled into the room, keeping her distance. "I've told him why I've never wanted this, and those reasons still hold true. Now more than ever."

Brett caught a glimpse at the wall clock and realized he had to leave or show up late. "We'll talk about this later. I've got to go."

She swept her hand toward the door. "By all means, go. Far be it for me to hold you back."

He hated leaving her this way—so damn angry at him. He put on his hat, picked up his keys and stood in front of her. "What are you going to do while I'm gone?"

"I've got a few finishing touches to put on the guest room."

The project she'd been working on in secret while he'd been taking care of business. "When am I going to get to see it?"

"I'll be done by tonight, so you can take a look then," she said. "I hope you like it."

"If you did it, I'm sure it's great."

"We'll see."

He wished she would yell at him, tell him he was a selfish bastard. He wished she'd say she still loved him, then maybe he'd have the courage to tell her he loved her, too. But that old saying about love sometimes not being enough was sure enough true.

He rested his palm against her cheek, expecting her to flinch or pull away. Luckily she didn't. "Cammie, when I come back from the rehearsal, we need to talk. I can't stand seeing you so unhappy."

She laid her hand on his and smiled, but it didn't make it all the way to her eyes, which were rimmed with tears. "You're right. We do need to talk if you can afford the time."

Brett sensed he couldn't afford not to make the time. "I'll try to get out of there early to give us plenty of time." Maybe even enough time for a little lovemaking. Time to show her how much she meant to him.

When Cammie said, "I'll be here," he wondered how long that would remain true. He took a risk when he took her into his arms, but she held on tightly like she didn't want to go. He didn't really want to go, either, but he didn't have much choice.

He released her and gave her a kiss, then hurried out of the house and into his truck. For a few moments he sat there immobile, keys dangling from the ignition. He should call Tim and tell him to find a way to get him out of participating tonight. He could ask him to accept any awards, if he actually earned any. Then he could stay home with Cammie and convince her that she was more important to him. But he had obligations that he needed to fulfill in order to stay afloat.

As he finally drove away, he had the strongest feeling that he might regret the decision. Little by little, he saw Cammie slipping away from him. And in some ways, she was already gone.

CHAPTER SEVENTEEN

SHE HAD A BORROWED CAR in the drive, her packed bags in the trunk and a burden as big as the Mississippi.

While she waited for Brett's return, Cammie sat in a chair on the deck counting the seconds and dreading each one, knowing that in a matter of minutes, she'd be leaving him for good. From her perch above the grounds, she saw the black truck traveling up the lengthy drive and swallowed around the threatening tears. For hours she'd considered what she might say. What she might do if he tried to convince her to stay. How she would feel if he didn't.

When Cammie heard Brett call her name, she swore her breaking heart skipped several beats. "Out here," she called back, her hands tightly clasped together on the tabletop.

He opened the glass door and walked toward her, a little slower than usual. "Is someone else here?" he asked.

"No."

"Then whose car is that in the drive?"

"It's a rental," she said. "For me."

He seemed confused for a moment before his expression turned somber. "Why do you need it?"

"Because I'm going home."

Brett raked the opposing chair back and sat. "For how long?"

He either didn't get it, or he was pretending not to. "Permanently."

He took off his hat and tossed it aside. "Why now? Are you trying to punish me by dropping this on me on the most important night—"

"Of your life," she finished for him. "And no, I'm not trying to get back at you for not inviting me to the party. I almost left you a note, but I thought you deserved to hear it from me face-to-face."

He stared off toward the lake, his dark hair ruffling in the warm breeze. "When did you decide?"

"I've been debating it since the night Tim came for dinner and you said if I could live one day at a time, you wanted me to stay. I can't do it anymore."

"You're giving up on me."

"On us, Brett. The other day I remembered something my grandmother once told me. She said never go into a relationship thinking you're going to change someone."

He finally turned his gaze to her. "I imagine you have a long list of things you'd like to change about me."

"Only your tendency to close yourself off to all the possibilities, but I do understand why you do it."

"Maybe you should enlighten me."

She ignored his sarcasm and continued. "You're so afraid people are going to leave that you drive them away, making it a self-fulfilling prophecy. You're also afraid of opening old wounds, so you keep everyone at emotional arm's length."

"I don't like to bleed."

"Sometimes you have to in order to heal."

He surprisingly smiled, a sincere one. "Did you minor in psychology?"

She smiled back even though she found it odd they could share a little humor in such a serious situation. Or maybe that spoke to the better part of their relationship. "I did take a few courses, but you don't have to be a psychologist to recognize someone who's in a lot of pain."

"I'm not when I'm with you," he said. "I haven't been able to say that in years."

Hearing him say that now gave her hope. False hope. "Maybe you temporarily suspend the pain when we're together, but it's always going to be there until you come to terms with your past."

"Our past makes us who we are, good and bad. That's something that can't be changed, Cammie."

"No, but if you don't learn from your mistakes and move forward, then you're not living. You're at an impasse, and no matter how much I love you or how patient I am, until you're willing to deal with it, I can't save you."

"I'm not asking you to save me, dammit. I'm just asking you for more time."

"And during that time, I'd be expected to remain in the shadows and pretend we're not together while you allow your career to dictate your personal choices. I can deal with your sullen moods and even your temper, but I won't play second fiddle while I'm hoping you'll eventually come around."

He fished his cell phone from his pocket. "I'm going to call Tim right now and tell him I'm bowing out tonight."

She laid a palm on his arm. "You can't do that. You've earned this night and you should be there."

"But you've already made it clear that my career is coming between us."

"I would never, ever ask you to choose between me and your career. Music's as much a part of you as that lucky buckle."

"Jana never understood that," he said. "She told me not long ago I cheated on her with my job. And she was right. But I had to keep going to provide for her and Lacey. I didn't have a choice."

"You have to find a balance, Brett," she said. "A lot of couples figure out how to do it. They tour together and even raise their kids on board the buses. It's not impossible."

He sat back and sighed. "Jana hated the road. After the baby was born, she refused to go with me, even on shorter trips."

She was taken aback that he decided to go into detail about his relationship with his ex-wife. "You and I both know it's not for everyone. They can't appreciate seeing sunrises and sunsets on the road or the excitement of seeing new places and meeting new people. Some folks are just happier staying home while the world passes them by."

"But you're not, which is why I don't understand why you're going back to Memphis to settle in a routine that doesn't make you happy."

Touché. "I told you why, Brett. I owe my grandparents so much."

"Then I guess that means we're both chained to our obligations and our pasts, doesn't it?"

He had her on that one. "Maybe it does."

He set the phone down and took her hand in his. "There's nothing I can say to change your mind about staying? Or at least get you to wait until I get home so we can talk more about it?"

If she did that, she could wind up back in bed with him, and she'd be right back where she started. "The longer I stay, the closer I'll get to you, and the harder it will be to leave. It's hard enough now as it is."

"Baby, it's about to kill me."

Cammie tried unsuccessfully not to cry, but when the first tear fell, Brett brushed it away with his thumb. "I want to hold you right now and tell you it's all going to be okay and promise I'll never make you cry again. I can't promise that. Life's full of tears, especially my life. But if you'll give me the chance, I'll try harder to make you happy."

She swiped at her face. "How would you do that, Brett?"

"I'll support you in whatever you want to do about singing. I won't ask you to do anything you're not comfortable doing. And I'll make good love to you whenever you want—all you have to do is ask. No more excuses."

"That all sounds great, but will this be as a permanent part of your life or as a live-in convenience?"

He let go of her hand and rubbed his jaw. "I don't know what's permanent these days. I see people who look like nothing could tear them apart and then they get married and it all goes to hell." He leveled his gaze on hers. "Why can't we just be together?"

How quickly he'd forgotten the conversation with Tim. "Best I recall, you agreed that as long as we're living together without the benefit of a license, it could damage your career. And since you've made it quite clear you have no intention of remarrying, that puts a kink in my plans. I'm too old to go steady the rest of my life."

His expression went hard, unforgiving. "I've been through one divorce. I don't want another one."

"You want a no-risk guarantee, Brett. That's not reality. If I thought for a second you might eventually change your mind somewhere down the road, I'd stick it out. But until you deal with your issues, including your relationship with your daughter, you're never going to be open to all the possibilities."

He shoved his chair away and walked to the edge of the deck, hands knitted together behind his neck. He remained silent for a while before he faced her again. "I'm spilling my guts to you, telling you the only way I know how that I need you in my life. But if that's not good enough, then go back to the family business. It's safe. Not very exciting, but safe. That's not me, Cammie. And it's not you, either."

"Sometimes safety is preferable to constant insecurity." She rose from the chair and pushed it under the table. "I have to go, Brett."

He took a few steps toward her and paused. "First, I need you to do something for me."

"What?"

"I want you to sing with me one more time."

That meant saying goodbye a second time. "Brett, I don't think—"

"It's two weeks from tomorrow," he said, ignoring her impending protests. "A few years back, I started a foundation to provide funds for organizations that support at-risk kids with music lessons and therapeutic horse programs. This is the annual benefit concert."

Cammie began to comprehend exactly how much she still had to learn about him, and that she wouldn't have the chance. "It sounds like a great cause, Brett. I'm glad you're willing to give your money and your time."

"I've been lucky. I just want to give back when I've been handed a lot in my lifetime. It's important to me, and that's why I need you there."

She scraped her brain to come up with a good excuse to bow out. "As much as I'd like to contribute,

Sundays are busy. I'm positive my grandfather will have me scheduled to drive. But I'm sure you'll do just fine raking in donations without me."

"I need someone to sing backup," he said. "Jerry Neill's signing on but he can't join us until Jensen releases him, and that might be a while. Technically you're still under the original contract, so I could force you to do it. I'd rather you do it because you think it's the right thing."

She paused for a moment to consider the risk in joining him onstage again. But she couldn't in good conscience refuse a good cause. A cause that obviously meant a lot to him. "Okay. I'll do it."

"I'll have the information faxed over to you and arrange for transportation to and from Memphis."

She would have expected him to sound less official and more pleased. "I'll drive myself."

"How do I know you'll show up?"

"You'll just have to trust me."

"Guess I can do that." He smiled, a sad one. "Like I've said before, I trusted you with my life every time you drove my bus."

She only wished she could trust him to make the necessary changes so he could finally have some peace. "Well, I better get on the road and you better get dressed."

"Yeah, that's probably a good idea."

Yet neither of them made a move. They just stood there for a long moment and stared at each other. Cammie wanted so badly to hold him one last time, but she feared she might not let go. But when Brett pulled her into his arms, she put aside her worries and captured these moments to add to her memory bank. Memories of the first time he'd held her, that first awkward kiss, that night they'd made love and every time since. She would have to rely on those recollections to get her through the next few weeks without him. And in order to start the process, she needed to leave immediately.

But when Cammie attempted to end the embrace, Brett held on tighter, brought his lips to her ear and whispered, "I do love you, baby. I just wish I could love you better."

The waterworks started then, hot tears that fell from her eyes, dampening Brett's shirt where she rested her cheek against his chest. And he continued to hang on to her until she found the strength to compose herself, and prayed for the strength to walk away.

"I have to go," she said as she worked out of his grasp and backed toward the door.

He didn't put up a fight or beg her to stay. He did look resigned. "Drive safe, Cammie. I'll see you in a couple of weeks."

He suddenly seemed so civil, and so detached. Maybe that was best for both of them. But before she left, Cammie had a request for him. "Please call your daughter, Brett, and don't wait too long."

She saw a flicker of pain in his blue eyes. "I'll think about it."

As she turned to go, she remembered something else she needed to say. She faced him again and smiled. "And good luck tonight. I hope you win."

"AND THE WINNER IS...BRETT TAYLOR."

For a moment—it seemed like hours—Brett didn't move. He'd been practically paralyzed from the reality of earning the industry's top honor. Then Tim appeared from nowhere and shook his hand. With Rusty, Bull and Jeremy trailing behind him, he realized he was moving in the direction of the stage, although he didn't remember standing. People slapped him on the back, shook his hand, hugged him. He ascended the steps and somehow made it to the podium, running on autopilot. He took the award from the woman onstage and greeted the presenters, who backed away so he could speak.

Funny, he hadn't even prepared a speech. But he knew what he needed to say before all these people now waiting for his words of gratitude.

He cleared his throat before he spoke. "I want to thank everyone involved in my career..." He listed his manager, producers, the fans, the band now standing behind him and, lastly, Pat. After he was done, he paused to look over the masses. With the exception of a random cough or the occasional whistle coming from fans seated in the balcony, the crowd remained quiet. He looked at the faces with detachment, not really seeing anyone. Cammie's face was the only one he cared to see. But she was long gone, from town and his life.

Then it struck him. None of this mattered much anymore. Not the accolades. Not the fame or the fortune. Only the woman he loved like crazy and the daughter he'd left behind.

Brett lowered his eyes and ran his hand over the award's solid metallic surface before lifting his face to the camera. "Life changes on a dime, and I've learned you've just got to change with it before you wake up and realize you've missed out on what real living is all about." He held the statue up and hoped she was watching. "Cammie, this one's for you."

After he left the stage, Brett didn't wait for the usual backslapping from the guys. He even bypassed the press area for the required postaward interviews. He just wanted to get out of there now and deal with the consequences later.

Brett pushed through the side doors, bent on making a quick getaway so he could get home to take care of some personal business.

"Too bad I beat you out for the male vocalist award, Taylor. Better luck next time."

He paused when he heard Mark Jensen's snide comment, but he didn't bother to turn around. He did hold the award high. "Hey, I have this one and it's bigger and better. So better luck next time, you bastard."

"Yeah, you've been stealing awards from me for

years, just like you stole my bass player and my woman."

He should just keep walking, but the anger simmering below the surface had reached the boiling point. He spun around, walked right up to Jensen and pointed a finger in his face. "Let's get one thing straight. Jerry's joining me because you're an egotistical prick, I earned this award by singing instead of shaking my ass and Cammie was never your woman to begin with."

Mark shoved Brett's hand away and glared at him. "One day, Taylor, you and me are gonna get some things straight, and it ain't gonna be pretty."

Even though he wanted to knock the hell out of Jensen, Brett sent him a look of disgust and went on his way. Causing a scene wasn't worth it, not with the press hanging around. They'd go on a media feeding frenzy if he did what he'd wanted to do to the jerk since the first time he saw him touching Cammie.

"Hey, Taylor, now that you broke Cammie in, think I'll get a little piece of that action. And this time you won't be able to stop me."

The threat plunged into Brett's gut like a switchblade. The fury—the disappointment and futility—tore through him all at once. He had enough wherewithal to switch the award into his left hand before he whirled around and charged the bastard. And with one furious, frustrated blow, expended all his hostility on an unprepared Mark Jensen.

Brett flexed his bruised fist and glared down on Mark, who'd landed on his ass at the bottom of the steps. "I'll see you in hell before I see you lay one hand on her again. Don't forget, I was the man she chose to be her first. Me, not you. And I'm going to spend the rest of my life making sure I'm her last."

As Brett turned to go, he noticed a doe-eyed female reporter coming after him. He picked up the pace but she caught up with him, anyway, microphone in hand, cameraman bringing up the rear.

"Brett, care to comment on what that was all about?"

No, he didn't, but he would. "Just taking care of a problem that should've been handled a long time ago." He took off at a sprint in search of his truck and a fast escape.

After Brett drove away, he hadn't made it out of the parking lot before his cell started ringing. He pulled the phone out of his jacket pocket and barely answered before he heard, "Where in the hell are you, Brett?"

"I'm heading home, Tim."

"You're expected to attend the after-parties and a press conference."

"Just tell them I'm sick." Sick of the whole scene. "And while you're at it, call my attorney and put him on notice. I might be needing his services." And the image of Jensen holding his broken nose was worth every penny.

"Mind explaining why that's necessary?"

"You'll figure it out soon enough."

He hung up, turned off the cell and slipped it in his jeans pocket. All the way home, he thought about Cammie. He thought about the changes he needed to make in order to have her in his life, and he was ready to make them. If luck was on his side, he'd find a way to win her back, but it was going to take more than a lucky buckle—like careful planning and good timing.

First, he had a phone call he had to make to another woman who'd probably give him hell for calling so late, even on a Saturday night.

After shutting down the truck, Brett entered the house, pulled off his jacket and tossed it onto the sofa on his way to the kitchen for some liquid courage. He set his keys next to the digital recorder attached to the phone set out on the granite bar. The red indicator showed he had twelve voice mails—two from Tim, one from his mother, the rest from various well-wishers. He'd eventually return the calls, but first things first.

He went to the refrigerator for a beer and spotted a handwritten note attached to the door with a magnet.

Don't forget to look at the guest room. You can change it if you have to, but I hope you don't have to. Love, Cammie.

He thought about waiting until he made the call, but that was where he headed next, leaving the beer and the note behind. He sprinted up the stairs and traveled past his bedroom to the end of the hall. He wasn't sure why she thought this was so important, or exactly what to expect. But when he opened the door, he finally understood.

Two weird overstuffed chairs—one orange, one purple—sat in the corner of the room next to the double window. Opposite the door, a queen bed covered in a purple spread hugged the wall. And above the white tufted headboard, a plaque bearing the name of the little girl he'd made.

Lacey.

Cammie had managed to leave a hint as big as the empty space in his heart. And if ever he'd had any reservations about making the phone call, they'd all disappeared.

Brett crossed the room, took a seat on the edge of the bed and noticed the picture on the nightstand—a framed photo of then three-year-old Lacey propped on his shoulders, wearing a pink T-shirt that read Daddy's Girl and the sweetest smile. He'd kept the memento of a better time tucked beneath his underwear in the dresser's top drawer. He should be mad that Cammie had gone through his stuff, but he couldn't be mad at her. Not after she'd gone to the trouble of doing this for his daughter. For him.

More determined than ever, he pulled out his cell and dialed the number that could put an end to at least some of his misery, or it could very well add to it.

Regardless, he planned to issue a few demands to Jana, tell her he still had rights and he'd see his daughter come hell or high water, even if he had to camp out on the doorstep. He'd tell her that she had no right to keep him—

"Hello?"

The voice on the other end didn't belong to his ex-wife, and although he hadn't heard it in a long time, he still recognized it. "Lacey?"

"Yeah. Who's this?"

Apparently she didn't remember his voice, and that ate at his soul like acid. "It's Brett. Your dad."

"Is this a joke?"

He couldn't help but smile. "Nope. It's me."

"I just watched you win that award on TV."

Fortunately, he hadn't woken her up, but he doubted she still went to bed at nine, especially on the weekend. She was already halfway grown, and that made his heart hurt more. "Where's your mom?"

"Out with Randy. I can give you her cell number."

The fact she called her stepdad by his first name gave him a strong sense of satisfaction. Maybe he hadn't lost her, after all. "That's okay. I wanted to talk to you, anyway."

"Okay." She sounded unsure, maybe even a little nervous.

He'd start with the most obvious reason for the call. "I got your letter. I'm sorry it's taken me so long to get in touch with you." Sorry it had taken him so long to try and make things right between them.

"That's okay," she said. "I know you're busy."

What now? "I was surprised you remember that song I used to sing to you."

"It's downloaded on my MP3 player. I put on my headphones at night before bed and listen to it. It helps me remember. I mean, I see you all the time on the internet and in the record stores, but I like to remember you before you got so famous."

And that fame had cost them both. "I just want you to know that none of this is your fault, Lacey. It's my fault for not fighting harder to be in your life. I just gave up because I thought it was best for you. But I never stopped thinking about you. I never stopped missing you."

"I missed you, too. I missed all those times when you showed me how to ride Daisy. I really missed going to get ice cream when you came to see me after you and Mom divorced."

A divorce that had damn near ruined both their lives. But then he wouldn't have met Cammie. "I'd sure like to see you again real soon."

"I'd like that, too. A lot."

An idea suddenly occurred to Brett. A great idea, if she agreed to it. "Would you like to come here to Nashville for a few days? I have a concert coming up and I'd like for you to be there."

"Really?"

"Really."

"Can I bring a friend?"

"I was thinking maybe you could come with your

grandmother. It might be the only way I can get her on a plane."

"Nana's cool. She lets me eat in front of the TV. Will I get to meet Cammie?"

"How do you know about her?" he asked, although he suspected he knew the answer.

"I heard Nana talking to Mom about her. She reads all the articles about you online and in the magazines. She says it's the only way she can keep up with what you're doing since you don't call her enough."

Another change he needed to make. "I'll introduce you to Cammie at the concert." If she didn't bail on him.

"Are you gonna marry her?"

"If she says yes when I ask her." He couldn't believe how easily the words had come out of his mouth. How quickly he'd made the decision.

"All the girls think you're hot, so she'll say yes."

He appreciated Lacey's vote of confidence, even though Cammie could tell him to ride out on the horse he rode in on. "Then you're okay with it?"

"Do you love her?"

No sense in denying it now. "Yeah, I do."

"Then it's okay."

He experienced a strong since of relief. "Then it's settled. If your mom's fine with you making the trip, I'll make all the arrangements." And that was a major hurdle they still had to clear.

"I'll talk her into it," she said. "I'll promise to

clean my room and do the laundry and not talk back. Much."

He couldn't help but laugh. "Between the two of us, we might be able to convince her to let you come."

A span of silence passed before Lacey spoke again. "Are you going to sign the papers?"

Not on her life. "No, sweetheart, I'm not. You're stuck with me."

"I love you, Daddy."

His mom had once told him a child would forgive almost anything if you gave them your love. Now he knew she was right. "I love you, too, kiddo. And I'll see you real soon."

After Brett hung up, he felt a solid sense of satisfaction mixed with more than a few regrets. He regretted all the time he'd wasted to get to this point. He'd never believed he deserved to be a part of his daughter's life, but he did deserve it, and Lacey did, too. She deserved a dad who'd be there for her through thick and thin, and he'd be that dad from now on. Cammie had taught him that.

He realized his drive to succeed had been influenced by his own dad's failures as a musician and a father. But he couldn't condemn him for that. Not after he'd gone down the same path with Lacey. He also regretted he had been so full of anger and pride that he hadn't told his dad goodbye when he'd had the opportunity. That he hadn't told him he loved him, because he had loved him in spite of his flaws.

He guessed that was what love was all about—forgiving and forgetting in the face of failure. Exactly what Cammie had been trying to tell him. Exactly why she loved him, although sometimes he didn't see what he'd done to warrant that love. And he didn't know what he'd do if he lost it—and her—for good.

The regrets and loss and sorrow from years past, the victories and defeats from today, bore down on him like a runaway train. And in the silence of the room reserved for his child, a gift from the one woman strong enough to slay his biggest demon—fear of commitment—he did something he hadn't done in over a decade.

He cried.

CHAPTER EIGHTEEN

SHE WOULD BE LUCKY if she made it on time.

Cammie took two wrong turns before she finally located the concert site set up on rural land west of Nashville. She showed her credentials at the gate, gained immediate admittance and navigated the company truck down a gravel drive past tons of cars and trucks parked on the grass. She hadn't expected some fancy venue befitting of an upscale fundraiser, but out in the middle of nowhere? Of course, this was Brett Taylor's concert, and definitely his cup of tea—performing in a glorified pasture.

But the closer she came to the location, the more she realized he'd gone to a lot of expense—from the gigantic video screen hovering above the semicircle of temporary bleachers filled with fans, to the towering lights illuminating numerous refreshment tents set about the area. After she pulled the truck next to an eighteen-wheeler, she grabbed her tote bag, slid out of the cab and drew in a deep breath. Time to literally face the music—and Brett. First, she needed to see if her surprise had arrived.

Cammie visually scanned the area behind the

makeshift stage, but the place was too dark to see much more than a few shadowy figures. She did see the bus parked in the distance and assumed Brett was hiding away in there.

"Hey, good lookin'. Can I buy you a beer?"

She didn't have to look behind her to know who'd delivered that tired come-on line. Her surprise had definitely arrived. She turned around, dropped her bag at her feet and practically hurled herself into Pat's arms, nearly knocking him backward. "You made it!"

After giving her one heck of a bear hug, he set her back and grinned. "I told you I'd be here, didn't I?"

Yes, he had, during their phone conversation a week ago when she'd asked him to temporarily come out of retirement. "Did you bring Sadie with you?"

"Nah. Her daughter came in with the boys today, so she stayed home. And get this. They're calling me Grandpa. Never thought I'd hear that."

Cammie was tickled over the absolute pride in his voice. "That's wonderful, Pat. And it looks like you've gained a little weight, which is a good thing. Sadie must be a good cook."

He patted his belly. "Yeah, she cooks good, but she's a better kisser. It's a damn good feeling to get a second chance with her. And if Brett was smart, he'd follow my lead."

Since she'd already filled Pat in on some of the details, she'd known it would be only a matter of time before that subject came up. "Have you seen him yet?"

"Nope. I just got here a few minutes ago. I figured I wouldn't make an appearance until the second set. Walker knows what's going down and he's on board with the plan."

Cammie signaled Pat to join her behind the metal support in case Brett suddenly appeared without warning. "I've been instructed to perform in the second set, too. And I can't wait to see Brett's face when he sees you onstage." She couldn't wait to see his face, period. That gorgeous face that had haunted both her waking and sleeping dreams.

When she heard the recorded version of their special song begin to play, followed by a cheer from the crowd, her heart fluttered, then fell under the weight of regret. She'd only been there for a matter of minutes and already the memories had begun to attack her.

"Well, I'll be damned. Look at that."

"What?"

Pat pointed toward the stage. "On the video screen."

Cammie came from behind the support to see the video she'd made with Brett splashed across the screen. She hadn't seen the final edit, and now all she could do was watch in wonder. The film flashed from Brett standing in front of a studio microphone, eyes closed as he sang, to the scenes depicting a couple's developing relationship among the notable

Seattle sites. A relationship that in some ways paralleled theirs. A first meet at a café, holding hands at the waterfront, holding each other on the boat, and then the final scene on the rocky beach.

She was thrilled with the sheer beauty of the pine trees providing the backdrop, and surprised by the way the camera panned in on them to capture each shared touch that conveyed the chemistry she'd experienced firsthand. She was completely mesmerized watching Brett kiss her, just as she had been when he'd actually done it. To any casual observer, it would appear they'd played their roles to a tee. But they hadn't been acting at all.

She swallowed around the knot in her throat and tried hard to hold back the tears. She'd sworn she wouldn't cry over him again, and she planned to keep that promise to herself.

"I've never seen two people so meant to be together, Cammie."

No tears…no tears…no tears… She turned to Pat and faked a smile. "I wish that were true. But I guess I shouldn't be so surprised it wasn't meant to be. We've only known each other four months."

Pat draped an arm over her shoulder. "Let me tell you a little story, Cammie. My grandma and grandpa met at a church social. Two weeks later, they ran off and got married. That marriage lasted through five kids and sixty-five years until the good Lord called my grandma home. My grandpa passed three days later. So don't tell me four months ain't enough time to fall in love with your soul mate."

If only Brett saw her in that light. "Sometimes love alone can't carry a relationship."

Pat gave her a squeeze before he let her go. "Love's been known to fell countries and kings, so I figure the current king of country music will eventually come around. And speaking of the king, there he goes."

Cammie looked to her left to see Brett approaching the stairs leading to the stage, a contingent of guards surrounding him and a group of people trailing behind him. They were all set in shadows, but she could still make out Bull, Rusty and Jeremy by their gaits alone. Luckily she and Pat were far enough away not to be noticed.

"Ladies and gentlemen, give it up for the man responsible for this worthy event, the reigning Performer of the Year and one of the country's most revered country singers, Brett Taylor!"

Cammie realized she was holding her breath when Brett appeared onstage to a standing ovation and deafening applause. Dressed in a black long-sleeve shirt, jeans and black hat, she couldn't recall when she'd seen him look so darn good, even if he'd apparently lost his razor that morning. A light shading of whiskers surrounded his mouth and set off the smile he sent to the overexcited crowd. A genuine smile that said he was truly happy to be there.

Maybe he would be equally happy to see her. Maybe pigs could fly.

He stepped up to the microphone and held up both hands in order to silence the masses. "First of all, thanks to everyone for showing up tonight to support the cause—from the bands that volunteered to open the show earlier today, to the radio stations who gave tickets away and the fans who gave up some hard-earned money to be here…."

As Brett explained the foundation's goals, Cammie leaned closer to Pat. "I don't think I've ever seen him this pumped up."

"I agree. Maybe he's excited because he knows you're going to be singing with him again."

"I doubt that. Maybe he has a new girlfriend."

"And I doubt that. Not when he dedicated his win at the awards show."

She had to admit she was stunned when she'd heard about it. She'd wished she'd actually seen it. Unfortunately, by the time she'd arrived home that evening, she'd endured a two-hour interrogation about her relationship with Brett, led by her grandfather. However, dedicating an award and dedicating your life to someone were two different things.

"…so the foundation will be called the Lacey Project from this point forward. And now I'd like to introduce the person responsible for that change, my daughter, Lacey Taylor."

Cammie couldn't stifle a gasp, nor could she believe the uncanny resemblance between father and daughter as Lacey walked onstage, her waist-length near-black hair bouncing in time with her gait. She wore jeans and a purple T-shirt bearing her father's name and a wide smile that revealed a shiny set of braces. When the camera panned in on Lacey's pretty face, highlighting her vibrant blue eyes, Cammie realized Brett couldn't deny she was his even if he tried. She was so glad he'd stopped trying.

"Did you know about this?" Pat asked.

"No, but I knew about her," she answered. "And I'm happy he finally found a way to be with her again." Thrilled that he'd obviously taken her parting advice.

Brett pulled up a stool for Lacey and after she was seated, he started to strum his guitar. "Now I'm going to sing a song that used to put my little girl to sleep at night. It's not exactly your typical bedtime song, but for some reason it worked."

Then he went into his rendition of the classic country tune that garnered more than a few whoops and hollers from the crowd.

"What the hell?" Pat shouted above the din. "Who sings a lullaby that involves cheatin' and drinking?"

Cammie could only laugh, and so did the fans when the song took a rowdy turn. Lacey didn't seem to be the least bit self-conscious, yet she did seem totally enthralled with her father. And when the number had ended, she slid off the stool and slipped her arms around his waist. He leaned down, kissed the top of her head and sent her on her way. But before the girl left the stage, she stopped and waved, earning loud approval from the crowd. Definitely a performer in the making—Cammie's first thought. And she wouldn't be a bit surprised if she could sing—her second.

Brett and the band moved smoothly into a round of boisterous country hits without taking a break. He did take the time to lean over and shake a few hands, creating havoc for the guards attempting to hold the masses at bay. Cammie looked on as women— young and old—fanned their faces and some even screamed his name. He was a wanted man, and no one wanted him more than she did at that moment.

When the set appeared to be winding down, Cammie realized in a matter of minutes it would be her turn to take the stage with him. But she found out she was mistaken when he traded his electric guitar for the acoustic and took a seat on the stool. "I'm going to do a song that I cowrote with a very special lady. Hopefully I'll be recording it soon."

Cammie stood in stunned silence as Brett began to sing the song she'd all but given up on. He'd kept the melody as is, and the lyrics stayed the same until he reached the final refrain. A refrain that spoke of changes and second chances and the road back to love.

By the time he'd finished to a resounding show of approval from the audience, Cammie's emotions were so on edge she wasn't certain she could perform. She just needed to pull herself together and get with the program.

"We'll be back in a few minutes, folks," Brett said into the microphone. "In the meantime, enjoy the food and drink and don't forget to bid on the silent auction items."

After Brett exited the stage, he walked down the stairs with Lacey along with a fifty-something woman. "Who is that with Brett?" she asked Pat as the group headed toward the bus.

"That would be his mom, Linda. Guess she came with Lacey."

Cammie wondered if the ex-wife was squirreled away in the bus, waiting for their return. For some reason that bothered her, even when it shouldn't. But she didn't have time to ponder it when Rusty spotted her and came rushing over.

"Now, here's a pretty lady," he said as he gave her a voracious hug. By that time Jeremy and Bull had made it to her side.

"Hey, you guys, did you miss me?" she asked.

"We all missed you," Bull said, giving her a kiss on the cheek.

Pat cleared his throat to garner their attention. "Did any of you no-accounts miss me?"

Cammie thoroughly enjoyed the shock in their faces followed by grins and macho hugs.

"We didn't know you were going to be here," Bull said. "Does Brett know?"

"No, he doesn't," Cammie blurted a little too

loudly. "It's a surprise. He's taking Bob's place during the second set."

Pat chuckled. "We'll see how long it takes him to figure it out."

"Are you ready, Cammie?" Bull asked with concern.

That remained to be seen. "Sure. I'll be fine after the first few missed notes. It's been a while since I've done this."

"You'll be great as usual," Rusty said before he turned to Pat. "As much as we missed you, she had a way of calming Brett down."

"He's gone back to being his usual pain-in-the-ass self," Bull said. "The way he's been acting, all of us are about to jump ship."

Cammie tugged on Bull's beard. "He depends on you guys. Just hang in there. He'll be fine."

"But will you?" Rusty asked.

"Oh, yeah. I'm doing great." A necessary lie.

"Ten minutes, folks," someone called from the bottom of the stairs.

"You all go ahead," Cammie said as she picked up the discarded bag. "I need a few minutes to change." And to deep breathe.

Rusty pointed to his left. "The yellow tent's for the crew. It's set up with a dressing room and private bathrooms."

That sounded preferable to changing in a Porta Potty, although she really wasn't a member of the crew any longer. "Thanks. Guess I'll see you all onstage."

After the trio delivered well-wishes and walked away, Pat remained by her side. "Just so you know, I've got pretty good instincts, and my gut says Brett might not be done with the surprises tonight. Be prepared because my guess is they'll have something to do with you."

Cammie would be extremely surprised if that turned out to be true. "I haven't even heard from him since the day I left."

Pat winked. "You know what they say about absence and the heart growing fonder. I figured that one out firsthand."

Well, if that wasn't true for Brett, then tonight she'd say goodbye to her friends, to this way of life and the man she'd never forget.

And it would be the most painful experience of her life.

BRETT HADN'T SEEN HER YET, but thanks to Rusty's recent announcement, he knew she was there. That gave him some measure of relief, and a whole lot of cause to be as nervous as a cat in a pen full of pit bulls.

After leaving Lacey and his mom back in the bus to cool off, he'd claimed a folding chair not far from the stage, drank half a beer and waited for the second part of a performance he wasn't at all sure he could get through.

"How's it going, Brett?" one of the road crew asked in passing.

"Hanging in there." Barely.

When the prerecorded version of one of his infamous love songs started playing over the speakers, he immediately thought about Cammie. Always Cammie. Since that day she'd said goodbye, she'd never been more than a thought away. He'd picked up the phone to call her probably a thousand times, only to hang up knowing he wasn't quite ready yet. On the nights when he hadn't been able to sleep—and there had been plenty—he'd rehearsed what he would say when he saw her. He'd planned this whole evening down to the last detail so it would come off without a hitch. That didn't mean it might not go to hell in a handbasket if Cammie didn't cooperate. Regardless, he couldn't turn back now. He didn't want to.

While he stared at a bolt in the metal scaffolding that comprised the assembled stage, Bull invaded his field of vision. Then Rusty and Jeremy gathered around him and stared like he'd grown a third eye. He supposed he should get up and get on with it, but concerns kept him cemented to his seat.

"You ready?" Bull asked.

"Yeah. Where is she?"

"She'll be here in a minute," Rusty said. "She's changing clothes."

"Guess this is it." Brett downed the rest of the beer, then tossed the bottle into a nearby bin. He couldn't remember the last time he had a drink before he went on. Alcohol tended to take away his energy. But tonight he was strung as tight as the strings on his guitar, so a case of whiskey probably wouldn't affect him.

He did feel a little better. Yeah, he was going to be fine, after all. The routine was rote. He'd have no trouble singing the songs. Except for one. He just hoped he could pull that one off. Sure he could. It was all going to be okay.

Then he heard her voice and he was anything but okay. When she said something to one of the roadies and laughed, his chest felt like he'd taken a blow to his ribs and one of them had impaled his lungs. And that was after *hearing* her. How the hell was he going to feel when he saw her?

He decided to take his first look at her onstage. Might be nice if he could actually move.

"Are you coming or are we going to have to carry you?" Bull asked when he didn't immediately stand.

"I'll be there in a minute. I need to tell Mom and Lacey we're about to start the show." And that was a lie. One of the security guards was already heading to the bus to summon them, per his earlier instructions.

"Try to make it before tomorrow morning," Rusty said as they headed away.

Brett waited a few seconds, and when he thought it was safe to look, he ventured a glance. Big mistake. Cammie stood at the bottom of the steps, chatting with the guys like this little reunion was no big deal. She wore tight black jeans and a silky white top that tied at the neck and showed a whole lot of bare shoulder. And damn if she wasn't wearing a sexy pair of black platform heels, something he noticed as she climbed the stairs before she moved out of sight.

At least he was prepared now. Not that it would matter. He'd be lucky if he remembered how to play his guitar or if he could even get one word out of his dry mouth....

When the announcer called ten minutes until showtime, Brett was jolted back into reality. He needed to get a move on, then remembered he'd left his hat in the hospitality tent where he'd gone to get the beer. He sprinted to the tent, grabbed the hat from the table and then ran smack-dab into a groupie with something other than his stage performance on her mind.

"Hi, Brett." She gave him a painted-on smile that didn't conceal the fact she was way too young. "You about to go on?"

"That's right, and I'm late." He positioned his hat in place and tried to move around her but she blocked his path.

She inclined her head to one side and grinned. "After it's over, why don't you and I have a beer together?"

Her kind would be a thing of the past after tonight, if all went well. He tried not to look too put out, although he was. "Don't think so, sweetheart. Look, I've got to go—"

She adjusted his collar where it was riding up at the fold. "There." She patted his chest and wet her lips. "I'm good at helping men get dressed. And undressed."

He thought about the likes of Mark Jensen and decided she needed a quick lecture. "What's your name and how old are you?"

She looked highly insulted. "My name's Kinsey and I'm eighteen."

And he was twenty-one. "Honestly."

"Seventeen, but I'll be eighteen next January."

Brett didn't have time to set her straight, but he was going to take the time, anyway. "Let me give you a few words of advice. Finish school and learn some self-respect. What you're doing is all kinds of dangerous."

She stuck out her lip in a pout. "But I want to be a singer like you."

"Sleeping your way to the top might take you places you don't want to go." Man, he sounded like a dad, and that was a good thing. "If you've got talent, learn how to go through the proper channels."

When the intro music began, Brett pushed past her and headed to the stage. He hoped the girl took his advice, and that made him smile. Maybe he was getting this dad thing down, after all.

He climbed to the top of the stairs and stopped off where his daughter and mom were seated. Lacey looked up at him, her eyes wide. "Daddy, she's beautiful."

"I agree," his mom said. "She looks like an angel."

Probably too much of an angel for a devil like him—except in his bed. "Yeah, she's pretty inside and out." He regarded Lacey again. "Do you have it?"

She patted her jeans pocket. "Right here."

"Good. Remember what I told you?"

She gave him a good eye-rolling. "Yes, Dad. I'm not a baby."

No, she wasn't, but she'd always be his baby girl. He leaned down to dole out hugs, straightened and exhaled. "Wish me luck."

He signaled the announcer he was ready and took his guitar from the roadie.

"Once again, put your hands together for Brett Taylor!"

As soon as he stepped onto the stage and moved in front of the microphone, his attention immediately went to Cammie standing to his right. And dammit, she smiled at him. He would've been better off with a go-to-hell look. He would've been better off if she wore a bag over her head.

When he turned to Bull to count down the beat, he did a double take. Standing in Walker's stead was the best man Brett had ever known. The man he'd always wanted to be. The man he still wanted to be.

The band began to play but he didn't care. He couldn't jump into a song without a greeting for Pat.

He walked over to him, shook his hand and gave him a brief guy hug. "How? Why?"

"You can thank the little gal over there." He pointed toward Cammie and grinned. "She thought you could use a little pick-me-up."

Brett turned around and saw she was smiling again, soft and so damn sweet, looking like the angel his mother thought her to be. In that moment, he couldn't have loved her more.

As the band continued to play, he claimed his spot behind the microphone and gave her a thank-you smile. He wanted to do more than that. He wanted to hold her and say what he'd needed to say to her a long time ago. But there would be time for that later, and the damn show must go on.

He picked up the song from the beginning without missing a beat, like his heart wasn't about to pound out of chest and he wasn't sweating bullets. Big ones. Somehow, someway, he managed to get through the eight-song set without stumbling over the lyrics, or himself when he shook a few hands. Yet in the back of his mind, he couldn't forget what was about to happen. If all went as planned, he'd be changing his life forever. If it didn't… Nope, he wasn't going to borrow trouble.

When it came time for the final song, he stepped up to the microphone and gathered every ounce of strength he owned. "I know most of you saw the debut video for 'When You Know It's Real' earlier this evening. Well, we're going to show it again, only this time I'm going to sing it live the way it's supposed to be sung." He stepped back and gestured toward Cammie. "I'm going to sing it with the star of the video and the best backup singer in the country, Camille Carson."

As the audience applauded like mad, Cammie took a little bow but remained planted in place. Brett set his guitar against a speaker, then came back and crooked a finger at her, indicating he wanted her to share his microphone. She dragged her feet getting there, like she wasn't sure she wanted to be that close to him. But he wasn't going to let that discourage him. He planned to get real close to her in a matter of minutes.

After the lights dimmed, the crowd quieted and the video began to play, Brett slid one arm around Cammie's waist, and she didn't make the slightest indication she didn't want the contact. One victory down, one to go. As always, they sang perfect two-part harmony, looking into each other's eyes. And when they came to the final refrain, Brett didn't care if the whole world was watching, he was going to kiss her. And he did. And she kissed him back like they'd never been apart.

He wasn't sure if the roar from the crowd resulted from the kiss, or the other part of his master plan. Maybe both. Now that the song was over, the fun had just begun.

When he pushed the microphone aside with the

hand that wasn't balanced on Cammie's waist, the audience went silent as a tomb.

She looked to be in that state known as confusion. "What are you doing?"

He slid his other arm around her and pulled her close. "I have something to say, and I'm going to say it."

"Now? What about the audience?"

"Believe me, they'll wait." He sucked in a long breath and let it out slowly. "Cammie, I've made a lot of mistakes in my life, and letting you go was one of the biggest ones to date. I've done a lot of soul-searching while you've been gone, and I figured out I'm not scared anymore. In fact, I'm ready to go all in."

She frowned. "Meaning?"

"First, I have a question for you. Do you still love me?"

"Of course I do. A couple of weeks didn't cure me of that. I'm not sure a couple of decades will change that."

He gave her a soft kiss, took her by the shoulders and turned. "Now look up."

Cammie, Will You Marry Me...?

She blinked twice before the words registered. She blinked again, then stared at Brett. "Are you serious?"

"Oh, yeah, I'm serious. I don't think I'd plaster

a proposal across a giant video screen if I wasn't. And to show you how serious I am—" he waved a hand over his shoulder "—I have something else to prove it."

Lacey came bouncing out holding a royal-blue velvet box in her hand. She gave it to her dad, stood on tiptoe and kissed his cheek, then bounced away again.

When Brett stepped back, Cammie's hand immediately went to her chest where she felt the rapid-fire beat of her heart. The moments were so surreal, she felt as if she might be having an out-of-body experience.

"On your knees, son," Pat yelled, sending her out of her momentary stupor.

"Hold your horses, I'm getting to that." As Brett knelt on one knee and opened the box to reveal an unbelievable diamond ring, the crowd went wild and Cammie started to cry. "Camille Carson, will you do me the honor of marrying probably the most flawed man you've ever met? But flaws and all, I love you more than all the fame and the awards and this insane career."

She could never have imagined this beautiful gesture would come from the love of her life, who now wore his heart on his sleeve and in his incredible blue eyes. However, that didn't mean she was beyond drawing out the suspense. "Do you promise I don't have to sing if I don't want to?"

"Yeah, if you'll promise to help me write my songs."

"Agreed. Babies?"

He gave her a winning grin. "You bet. Five or six."

"I'll settle for two or three."

After someone yelled, "Hurry up," they both laughed.

"Baby, you heard the man. Give me your answer before my knees permanently lock up. And it better be yes. Otherwise, I'll never be able to show my face again in Nashville, much less the rest of the good old U.S. of A."

Deciding to put him out of his misery, Cammie held out a hand to him that he took without hesitation. She considered the only word that came to mind. The only word that mattered at the moment. "Yes."

Brett leaned over to the microphone. "Hell, yeah, she said yes."

Cammie was sure the thunderous outcry from the crowd was sufficient enough to wake every dog in the county. The kiss Brett gave her was hot enough to set the stage on fire.

When Bull hollered, "You forgot the ring, Brett!" they finally parted.

As he pulled the ring from the holder and pocketed the box, Cammie held out her left hand for him to slip the emerald-cut diamond on her finger. Once that important act was done, he went back to the microphone. "The show's over, folks, but the champagne's on the house."

Just one more reason for the fans to get whipped into a frenzy, and an expensive reason at that. But Cammie only cared about finding out where Brett was leading her at the moment. They stopped behind the stage where Lacey and his mother were waiting, both looking tremendously pleased.

Brett tugged her forward and rested his palms on her shoulders for the official presentation. "Lacey, this is Cammie."

"It's great to meet you, Lacey," she said. "And thanks for assisting your dad."

Taking Cammie by surprise, the girl gave her a hug. "Nice to meet you, too." When she stepped away, she rocked back and forth on her heels as if she had a live wire attached to her purple flip-flops. "That was pretty cool, huh? I can't wait to tell my friends about it back home. Can I be in the wedding? We could wear purple dresses. Oh, and I love my room at Daddy's house—"

"Simmer down, motormouth." A woman stepped forward, her eyes the same color as Brett's, a shock of white running through one side of her black hair. "I'm Linda, Cammie, Brett's mother, and please excuse my son's and granddaughter's lack of manners."

"It's so nice to finally meet you, too."

Linda took Cammie's offered hand and pulled her into a tight embrace. "We're huggers," she said after she released her. "And welcome to the family."

She truly felt welcome. "Thank you."

"And while we're at it, let me say a few words regarding my son—"

"Careful, Mother."

Cammie glanced back to see Brett's scowl before she gave her full attention to Linda. "Please. I'm all ears."

"Make him put up his own laundry because that's what he's been taught to do. If he pouts, just ignore him because he'll eventually come around. He's really ticklish right around the ribs, so that's a good weapon. And if he gives you any crap, call me and I'll give him what-for."

Cammie laughed. "Thanks so much for the info."

"You forgot the part about me burping the alphabet when I was in junior high," Brett said, a hint of annoyance in his tone.

Linda reached up and patted his cheek. "I'm sure I'll fill in the blanks for Cammie when you bring her home to meet the relatives."

"That's our cue to leave," Brett said. "Otherwise, she'll start listing them, including the cousins three times removed."

"Can Cammie ride back to the house with us on the bus?" Lacey asked.

"Actually," Cammie began, "I have to head home because I'm in the company truck."

"It's late so you should come back to the house," Brett said. "Besides, I plan to go back with you to

Memphis in the morning to officially ask your granddad for your hand."

Cammie hoped Jed had put the shotgun away. "I'm sure he'd appreciate that." And she'd like nothing better than to spend the night with Brett, but with an impressionable preteen in the house, not to mention a future mother-in-law, the sleeping arrangements could get complicated. "I suppose I could sleep on the sofa in the great room and head back in the morning."

"Nonsense," Linda said. "I'll sleep with Lacey and you can have the other guest room closest to the master bedroom. Of course, it doesn't actually have a bed, but I imagine the two of you can figure something out." She topped off the comment with a wink, flooding Cammie's face with heat.

Rusty, Bull, Pat and Jeremy, who'd been waiting nearby, came up and offered their congratulations where they joined together in a group hug.

"I just have one question for the two of you," Rusty said.

Cammie worried over what that might be. "Ask away."

"Who's going to call Bud and tell him?"

Brett laughed and slipped his arms around Cammie's waist. "I think we'll just wait and let him find out when he rejoins us on the next tour."

"Or sees it in some magazine," Cammie said. "I'll call him after I call my grandparents." She might as well get the fireworks over with all at once.

After Brett sent Linda and Lacey back to the house on the bus, he led Cammie to a secluded spot behind the tent while they waited for the last of the fans to disperse.

"That was quite a proposal, Brett Taylor," she said. "And I love you for it."

He gently touched her face. "I love you better. Not better than you love me. Just better than I ever thought I could."

If she'd had any doubts about that, they'd all been dispelled. "You know, that sounds like a song."

"You're right, and we can write it together. Just so you know, I'm going to kiss you and seal the deal."

And he did kiss her, softly at first, then a little deeper until Cammie began to feel weak in the knees and worried someone might see them.

"You two need to get a room, or at least go in the woods."

Somewhat embarrassed, Cammie broke the kiss and looked to her right to see Pat standing nearby. "I thought you'd already left."

He approached them, hat in hand. "Not without saying an official goodbye, and not before I tell the two of you a few things."

Brett groaned. "I don't think I can handle any more advice tonight."

"Too bad, because you're going to get it." Pat's expression turned somber. "Don't ever forget the way you're lookin' at each other tonight, and when you fight, remember that makin' up is truly the best part.

Most important, real love doesn't come along often, so don't go squandering it like I did." He hooked a thumb over his shoulder. "Now I'm heading home to my lady and, if I'm lucky, I'll get some of what you two have been gettin' only I'll make sure we're not putting on a show out in the open."

"One more thing," Brett said. "I want you to be the best man."

Pat sent him a cynical look. "I am the best man so I expect nothing less. But, son, you're well on your way, too. That means I did something right when I raised you." With that, he turned around and laughed as he walked away.

Brett faced Cammie again and studied her eyes. "You know, four months ago if you'd told me this day would come, I would've said you're crazy. But then, a lot of people are going to call us crazy for getting engaged after such a short time."

She kissed him softly and smiled. "Did Pat tell you the story about his grandparents?"

"Not that I recall."

"Then I'll tell it to you on the way home. And by the way, someday I will get you back for that whole video-screen proposal…."

As they walked, arms around waists, toward the truck, Cammie agreed they were definitely crazy. Crazy in love. Still, she had no illusions about their future. She expected their life to be filled with as many peaks and valleys as a Smoky Mountain road, along with an abiding love and a passion that knew no bounds. She did have high hopes of how it would end—making beautiful music together for at least sixty-five years.

EPILOGUE

BRETT TAYLOR STOOD at the open door, remaining partially concealed while mentally plotting his course from the tour bus to the rear entrance of the coliseum. As usual, it was near to impossible to sneak past a crowd during a stock show, particularly when parked in wide-open spaces in broad daylight—in the same place where it had all begun two years ago.

After he slipped the new photo into his pocket, he descended the stairs and stepped out onto the lot where the shouting and shoving commenced, sending his security team into action, their beefy arms attempting to hold the crowd at bay.

Fans were good, though. Fans helped pay for college funds and dance lessons and, someday, diapers. But these fans would have to wait until after the show. He was already late and impatient to get to the stage to see his lady for the first time in two weeks.

Brett strode into the back entrance of the arena, past the catch pens and the same cowboys seated on the rails. This time he didn't have the urge to borrow a horse and ride away like an Old West hero.

And he still wasn't a hero, except maybe to his little girl, who wasn't so little anymore.

The guards pushed open the heavy metal door, led him down a corridor and then up the stairs to the backstage jungle. After he took his guitar from the roadie, he scanned the area in an attempt to locate the woman behind his reason for hurrying.

He finally spotted her standing near the curtain, wearing her hair piled into a ponytail and a T-shirt that read I Know Joe—the same words that had been painted beneath the Just Married sign plastered to the rear of the bus some eighteen months ago. She still looked as beautiful as she had the day they'd exchanged vows with a song.

After fitting the guitar strap over his shoulder, he bypassed the outskirts of the stage. He no longer needed to see the eager faces to prepare for a performance, only Cammie's face. He didn't have to draw energy from the spirited roar or the passionate applause because he had the love of a good woman to sustain him. He still knew all his songs by heart, but better still, he now knew his own heart. And he'd learned to accept life's crazy turns and unexpected changes, because sometimes changes were good. Damn good.

Without regard to the backstage chaos, he walked right up to Cammie and laid a long kiss on her. Once he was done—for now—he stepped back and frowned. "Are you going to wear that onstage?"

She grinned, pulled the shirt over her head and

tossed it behind her, revealing a sleeveless shiny purple blouse. "Lacey picked it out."

He let go a tuneless whistle. "Yeah, I like it."

Cammie took his hand into hers. "Are you ready?"

"Question is, are you? That flu hung on a long time."

"I promise I'm fine, and I'm more than ready."

As the lights went down, darkening the stage, Brett led Cammie to the microphone and waited to be announced.

"Ladies and gentlemen, please give a big Houston welcome to two-time Performer of the Year and multiplatinum country-music superstar Brett Taylor, performing his brand-new number-one hit, 'Better Than I Ever Thought I Could,' with his wife and cowriter, Camille Carson-Taylor!"

Brett waited for the shouts to subside, the applause to die down and for the band to start playing, but none of that happened. In fact, the applause just got louder.

He looked at Cammie to find she was giving him an ear-to-ear grin. "What's going on?"

She stepped behind him, took him by the shoulders and turned him around. "Look up."

He did as she asked and had to blink twice to make sure he'd correctly read the words spread across the video screen.

We're Going to Have a Baby.

After the initial shock wore off, he turned back to Cammie. "Seriously?"

She nodded. "I told you I'd get you back, didn't I?"

He kissed her then, not caring if the whole world witnessed how much he loved his wife. After he let her go to sing the song that summed up their relationship, he counted down the beat as he counted his blessings. All the accolades, sold-out crowds and numerous hits couldn't compare to the gifts she'd given him.

Thanks to one former feisty bus driver, with the face of an angel and a voice to match, Brett Taylor—the better man—had finally arrived.

* * * * *

LARGER-PRINT BOOKS!
GET 2 FREE LARGER-PRINT NOVELS PLUS
2 FREE GIFTS!

HARLEQUIN®

super romance®

Exciting, emotional, unexpected!

ReaderService.com

Manage your account online!

- Review your order history
- Manage your payments
- Update your address

Enjoy all the features!

- Reader excerpts from any series
- Respond to mailings and special monthly offers
- Discover new series available to you
- Browse the Bonus Bucks catalog
- Share your feedback

Visit us at:

ReaderService.com

RS13